Roaring Fork

ROCKSTAR

HEATHER SLADE

Table of Contents

1

Keltie

I should have known something was up the moment the Wheaton siblings huddled together and bolted for the door. But on the twenty-first of December, with the Goat packed wall to wall for our early Christmas bash, I had other concerns—like keeping the bourbon flowing and making sure no one fell off the mechanical bull we'd rented for the night.

Taking over my family's old bar in this small mountain ski town wasn't the career path I'd imagined after years of mixing sound for touring bands, but the money my father had promised I'd make would help with Luna's medical bills.

"Another round for table six," I told Miguel, my most reliable employee, sliding the empty glasses across the polished wood. The holiday crowd pressed in from every direction, a sea of flannel and denim, cowboy hats and boots. Through the crush, I spotted him again—Holt Wheaton—the local musician who'd been playing regular Thursday- and Saturday-night sets since I reopened. The man was unfairly gorgeous, with intense blue eyes and dark hair that he kept long enough to run fingers through. Not that I was looking. Not with Luna at home with Mrs. Lopez, my elderly neighbor who charged half her going rate because she adored my daughter.

His voice, though—that was something else entirely. The first time I heard him sing, I nearly dropped an entire tray of drinks. There was a raw, haunting quality to it that made the hair on my arms stand up. The locals told me he was part of a famous band that toured internationally, but he never mentioned it when he showed up every week, guitar case in hand, asking if the stage was ready.

"Keltie!" One of the waitresses—Jenna, I think—waved frantically from across the room. "We need more napkins!"

As I ducked beneath the bar to grab a stack, my phone buzzed with a text from Mrs. Lopez, confirming Luna was asleep. I allowed myself a small breath of relief. The good nights were becoming more frequent, but I never took them for granted.

I checked the time—three more hours before I could relieve the sitter and hold my little girl close.

I hated being away from my daughter at night, but the stack of her medical bills grew faster than I could pay them down.

I glanced over at Holt again, reminding myself there was no time to fantasize about blue-eyed musicians when my four-year-old needed specialized care I could barely afford.

The Wheaton family had caught my attention earlier, a boisterous group celebrating near the fireplace. I'd recognized Holt immediately, of course, but hadn't met the others until they approached the bar. The introductions had been casual enough—Cord and his wife, Juni, her parents, and another woman, named Samantha, who came to stand near them.

That's when everything shifted.

"Hey, Cord," the one called Juni had said, pointing to a picture on the wall. "And, Sam, did you see this?"

They were all staring at a photo I'd hung, of my father with his sister Ursula outside the original Goat.

"How do you know my aunt Ursula?" I asked, moving toward them.

The older man—Jay, Juni's father—looked over his daughter's shoulder. "That looks like the guy I bought our place from."

My forehead scrunched. "That's my dad."

"What's his name?" Jay asked.

"Victor Marquez."

The one called Cord muttered something under his breath while his wife spun around, her eyes wide with shock.

"So, uh, anyone wanna fill me in?" I asked, feeling like I'd walked into the middle of a movie.

That's when Samantha stepped closer. "Pilar Marquez was my grandmother. I'm Samantha."

The revelation hung in the air between us, a connection neither of us had known existed. I grabbed the bourbon without thinking, lined up shot glasses, and asked who was in. All five raised their hands.

"To the Goat," I toasted, the whiskey burning a path down my throat.

"To the Goat!" they echoed.

I noticed Holt watching from several feet away, his expression unreadable. When our eyes met, he didn't look away. Their intensity wasn't just for show on stage.

"Did your dad ever mention anything about East Aurora?" Sam asked, leaning across the bar.

I shook my head. "Not really. Only that he and Aunt Ursula ran a place there before I was born."

"And he never mentioned the Wheaton family? Or the Rookers?"

"No," I said, trying to recall hearing any random comments about either. "He's not exactly the reminiscing type."

Holt approached then, resting his hand on Cord's shoulder, and whispered something in his ear. I watched them move through the crowd, collecting what I assumed were his other siblings. They gathered near the door, heads bent together in conversation.

"Excuse me," Cord said, setting his empty glass on the bar. "We need to step outside for a minute."

Juni looked torn, glancing between her husband and her parents.

"Go," said Juni's father. "We'll be fine."

I watched them leave, Holt holding the door as the others filed out into the softly falling snow. Something told me they wouldn't be back—at least not tonight.

"Your father might have the answers we've been looking for," Sam said, handing me a napkin where she'd written her phone number. "Would you mind asking him to give me a call tomorrow?"

"Sure," I replied, tucking the number into my pocket. "But I'm not promising anything. Dad can be…selective about what he shares."

Hours later, after Sam and her husband had also left and the bar emptied, I counted out the register while thinking about Luna. Four years old and already braver than most adults I knew. The recurring doctor visits for her unexplained fevers were adding up—meaning I needed to earn a *helluva* lot of money.

I rolled my shoulders, willing the stress away, then locked the cash in the safe and grabbed my coat.

"You heading out, boss?" Miguel called out.

"Yeah. You good to finish up?"

He stopped sweeping. "Hey, what was that all about earlier? With the photo?"

I shrugged. "Family stuff, I guess. Turns out my dad has more connections to this town than he let on."

"Mysterious." Miguel grinned. "Like a telenovela."

"God, I hope not." I laughed, though part of me wondered.

Outside, the temperature had dropped to well below freezing. The snow crunched under my boots as I made my way to where I'd parked. Downtown Crested Butte sparkled with Christmas lights, and for a moment, I let myself enjoy the beauty of it—the white-peaked butte, visible even in the darkness, the quiet of a small town long since closed up for the night.

I climbed into my truck and turned the key, waiting for the engine to warm. Tomorrow, I'd call my father and demand answers. But tonight, I needed to get home to Luna. Whatever secrets lingered in the walls of the Goat would have to wait until morning.

As I pulled away from the curb, I caught a glimpse of a tall figure standing under a streetlight across the street—Holt Wheaton, watching as I drove past. Our eyes met for a brief moment before I turned the corner, heading for home. What was he doing, standing out in the cold? Did he need help? What had happened to all his siblings?

I couldn't stop myself. I spun the truck around and pulled up beside him. "Everything okay?" I asked.

He stepped over and rested his arms on the window I'd lowered. "Favorite time here in town," he said. "When everything's quiet enough that you can hear the snow falling."

"Well, it's actually my favorite time to be in bed. Err, I mean, asleep."

He chuckled and stepped away. "You got me there. Being in bed is my favorite thing too—and I don't mean to sleep," he added with a wink.

I shook my head, raised the window, and drove the three blocks home, knowing damn well that as soon as I crawled under my covers, I'd fall asleep wondering what sharing my sheets with the rock god Holt Wheaton would be like.

2

Holt

My stomach knotted as I stared at the text from Six-pack that had arrived at nine this morning.

Meeting at my office, 1:00 PM today. All Wheaton siblings required. No exceptions.

The snow swirled outside my cabin window as I sipped coffee that had gone cold. Less than twelve hours ago, we'd been at the Goat, celebrating Cord's return from New York and his marriage to Juni. Now, this.

I'd known this day would come. But knowing didn't make it any easier.

I shook my head, trying to focus on the view outside my window rather than the dread spreading through my chest. The mountains stood indifferent, snow-capped and silent, unconcerned with the games a mysterious LLC was playing with my family.

When I arrived at Six-pack's office in Gunnison, all my siblings were already gathered in the conference room. Six-pack stood at the head of the table, manila folder in hand, wearing the same expression he'd had when delivering the news to each of my three brothers before me.

"Holt," Six-pack greeted me. "Seeing as we're all here, we can begin." Flynn, the youngest of the five of us and our only sister, and I took the two open seats. Now that she was married, with twin sons, I hoped whatever this asshole was about to tell us would be something required of me, not her.

"Let's get this over with," I said, hating how my voice sounded. "What impossible task do I need to perform?"

Six-pack adjusted his glasses. "I've received instructions from the Roaring Fork Trust LLC regarding the next codicil."

"Get on with it, Six-pack," Buck snapped.

"It reads as follows. 'The Roaring Fork Trust further stipulates that Holt David Wheaton must live in Crested Butte, Colorado, for a period of three hundred and sixty-five days, defined as not being absent from the boundaries of the town for a period longer than forty-eight consecutive hours.'"

I frowned. "That's it? Stay in CB for a year?" It sounded suspiciously simple after what my brothers had been through.

Six-pack cleared his throat. "There's more. 'During this period, he must perform musical sets at local establishments no fewer than three times per week and donate fifty percent of all earnings from these performances to the Miracles of Hope Children's Charity of Crested Butte, Colorado.'"

It was the same charity that would get everything if I didn't do what the codicil demanded. I felt my jaw tighten.

"So I'm trapped in town, playing dive bars for a year," I said flatly.

"That appears to be the requirement, yes," Six-pack replied.

I laughed, but not because it was funny. "Any specific songs they want me to play? Any venues I have to avoid?"

"The codicil doesn't specify further details about the performances," Six-pack said, "only that they must be public, paid engagements and properly documented for verification purposes."

I stood up, unable to stay seated. The walls felt too close, the air too thin.

"If the terms of the codicil are not met, then the ranch will be sold and the proceeds given to—"

Buck stood like I had. "Shut the fuck up, Six-pack. We know all this shit. Holt doesn't do as he's told, we lose everything. Is there anything else we don't know? Other than who the asshole behind the scenes calling the shots is?"

The attorney—a guy we all went to high school with—shook his head.

"Then, we're outta here," Buck added.

"When do I have to start?" I asked, the question sounding strange even to my own ears.

"Immediately," Six-pack replied. "The clock begins ticking today. You have twelve months."

I turned and headed for the exit, not trusting myself to say anything more. My hand trembled on the doorknob—not from fear, but from the effort of containing everything churning inside me.

Once outside, I stood by my truck, resting my hands on the hood, trying to steady my breathing.

"You okay?" Cord's voice came from behind me.

I straightened, not turning around. "Were you a year ago when you found out you had to drive across the country to a place you'd never heard of?"

Cord shook his head. "You know I wasn't."

"To tell you the truth, I wish I had to go somewhere."

"I get it, man."

We all did. Buck, Porter, Cord, me, and even Flynn. We were powerless against a nameless, faceless trustee who pulled our strings like a puppet master. "Sorry. I know you do. Listen, I need some time."

I hugged each of my siblings, then got in my truck. It was a thirty-minute drive to the Roaring Fork—a ranch that had been in our family for generations. It was worth millions, and if I didn't do my part, every penny of it would be gone.

My brothers had done their share. Now, it was all on me.

The envelope in my pocket—the one with CB Rice's official logo and tour schedule that included forty-eight cities in eighteen countries—felt like a brick. The tour I'd spent my whole life dreaming about, the kind that made songwriters legends, was now something I couldn't be a part of.

I needed a fucking drink. And I knew exactly where to get one.

"Hey, Holt," said Keltie when I walked into the Goat. "I didn't expect you to be here today. Something I can do for you?"

I motioned over to the small stage. "Mind if I play a while?"

Her head cocked for a second. "You're welcome anytime someone else isn't on the schedule."

"Thanks, darlin'."

"Get you a drink?"

"I'd appreciate it." I watched her walk away, unable to take my eyes off her. Keltie's five-foot-seven frame commanded the space behind the bar like she'd been born to it. She'd tucked her flannel shirt into a pair of worn jeans that hugged her curves in all the right places—ample breasts, narrow waist, proportionate hips. The kind of body that made a man's hands itch to explore.

But it was her eyes that got me. Big, round, and a light brown that looked almost amber under the bar lights. They held secrets—I'd bet my guitar on it. Her wild, curly, dark-brown hair framed her face, a few strands escaping the loose ponytail she'd pulled it into for work.

I couldn't help but remember our exchange of last night. "Being in bed is my favorite thing too—and I don't mean to sleep." I'd winked, and her cheeks had flushed before she raised her window and drove off. That blush had stayed with me all night.

When she returned with my drink, her smile lit up her whole face, transforming her from merely beautiful to breathtaking. Her square-toed cowboy boots clicked against the hardwood floor as she set the glass in front of me.

"There you go. On the house," she said, seemingly unaware of the effect she had.

"Thanks," I said, feeling more parched than when I'd walked in, but not for the whiskey in my glass. "But lemme start a tab, Keltie. I'm not going anywhere for a while," I said, thinking about the codicil's requirement. *Three hundred and sixty-five days.* Maybe being stuck here wouldn't be as bad as I'd thought.

I picked up my guitar case and headed for the stage, feeling her eyes on me as I walked away. At least I'd have something worth looking at while I played my forced sets for the following year.

For the next couple of hours, my Gibson hummed under my fingers, a familiar comfort amidst the biggest disappointment of my life.

My phone buzzed again—probably Remi, CB Rice's manager, asking for the hundredth time where the hell I was and when I'd get my ass over to the band's recording studio, sign the contract, and start practicing with the rest of the guys. The hardest part about responding was that I had no idea what I'd say. How I'd explain that, even though my share of the money CB Rice would make on the road would have given me the means to launch my own tour, record my own music, now, I had to watch my dreams slip away. While, at the same time, donating half my local gig money to a children's charity that stood to get my inheritance should I fail.

I glanced over at the bar, and my eyes met Keltie's. She was drying glasses and looking at me like she could see right through me. That was the problem with small towns—everyone thought they knew your story, even people you hadn't known all your life. Not that anyone outside our family was aware of the trust. All of us agreed that it was nobody's business.

As I thought about what to play next, my father's voice sounded in my head. "Music won't feed cattle, boy." He was as right as he was wrong. It sure as hell wouldn't now that my one chance to make it big was gone. No way would Ben Rice, the band's lead singer and founder, give me another shot next year. Why would he? By then, he'd find a line of guys ready, willing, and able to replace me.

When Keltie dimmed the stage lights as evening fell, they cast shadows across the bar's worn floorboards. From here, I could see the old photograph of the Goat's original opening day. Something about it nagged at me like a wrong note in a familiar song.

"What's up?" she asked, sliding another whiskey closer, which I downed in one gulp.

"Nothin'," I replied, running my fingers across the guitar strings once more. The emerging melody was unfamiliar, something sad and sweet and ancient, like a lullaby half remembered from childhood.

Keltie stilled, and her eyes widened. "Where did you learn that?"

"I didn't," I said, but my fingers kept playing, a muscle memory I shouldn't have—like a secret someone had whispered almost too quietly for me to hear. "You know it?"

"It sounds familiar, but I can't place it." As she turned and walked away, I couldn't help but wonder why music neither of us knew seemed to have such a profound effect on us both.

My mind was elsewhere as the bar filled with people, most of whom I'd known all my life. I'd wave when they did, but otherwise, I couldn't stop myself from thinking there was something I was missing with the trust—obvious like a word on the tip of my tongue that I couldn't pull out of my head. All I knew was that whatever it was would shake me, my brothers, and my sister to our collective core.

I couldn't explain the premonitions that had started coming to me when I was a kid. The first was that my mama was going to die. To this day, I hadn't told anyone that, at seven years old, I knew our mother had cancer before she or our father breathed a word of it.

I looked up at Keltie, who, like me, appeared lost in thought. I was about to take a break, walk over, and talk to her when a feeling—like one of those premonitions—came over me that I couldn't ignore. As if she felt it too, she walked toward me. "Sorry, I need a minute," I said when she was within a foot of me. I set my guitar on its stand and raced out of the bar's rear entrance and into the frigid cold.

"Hello. Who are you?" said a little girl I'd almost knocked down when I barreled outside.

"I'm, uh, Holt Wheaton," I said. "Who are you?"

"I'm Luna. My mommy owns this bar." I should've known she was related to Keltie. Like her mama's, the girl's dark curls were wild around her face and her brown doe eyes bored into mine as if she could read my every thought.

"Vete para adentro ahora, pequeñina," said the older woman with her, who I didn't recognize. Since I spoke Spanish fairly well, I knew she'd said something like, "Go inside now, little one."

"It was nice to meet you, Mr. Wheaton," Luna said, holding her hand out for me to shake. It was tiny and fragile when I grasped it. But worse, the feeling that had sent me outside in the first place intensified. Something was wrong with her, something bad. I was as certain of it as I was of my own name.

3

Keltie

The rear door swung open, and I spotted Luna with Mrs. Lopez. My stomach dropped. It was a few minutes after seven—right when I'd expect my daughter to be having dinner at home, not at the bar.

"Luna? Is everything okay?" I hurried toward them, concern rising in my chest.

"Mommy!" Luna brightened when she saw me, breaking away from Mrs. Lopez to wrap her arms around my legs. "I met Mr. Wheaton! He's super tall, and he has long hair like we do!"

I shot a questioning look at Mrs. Lopez, who shrugged apologetically. "She insisted on seeing you tonight. Said she couldn't sleep without a good-night kiss."

"Where is Mr. Wheaton now?" I asked, looking past them.

"He left," Mrs. Lopez said. "Seemed in a hurry after we bumped into him. Almost like he'd seen a ghost."

I knelt down, bringing myself to Luna's level. Her flushed cheeks and unusual energy worried me, especially considering how tired she'd been this morning.

"He was nice, Mommy," Luna continued.

I pulled my daughter close for a hug, pressing my lips to her forehead. The warmth radiating from her skin confirmed my fears—another spike. Not emergency-room hot, but definitely higher than normal.

Mrs. Lopez caught my eye and tilted her head. "She seemed tired earlier, but perked up outside," she said with concern.

"Thanks for bringing her," I replied softly, squeezing the older woman's hand. "I've got her now."

After Mrs. Lopez left, I guided Luna to a corner table with a clear view of the bar. "Do you feel like coloring while Mommy finishes work?" I suggested, pulling out the activity books and colored pencils I kept stashed under the counter for nights exactly like this.

"Can I have apple juice?" Luna asked, already reaching for her favorite purple pencil.

"Of course, baby." I kissed the top of her head, trying to ignore how my hands shook as I poured her juice into a plastic cup with a lid.

I looked over at the stage, where Holt's guitar still rested on its stand, abandoned. When he'd rushed out earlier, I assumed he'd be back. Now, customers were asking what had happened to the music. I'd have to put something on the sound system to fill the silence.

I found it strange that Holt had left his prized guitar behind. In the month I'd known him, he treated that guitar like it was made of gold—never letting it out of his sight. Something had clearly rattled him enough to make him forget it entirely.

Miguel approached as I was setting up a playlist on the sound system. "Where'd our entertainment go?" he asked, motioning toward the empty stage.

"No idea," I said, selecting a mix of country and classic rock that would keep the crowd happy.

"That's weird. First time I've seen Holt Wheaton bail on a gig." Miguel's brow furrowed. "And definitely the first time I've seen him leave his Gibby behind."

"I know," I agreed, glancing over at my little girl, who was contentedly coloring at her table. "Do me a favor and keep an eye on the bar for a minute? I need to check on Luna."

"Sure thing, boss."

I made my way across the crowded floor, saying hello to regulars as I passed. The Goat was filling up fast—Sunday nights were always popular, especially at this time of year.

Luna didn't look up as I approached, absorbed in her artwork. I slid into the chair beside her, watching as she colored an animal purple with green spots.

"That's a beautiful horse," I said, gently brushing a curl from her forehead. Still warm.

"It's not a horse, Mommy," she corrected with the exaggerated patience four-year-olds reserve for clueless adults. "It's a unicorn. See the horn?" She pointed to what I'd taken for an ear.

"Of course. My mistake." I smiled, but my mind was racing, calculating the hours until I could reasonably leave and whether Luna's fever would climb higher in that time.

"Mr. Wheaton has a very nice face," she said before returning to her coloring.

"What did he say to you?" I asked, trying to sound casual.

Luna's tongue poked out of the corner of her mouth as she concentrated on staying in the lines. "Nothing, but he looked sad before he left." She frowned, picking up a blue pencil. "Do you think he has a tummy ache like I get sometimes?"

"I don't know, Luna-bug. Maybe." I kissed the top of her head and stood. "Let me see if Miguel can cover for me tonight, and we'll go home."

"Okay," she said, already absorbed in her art again.

Instead of going straight over to the bar, I walked to the stage, placed Holt's guitar in its case, then set it near the counter.

"Is that seat taken?" a familiar voice asked.

I turned to find Samantha Marquez—my newfound cousin—sliding onto a stool. She looked different than she had last night—more relaxed, in jeans and a sweater, her dark hair pulled into a loose bun.

"It is now," I replied, setting a napkin in front of her. "What can I get you?"

"Club soda with lime, please," she said. "I'm the designated driver tonight. Beau's over at the Eldo with guys he skied with today. I swear that man has never met a stranger."

I prepared her drink, aware of the growing headache behind my eyes. Between Luna's unexpected appearance and Holt's bizarre disappearance, the evening had veered far from normal.

"Sorry if I seem distracted," I told Sam, sliding her glass across the bar. "It's been a crazy day."

"Hey, I get it. Busy time of year." She took a sip, then gestured toward Luna, who was now yawning over her coloring book. "She yours?"

A mix of pride and protectiveness washed over me. "That's Luna. Four going on forty."

Sam smiled. "She's beautiful. Has your eyes."

"And her father's stubbornness," I added without thinking, then immediately regretted it when Sam's expression turned curious.

"Is her dad in the picture?" she asked, then quickly added, "Sorry, none of my business."

"No, it's okay." I busied myself wiping down the prep area. "He's not involved. His choice."

Sam didn't press the issue, which I appreciated. Most people couldn't resist digging for more details, as if single motherhood was an invitation for personal questions.

"Will you be going to New Mexico for Christmas?" she asked, changing the subject.

I shook my head. "Can't. The Goat's only closed on Christmas Eve and Christmas Day. Not enough time to make the trip worthwhile."

"That's too bad. But since you'll be here, I was hoping we might be able to connect more about the family stuff." She ran her finger around the rim of her glass. "We'll head to New York right after the holidays."

"Maybe we can grab coffee before you go," I offered, though we both knew it was one of those vague suggestions people make without real commitment. Between running the Goat and caring for Luna, my free time was nonexistent.

"Sure, that would be great." Sam finished her drink and stood, leaving a generous tip. "I should check on Beau. Good to see you again."

As she turned to leave, I found myself calling after her. "Sam, wait. I really would like to get coffee, if you have time."

"I'd love it." She pulled out her phone. "Text me, and we'll make a plan."

I remembered she'd given me her number, but I hadn't put it in my cell yet. "Sorry, I must've lost that napkin you gave me."

"No worries. Give me your number, and I'll put it in my phone."

After I recited it, she sent a message right away.

"I'll be in touch," she promised, sliding her phone into her pocket. "Take care of that little girl. She's precious."

After she left, I found myself drawn to the photo of my father and Aunt Ursula outside the original Goat, which had started this whole chain of events. They looked young and hopeful, arms wrapped around each other's shoulders, proud of their new venture.

Luna's small voice interrupted my thoughts. "Mommy, I'm tired."

I turned to find her standing beside me, coloring book clutched to her chest, her eyes heavy with fatigue. The burst of energy from earlier had clearly worn off.

"Let's get you home, sweetheart," I said, brushing her flushed cheek with my fingertips. Definitely still warm.

I signaled to Miguel across the bar. "Luna's not feeling great. Can you handle closing up tonight?"

"No problem, boss." He gave Luna a gentle smile. "Feel better, *pequeña*."

I gathered her things and my own, making sure to remind Miguel to lock Holt's guitar before he left.

The temperature had dropped steadily since sunset, and the night air was biting cold when we stepped outside. Luna shivered against me despite her wool coat, and I picked her up and carried her to my truck.

While I waited for it to warm up after I started the engine, I wondered again what had happened with Holt. The way Mrs. Lopez described it—like he'd seen a ghost—made me uneasy in ways I couldn't explain.

While the drive to our house took less than five minutes, Luna fell asleep in her booster seat, her breathing soft and even. I carried her inside, straight upstairs, and gently laid her on the bed. The digital thermometer confirmed what I already knew: 100.4°F. Not high enough for the emergency room, but another in the pattern of unexplained fevers that had plagued her for months.

I measured out the children's Tylenol, coaxing her to swallow it before changing her into pajamas. Her favorite stuffed rabbit—aptly named Bunny—was clutched tightly in her arms as she drifted to sleep.

Instead of going to my own room, I crawled into bed beside her, one hand resting lightly on her chest to feel the reassuring rise and fall of her breathing. Tomorrow, I'd call her doctor and see if I could bring her in.

As I watched Luna sleep, my mind wandered to how we'd ended up here. Five years ago, my world had been soundboards and cables, working as a sound engineer for touring bands. I'd been good at my job—damn good.

CB Rice's European tour was the highlight of my career. That's where I'd met Remi Gilbert, the band's manager—tall, charming, with an affected accent that made everything sound important. Our romance had been intense and fast. Then I missed my period. Twice.

When I told him I was pregnant, his expression had shifted from shock to cold dismissal in seconds. "It isn't mine," he'd said flatly. Just like that, I was off the tour, my replacement arriving before I'd even packed my equipment.

After returning to my father's place in New Mexico, I'd built a new life, saving every penny for Luna's arrival. Eventually, I moved to Albuquerque, where there were more jobs and better childcare. Then, eight months ago, Dad called about buying the Goat. I'd been skeptical—I had no interest in a small Colorado ski town I'd never visited. But the profit potential could help with Luna's mounting medical bills.

Since the move, Luna's health had deteriorated further. The costs without Colorado's health insurance had been staggering, and instead of getting better, she'd gotten worse.

My baby girl stirred beside me, her breathing changing rhythm. I stroked her hair, humming softly until she settled again.

Tomorrow, I'd call my father and tell him about Sam, his niece. Then, I'd contact Luna's doctor's office to make an urgent appointment. And I'd reach out to Holt, if only to tell him his guitar was safe.

But tonight, I listened to the winter wind whistling outside our window and tried not to think about the blue eyes watching me from across the bar or the strange certainty that, somehow, everything in my life was about to change.

4

Holt

The digital clock on my nightstand read a few minutes before eight. Outside my window, snow drifted down in thick, lazy flakes, blanketing the Roaring Fork Ranch in unblemished white.

"Shit," I muttered, running a hand through my hair as last night's events flooded my memory.

Luna. Keltie's daughter. Those enormous brown eyes that had looked right through me, and the overwhelming sense that something was wrong with her. The feeling had hit me so hard I'd bolted from the Goat without even grabbing my guitar.

I swung my legs over the edge of the bed, the wooden floor cold beneath my bare feet. The cabin felt emptier without the Gibson propped in its usual corner.

I grabbed my phone from the nightstand, checking for messages. Nothing new from Remi, which surprised me since, previously, he was relentless in trying to reach me.

After a quick shower, I pulled jeans and a flannel shirt on, then laced up my boots. The main house would be bustling by now. Sunday morning breakfast was a new Wheaton tradition since Flynn and her husband, Irish, had moved in with their twins.

For the last couple of years, as the rest of us moved out, we'd wondered if anyone would ever live there again. The best part was that Flynn and Irish were redoing the entire place, updating it, and making it their own. I hoped that by doing so, the bad memories of our asshole father would be scraped away like old wallpaper.

The walk from my cabin took less than five minutes, but the frigid air stung my lungs with each breath. I paused halfway, taking in the view.

Music drifted from inside as I approached—Flynn's playlist of indie folk mixed with the clatter of pans and the rumble of conversation. I stomped the snow from my boots on the porch and pushed the door open.

"Look what the storm blew in," Buck called from his position at the stove, spatula in hand.

"Morning," I replied, heading straight for the coffeepot.

The dining room table was already crowded. Cord and Juni sat side by side, their honeymoon glow still evident despite the early hour. Flynn and Irish's twins, Paxon and Rooker, babbled in their high chairs while Irish tried to convince them to eat their breakfast rather than wear it. Buckaroo—Buck and TJ's two-year-old son—smooshed his pancakes with pudgy fingers as TJ wiped syrup from his cheeks while Beau and Sam sat quietly at the end of the table, taking it all in.

"*Unca* Holt!" Buckaroo squealed when he spotted me, waving syrupy fingers in my direction.

"Hey, little man," I said, taking a seat.

"Miguel called the house phone, looking for you, this morning," Flynn said, one eyebrow raised. "Said you left your guitar at the bar last night. That's not like you."

Buck glanced in my direction, but I avoided his gaze, focusing instead on pouring maple syrup over my pancakes. Buck had always been able to read me better than the others—a talent that grew more annoying with age.

"Heard a rumor that CB Rice is headed out on tour next year," he said.

"You heard right."

Flynn put her hand on my shoulder. "I'm sorry, Holt."

I focused on my plate rather than the pity in my baby sister's gaze. "Yeah, well. It is what it is."

"I hate to butt my nose in, but the stipulations of this trust are highly manipulative," said Beau, shaking his head.

Given Sam had inherited the estate where Cord was sent last year, which we subsequently found out had been in our mother's family—and that Sam was our cousin—it didn't surprise me that Beau had heard the whole story.

A heavy silence fell over the table. Our father had ruled the ranch with an iron fist for forty years. What secrets he'd taken to his grave, we might never know.

"I'm not convinced this was Dad's doing," said Cord, clearing his throat. "Something tells me our mom was involved."

"Mom, who died years before Dad did?" Flynn objected.

"She kept her share of secrets," Buck countered. "And now, Keltie Marquez, who owns the Goat, has a photograph of her aunt and father from decades ago, and I'm convinced Mom was aware of it, somehow."

I set down my fork with an unintentional clatter. "Did any of you know of Victor Marquez?"

A chorus of nos answered me.

"I spoke with Keltie yesterday," Sam said, breaking the momentary silence. "She said she and her daughter are staying here for Christmas. Seems like they're on their own."

"She has a daughter?" Juni asked, surprise evident in her voice.

"Luna," I confirmed without thinking

"She's four," Sam added.

Six pairs of eyes turned to me with varying degrees of curiosity.

"I met her last night," I explained, uncomfortable under their scrutiny. "She came to the bar, looking for her mom."

"Was she alone?" Juni asked.

"No, with an older woman. Her babysitter, I think."

"Was she okay being in a bar?" TJ wondered aloud. "That's an odd place for a kid that age."

I thought about Luna's flushed cheeks and the something in her eyes that didn't seem quite right. "She seemed… I don't know. Not sick exactly, but not entirely well either."

Flynn and TJ exchanged a glance, the kind of silent communication that happens between mothers.

"What?" I asked, noticing the look.

"Nothing," Flynn said too quickly. "Just… kids that age catch everything. Especially at this time of year."

"What would you think of inviting them to spend Christmas with us?" Sam asked. "With Buckaroo and the twins, it would be fun for Luna. And then they wouldn't be alone for the holiday."

A murmur of agreement swept around the table.

"Someone needs to ask them," TJ pointed out, glancing meaningfully in my direction.

"Why me?" I asked, though I already knew the answer.

"Because you're already halfway in love with her." Buck smirked.

"I am not," I protested, feeling the tips of my ears burn. "I barely know her."

"Then, get to know her," Flynn suggested. "While inviting her to spend Christmas here."

I pushed away from the table. "I'll think about it."

Their knowing looks followed me as I retreated to the kitchen to refill my coffee mug.

"Don't let them get to you," Sam said, appearing beside me with her own empty cup. "They're typical siblings."

"I'm fine," I said automatically.

Sam gave me a sympathetic look. "I think inviting Keltie is a good idea, regardless of whether you're interested in her romantically. This is all new for her—new town, running a business, raising a child alone. Trust me, holidays can be rough when you're flying solo."

There was a weight to her words that suggested personal experience. I studied her face, thinking about how recently she'd discovered she was our cousin.

"I'll ask," I promised. "But no matchmaking attempts from any of you."

Sam smiled, a mischievous glint in her eye. "Would we do that?"

"In a heartbeat," I grumbled, but found myself smiling too. "Seriously, though. Can I ask you something?"

"Of course."

I motioned for her to follow me out to the screened-in porch. "So, we're cousins, and you and Keltie are cousins. Does that mean…?"

Sam shook her head before I finished the question. "I'm related to you on your mom's side and to her on my grandmother's side. She was a Marquez like Keltie's dad is. Your mom wasn't related to the Marquez family. Keltie's aunt married your mother's brother."

I cocked my head, not sure I followed everything she'd said.

"Holt, if you were cousins, I'd tell you."

That was good enough for me. "Thanks," I said before heading out to my truck. "Say bye to everyone for me, would you?"

"Are you going to invite her for Christmas?"

"Yes, Sam."

As I walked away, I heard her clap.

After breakfast, I returned to my cabin and dug out my laptop. With half my earnings this coming year going to charity, I wanted to know exactly where that money was headed.

The Miracles of Hope Children's Charity website was basic but functional. Founded twenty-two years ago by an anonymous resident whose child had been diagnosed with a rare blood disorder, the organization specifically helped families in Crested Butte with kids facing serious medical conditions.

Luna's face flashed before me—those big brown eyes, the flush in her cheeks, and that inexplicable feeling that had hit me like a truck when I shook her tiny hand. The certainty that something was wrong remained—a weight in my chest I couldn't dislodge.

My phone buzzed, Remi's name flashing on the screen. I'd been expecting this call since yesterday.

"Where the hell are you?" His voice boomed through the speaker, his New York accent thickening with anger. "We had a session booked yesterday. Ben's been waiting."

"I can't do it, Remi," I said, the words burning my throat on their way out. "I can't join the tour."

Silence hung on the line for several seconds.

"Is this your idea of a negotiation tactic?" he finally asked, suspicion creeping into his tone. "Because if you want more money—"

"It's not about money," I cut him off. "It's a family situation. I can't leave Crested Butte for the next year."

"A year?" Remi's voice rose in pitch. "The tour kicks off in three weeks, Holt. We need you in the studio now."

"I know the timeline." I paced the length of my cabin, boots thudding against the wooden floor. "I wish things were different."

"This is career suicide," Remi warned. "You know that, right? Opportunities like this don't come around twice."

The weight of his words settled in my chest.

"I know," I said quietly.

"What am I supposed to tell Ben? He considers you part of the family."

I closed my eyes, realizing I should've been the one to tell him. I'd known Ben Rice my whole life, and our families were close. I should've had the courtesy to tell him before Remi.

"Let me talk to him. This is personal, man."

Remi snorted. "Personal? What it is, is bullshit."

My grip tightened on the phone. "This isn't your business, Gilbert."

"I make it my business when someone throws away their shot, Holt. I've seen it before. Usually, it's drugs or alcohol."

"It's neither," I said, frustration building.

"Right," Remi sighed. "Look, I like you. You're talented. But I can't hold this spot. If you can't commit, we'll have no choice but to find someone to take your place."

"I understand. I hope the tour's a success."

Remi was quiet for a moment. "You're making a fucking mistake, Holt."

"Wouldn't be my first," I replied, trying to keep my tone light despite the heaviness in my chest.

After we hung up, I sat on the edge of my bed, guitar-calloused fingers running through my hair. The silence of the cabin pressed in around me, broken only by the occasional sound of timber settling in the cold.

My gaze fell on the corner where my Gibson usually rested. I needed that guitar—needed its familiar weight in my hands. More than that, I needed to see Keltie again, to understand why her daughter had sparked such a visceral reaction in me.

I grabbed my truck keys and headed out into the snow.

Fifteen minutes later, I parked in front of the Goat, surprised to find the lights off. The "Open" sign was flipped to "Closed," and the handwritten note taped to the door sent a chill through me that had nothing to do with the temperature.

Closed due to family emergency.

I sat in my truck, engine idling, staring at the darkened windows. What kind of emergency? Was it the little girl? The feeling that had sent me running last night was back, stronger now.

A tap on my window made me jump. Miguel stood outside, bundled against the cold, holding a familiar guitar case.

I rolled down the window. "Miguel. What happened?"

"Figured you'd come for your guitar. Keltie asked me to lock it up last night."

"Thanks," I said when he opened the rear passenger door and set it on the seat. "Where is she? The note says 'family emergency.'"

His expression turned somber. "Luna. She's in the hospital over in Gunnison. Fever spiked real bad last night after you left. Keltie texted me at seven, asking if I could let everyone know we'd be closed today."

My stomach dropped. "Is she going to be okay?"

"Don't know, man. Keltie sounded pretty scared on the phone when she called to check in an hour ago. Said something about tests they needed to run."

"Thanks for letting me know."

As Miguel walked away, I gripped the steering wheel and a familiar certainty settled in my bones. I'd been right. Something was wrong with Luna—something serious enough to warrant a hospital visit in the middle of the night.

Without consciously deciding to, I shifted the truck into drive and headed for the highway that would take me to Gunnison. Christmas invitation or not, I needed to see for myself that the little girl with those huge brown eyes was going to be okay.

And if I was being honest, I needed to see her mother too.

5

Keltie

It was a little after ten in the morning—six hours since I'd rushed Luna to the Gunnison Valley Hospital's emergency room with a fever that had spiked to 103°F. I sat beside her bed in the pediatric bay, watching her sleep fitfully after hours of tests and medications.

"Mommy?" Luna's voice was small and raspy.

I brushed a damp curl from her forehead. "I'm right here, baby."

"When can we go home?"

"Soon, I hope," I said, forcing a smile. "The doctors are running tests to figure out why you keep getting fevers."

Luna's eyelids were already drooping. "I'm tired."

"Sleep, Luna-bug. I'll be right here."

I watched as she drifted off, the steady beep of the heart monitor a metronome tracking each moment. My own heart felt like it might burst from my chest, hammering with fear I couldn't show her.

This wasn't our first hospital visit. Over the past three months, Luna had experienced recurring fevers, growing fatigue, and most recently, unexplained bruising on her legs that the previous doctor had dismissed as "normal childhood injuries." I knew something was wrong, but each time we visited her pediatrician, we left with a different explanation—a virus, a growth phase, childhood anemia.

The curtain rustled as Dr. Patel entered, clipboard in hand. The on-call pediatrician who'd examined Luna when we arrived was new to us. Unlike the others, he hadn't dismissed my concerns.

"Ms. Marquez? May I speak with you?"

I squeezed Luna's hand before stepping right outside the curtained area.

"We have some preliminary blood results," he said, his expression serious. "Luna's counts are concerning enough that I believe she should see specialists in Denver for a more thorough evaluation."

The floor felt like it tilted beneath me. "Are you saying…? What are you saying?"

Dr. Patel lowered his voice. "These symptoms, along with the blood work, could indicate several conditions."

"Right," I muttered, hating that I was once again dealing with someone unwilling to tell it to me straight. Maybe it was my sheer exhaustion or that hospitals didn't give a shit about the people who had to sit at their kid's bedside for hours on end, but something inside me snapped. "What do you *think* it is?"

"Given the symptoms, I'd like to determine whether her blood-forming tissues have been compromised. Further testing would help us do that."

Blood-forming tissues? What in the hell did that mean?

"Specifically certain kinds of cancer," he added before I could ask. His words struck me in the same way it would have if he'd reached out and punched me. My daughter—my bright, beautiful four-year-old— might have *cancer*.

"I've made some calls," the doctor continued, his voice fading in and out like a bad radio signal as my mind reeled. "There's an excellent pediatric oncology team at Children's Hospital in Denver. They can see Luna next week. In the meantime, we'll stabilize her fever and run additional tests here."

I was unable to form words.

"Ms. Marquez? Is there someone I can call for you? A family member or friend?"

"No." The word came out sharper than I'd intended. "No, thank you. I need a minute."

"Of course. Luna's sleeping now. I can ask one of the nurses to step in to give you a few minutes if you'd like."

I glanced at my daughter, her favorite stuffed rabbit tucked beside her. Bunny had been through every fever, every doctor's visit, every late-night terror. Now, it might be facing something far worse with her.

"I'll be right back," I whispered, though she couldn't hear me.

The walk to the exit felt endless. Nurses and staff blurred past as I moved on autopilot, walking through the automatic doors and out into the frigid December air.

Only when I reached my truck did I finally break. My legs gave way, and my knees hit the frozen asphalt with a dull thud. The tears came without sound at first, then built into gut-wrenching sobs that tore through my chest.

Luna. My baby. My entire world. The thought of losing her was unimaginable. Yet here I was, forced to imagine it.

Would our new insurance cover all these tests? What would happen to the bar while we were in Denver? The questions spiraled, each more overwhelming than the last.

A warm hand touched my shoulder, gentle but firm. I startled, looking up through tear-blurred eyes.

Holt Wheaton crouched beside me, his blue eyes filled with concern. Without a word, he embraced me.

I should have pulled away. I barely knew this man. Instead, I collapsed against his chest, my fingers clutching the fabric of his jacket as the sobs overtook me again. He held me, one hand stroking my hair, the other arm wrapped around me, saying nothing, asking nothing.

When the worst of it finally passed, leaving me hollow and spent, I wiped roughly at my face.

"What are you doing here?" My voice was hoarse from crying.

"I stopped by the Goat, and Miguel told me you brought Luna here." Holt's gaze was steady. "I thought you might need…" He trailed off, not finishing the sentence.

Need what? Need him? The thought should have annoyed me, but instead, a treacherous part of me whispered that maybe I did.

He handed me a bandana from his pocket. "Here."

I took it and wiped my face. "Thanks. I, uh, should go inside."

"Let me walk you." He stood, extending his hand. After a moment's hesitation, I took it.

As we passed his truck, Holt stopped. "Hold on a sec." He reached inside and pulled out his guitar case. "Maybe this will help. You know, kids usually like music."

The simple gesture—so unexpected, so thoughtful—nearly broke me again.

Inside, Dr. Patel was waiting near the nurses' station. His eyes flickered between Holt and me.

"Ms. Marquez, you're here. Good." He glanced at Holt. "Is this Luna's father?"

"No," I said quickly. "He's a friend."

Holt extended his hand. "Holt Wheaton. Here for support."

"I'd like a private word with Ms. Marquez, if you don't mind," said Dr Patel.

"No problem." Holt took a step away. "I'll wait over there."

As he moved, I heard Luna's voice from her bay— "Mr. Wheaton!"—her tone brightening in a way that defied how sick she was. Holt looked at me questioningly. I nodded, and he disappeared behind the curtain as the doctor led me over to the nurses' station.

"I've arranged an appointment with the oncology team in Denver for December 30," he said once we were seated. "I know that's a week away, but they're fitting us in as soon as they can. In the meantime, we'll monitor Luna closely. I'll send you home later with medication to manage her fever."

The word "oncology" made my stomach clench. "I thought you said you wanted to rule out cancer?"

"Based on her symptoms and the preliminary results, it's one possibility, but other conditions can present similarly. The specialists will conduct bone marrow tests and more comprehensive blood work."

I gripped the arms of my chair. "And if it is…?"

Dr. Patel's expression softened. "Pediatric acute lymphoblastic leukemia—or ALL—has one of the highest success rates among childhood cancers. Over ninety percent of children achieve remission with proper treatment."

"As in chemotherapy? Radiation?" The words felt foreign on my tongue.

"Potentially, yes. But let's not get ahead of ourselves. The first step is a definitive diagnosis."

"When can I take her home?" I asked, struggling to process it all.

"We'll keep her for a few more hours to make sure the fever stays down and to finish the IV antibiotics."

I paused outside the curtain of Luna's bay, struck by the scene inside. Holt sat in the chair by the bed, guitar balanced on his knee, playing a soft melody while Luna watched with wide, enchanted eyes.

"Then the unicorn said to the little girl, 'If you can find the secret pond where the stars swim at night, I'll show you how to hear the music of the forest,'" Holt was saying, weaving a story between gentle strums of his guitar.

"What happened next?" Luna asked, completely captivated.

"Well, the little girl searched high and low. She climbed mountains and crossed rivers. And when she was about to give up…"

"She found it!" Luna exclaimed.

Holt grinned. "How did you know?"

"Because she didn't give up! That's what Mommy always says. Don't give up."

Something in my chest cracked open at her words. I stepped into the bay, and Luna's face lit up further.

"Mommy! Mr. Wheaton is telling me a story about a magic pond!"

I smiled, the gesture pulling at muscles tight from crying. "I heard. It sounds wonderful."

Holt looked up at me, his eyes asking silent questions. I gave a small shake of my head, a promise to explain later.

"Can Mr. Wheaton finish the story before we go home?" Luna asked.

"Actually, sweetie, we need to stay a bit longer. The doctors want to make sure your fever stays down."

"But I feel better now." As if to prove her point, she sat up straighter, though the effort clearly cost her.

"I'm glad," I said, sitting beside her and taking her hand. "But we still need to listen to the doctors."

Holt stood. "I should let you rest."

"No!" Luna protested, her fingers reaching for his sleeve. "Please stay. Please finish the story."

He glanced at me, and I surprised myself by nodding. "Stay. Unless there's somewhere else you need to be."

The relief on Luna's face was worth whatever complications I was inviting by allowing this beautiful, magnetic stranger deeper into our lives.

Holt settled into the chair to resume his story. Luna's eyes grew heavy as he played, her body relaxing into sleep even as she fought to hear the end of the tale.

When he finished, she was sound asleep, her breathing deep and even. Holt placed his guitar in its case and stood again, gesturing toward the hallway. I followed him out.

"Thank you," I said quietly. "It was nice to see her smile."

His gaze was intense. "I overheard a bit of what the doctor said."

I stiffened. "You were listening?"

"Not intentionally." He ran a hand through his hair. "Look, I know this is presumptuous, but I want to help. I can drive you both to Denver for the appointment."

"That's really not necessary. We'll be fine."

He hesitated, indecision flickering across his face. "The thing is…" He stopped, then seemed to come to a decision. "I need to tell you something strange."

"Strange how?"

"I know we barely know each other," he said quietly. "And I don't want to overstep. But when I met Luna last night…" He paused, seeming to reconsider his words. "She's a special kid. I could tell right away."

"Thanks." I was tired but grateful for the acknowledgment.

"And when Miguel told me she was in the hospital, I thought you could both use a friend."

I studied his face, looking for ulterior motives, but finding only genuine concern. His showing up was unexpected, yes, but his support—especially the way he'd connected with Luna—felt like a lifeline on one of the worst days of my life.

He cleared his throat. "Anyway, the offer stands."

"Why would you do that? You barely know us."

The question seemed to surprise him. "Because you need help, and I can give it. Because Luna is…" He trailed off, then finished simply, "Because it matters."

We stood in silence for a long moment, the hospital sounds fading to background noise. Part of me screamed not to trust him, not to need anyone. That part had kept me safe, kept Luna safe, for four years. But a smaller voice whispered that Luna deserved every advantage, every kindness the world might offer.

"The appointment isn't until next week," I finally said. "December 30."

"Just let me know."

"I'll think about it."

"Good." He hesitated. "Actually, there was another reason I came looking for you tonight. Sam and my family wanted me to invite you and Luna to spend Christmas with us at the ranch. There's plenty of room, and with all the kids there now, it would be fun for Luna. One of the ranch hands dresses up as Santa every year."

The invitation caught me off guard. Christmas was two days away, and I'd planned for Luna and me to have a quiet celebration at home. But looking at my sleeping daughter, I wondered if a family Christmas—even with strangers—might be better than the two of us alone in our house with this new fear hanging over us.

"I'll think about that too," I said. "If Luna feels up to it."

"Fair enough." He glanced at his watch. "Can I get you anything? Something to eat or drink?"

His kindness nearly undid me again. "Coffee would be amazing."

"Coming right up." He squeezed my shoulder lightly, the touch sending an unexpected current through me despite my exhaustion. "By the way, you should know—Luna made me promise to teach her how to play guitar when she feels better."

A smile tugged at my lips, the first real one in hours. "Did she, now?"

"She's very persuasive. Must get that from her mother," he added with a wink.

6

Holt

After a restless night of worrying about Luna and her mother, one thought kept circling through my mind: I hadn't given Keltie my number.

How had I spent hours with her at the hospital—playing guitar for Luna, bringing coffee, offering to drive them to Denver—and somehow forgotten something so basic? I knew the Goat had my contact information, but it was Christmas Eve. Keltie had mentioned the bar would be closed today and tomorrow.

Rolling out of bed, I pulled on a clean shirt and jeans, grabbed my keys, and headed for my truck. I'd drive into town, maybe see if anyone who could connect us was at the Goat, or maybe stop by Miguel's and see if he'd put me in contact with her.

I'd gone out to my truck, gotten in, and was about to pull away from the cabin when I hit the brakes instead and put it in park. What in the hell was I doing?

I cut the engine and went inside.

For the next hour, I paced the wooden floors, picking up my phone and setting it down again, unable to decide on a course of action. I had Miguel's number, but if I called him, I'd have to explain why I needed to reach Keltie so urgently.

A knock at the door interrupted my spiraling thoughts. I pulled it open to find Sam and Juni standing on my porch.

"So?" Sam asked, pushing past me into the cabin. "Are they coming for Christmas?"

Juni followed with an apologetic smile. "Sam's been planning since you left yesterday."

"Planning what?" I asked, closing the door behind them.

"Operation Christmas Miracle," Sam declared, unwinding her scarf. "We need to know if Keltie and Luna are coming, so we can prepare. Did you invite them like you promised?"

"I mentioned it at the hospital."

"The hospital?" Juni gasped.

"Luna was, err, sick. Well, not really sick per se. At least not the contagious kind of sick."

"What do you mean?" Sam asked.

I hesitated, not wanting to share too much of Keltie's private business. "The doctors aren't exactly sure what's wrong. They're running more tests, and she has to take her to Denver next week."

"You're sure it isn't contagious?" Juni asked.

Based on what I'd overheard, it was much worse than that. "Positive," I responded instead of giving details.

Sam's expression softened. "All the more reason they shouldn't be alone for Christmas."

Before I could reply, she pulled out her phone and began typing.

"You have her number?" I couldn't keep the surprise from my voice.

"I do." Sam glanced up with a knowing smile. "Why? Did you want it?" She winked.

"No. I mean yes," I mumbled, watching her phone for Keltie's response. When no immediate reply came, I felt my patience wearing thin. "Maybe you should call her."

Juni laughed. "It's been thirty seconds, Holt."

"She might be busy with Luna," I reasoned.

Sam and Juni exchanged a look that made me want to crawl under the floorboards.

"Fine," Sam said, pressing the call button. "But only because you look like you might spontaneously combust if I don't." I could hear it ringing on the other end, then Keltie's voice.

"Hey, it's Sam. Holt mentioned you had to take Luna to the hospital last night. How is she this morning?"

As I listened to Keltie thank her for asking, then say her daughter seemed much better now, I shifted my weight, fighting the urge to grab the phone.

"Actually," Sam continued, "I'm with Juni and Holt right now, and he'd really like to talk to you. Mind if I put him on?"

She handed me the phone before Keltie could respond. I took it, shooting her a glare before stepping toward the window for some semblance of privacy.

"Hey," I said, my voice rougher than I'd intended. "I realized I never gave you my number. I wasn't sure if you had it from the Goat."

"Actually," Keltie replied, a smile in her voice, "Miguel called this morning to check on Luna. He gave it to me then."

"Oh. Great." I cleared my throat. "How is she doing today?"

"A lot better. The fever's down, and her energy is good. She's currently dismantling the living room to build a fort."

Relief flooded through me. "That's good to hear."

"It is," she agreed. "Though my sofa cushions might disagree."

I chuckled, then remembered why Sam had called in the first place. "Listen, about Christmas at the ranch—"

Sam snatched the phone from my hand before I could finish. "Keltie? Sam again. Sorry to interrupt. The schedule is dinner, followed by a visit from Santa. After that, Buck will read *the Night Before Christmas*. By then, we figured the kids will be worn out enough that they'll fall asleep before he gets to the end."

I watched Sam's face anxiously, trying to gauge Keltie's response from her reactions. When she smiled, I felt a weight lift from my shoulders.

"Oh, and I talked to Flynn. There's room for you and Luna to stay in the main house tonight," Sam continued. "It has loads of guest rooms. And she said that with Luna, Buckaroo, and the twins, it'll be the most exciting Christmas they've had in years."

Sam looked over at me. "Do you want Holt to come pick you up and drive you out here?" She paused, listening. "Oh, that sounds perfect. We'll see you later this afternoon."

She ended the call and shoved the phone in her pocket before I could ask her to send me Keltie's number. "I guess Luna's been pleading with her mom about having breakfast at McGill's, but after that, she'll get their stuff together and head out."

"It's settled, then," I said, trying to sound casual despite the ridiculous grin threatening to take over my face.

"Which means we need to get moving. Juni and I are going shopping for gifts for Keltie. You need to get stockings for her and Luna—they can be personalized at Lucy's Toy Shop—plus something for Santa to bring for Luna."

She scribbled the list on a notepad and handed it to me. "Get going. We have a lot to do before they arrive."

Thirty minutes later, I pulled up in front of the toy store, which happened to be next door to McGill's. After I cut the engine and jumped out, I spotted Keltie and Luna sitting at the table closest to the front window. The moment the little girl saw me, her entire face lit up, and she waved frantically.

I couldn't help but wave too, changing course and heading into the diner instead. I'd handle the shopping after saying hello.

"Mr. Wheaton!" Luna called as I approached their table. "We're having pancakes!"

"I can see that," I said, smiling at the maple syrup already smeared across her cheek. "They look delicious."

"Would you like to join us?" Keltie asked, gesturing to the empty chair.

"I'd love to," I replied, sliding into the seat. Stacey, who I'd gone to high school with and whose family owned McGill's, appeared almost immediately. "What can I get you, cowboy?"

I chuckled. "You know the drill. Coffee before I can even look at the menu."

"You got it," she said, turning on her heel to fetch me a cup.

"Aren't you hungry?" Luna asked.

"I am, actually," I admitted. I glanced at the specials board, deciding on the Smoked Salmon Benedict.

"Mommy said we might spend Christmas at your ranch," Luna informed me solemnly. "She said Santa will know where to find me."

"He absolutely will," I assured her, then remembered the errand I still needed to run. "Actually, I need to step next door for a minute. Business to take care of. But I won't be long, okay?"

Luna's attention was already on her pancakes.

I found Stacey near the counter and placed my order before rushing out.

"You want your coffee to go?" she asked.

"Nah, I won't be gone that long."

The bell above the door jingled as I entered the toy store that always smelled like cinnamon and pine. Holiday music played softly, and when Lucy emerged from behind a display, her face lit up. "Holt Wheaton! What brings you in? Last-minute shopping?"

"Hey, Lucy. I need some Christmas magic."

"What kind of magic are we talking about?"

I pulled out Sam's list. "Personalized stockings for two special guests at the ranch tomorrow—Keltie and Luna. And I need toys for Luna. She's four."

Lucy raised an eyebrow. "The little girl who comes in with the new owner of the Goat? Sweet child."

"That's the one," I confirmed, already moving through the aisles.

A stuffed unicorn with a rainbow mane and silver hooves caught my eye immediately. "This," I said, grabbing it. Nearby was a matching robe-and-slipper set with the mystical animal dancing across a starry sky. "And these."

I continued through the store, adding picture books, a children's keyboard, art supplies, and a doctor's kit. Something about the last item felt right—maybe it would help Luna process her hospital experience.

"Holt," Lucy called, laughing. "I think that's enough to keep any child occupied until next Christmas."

I looked down at the growing pile in my arms. "Too much?"

"Well, it's not my place to say, but…" She gestured to the mountain of toys.

"I'm gettin' it all," I decided after thoughts of what I'd heard the doctor tell Keltie last night echoed in my head.

I handed over my credit card without asking for the total.

"It's nice, what you're doing," she said as she rang up the purchases. "Keltie and her daughter are new in town. No family around for the holidays."

"They're not alone anymore," I said, the words coming out before I could think about them.

She smiled. "I'll get this delivered by midafternoon," she said, handing me the receipt and my card.

"You're the best, Lucy."

I hurried over to McGill's, where Stacey was setting my breakfast on the table. "Sorry for the delay," I said, sliding into my seat.

"Where did you go?" Luna asked immediately, curiosity shining in her eyes.

I glanced at Keltie, then leaned conspiratorially toward Luna. "Well, I happened to run into Santa at the toy store. He asked if I knew whether a girl named Luna would be at the Roaring Fork Ranch tonight, and if he should bring her presents there."

Luna gasped, her eyes growing impossibly wider. "Really? *You saw Santa?*" She turned to her mother, bouncing in her seat. "Mommy, Santa knows I'm gonna be there!"

Keltie shot me a look that was half amusement, half exasperation. I mouthed "sorry" over Luna's head, realizing I might have overstepped. But when she rolled her eyes and smiled, I knew we were okay.

"Can we go now?" Luna asked, already done with her pancakes. "Please, Mommy?"

"We need to go home and pack first," Keltie said, then looked at me. "If you don't mind giving us a ride afterward…"

"I'd be happy to," I replied. "Just tell me when and where."

Keltie wrote her address on a napkin and slid it across the table. "Give us about an hour?"

When the check came, I grabbed it before she could reach for it.

"Holt, you don't have to—"

"My treat," I insisted, handing my card to Stacey, whose knowing grin made my cheeks flush. Yeah, I was smitten, and I knew damn well it was obvious.

As I was walking to my truck after finishing my breakfast, something in the window of the store on the opposite side of the toy shop caught my eye. I went in and made the purchase, but rather than having it wrapped, I decided this one I wanted to take care of myself.

I glanced at the address Keltie had given me, then up at one of my favorite houses in downtown Crested

Butte. Situated a couple of blocks from the Goat, it was painted a deep-red color with white shutters and had a porch with a swing that, today, appeared buried in snow.

I pulled up in front, cut the engine, and when I jumped out, noticed a familiar figure walking down the street—Remi Gilbert, CB Rice's manager. What was he doing here? He lived on the East Coast, as far as I knew, and I doubted Ben would've invited the guy to spend the holidays with his family.

Remi raised his head and waved, then walked in my direction. I met him halfway.

"Holt," he said with genuine surprise in his voice. "What brings you into town?"

"Visiting a friend," I replied vaguely. "You?"

"Same." He shrugged.

An awkward silence stretched between us.

"Listen," he finally said. "The band's hit a snag with your replacement. Ben's not happy with any of the candidates."

I shifted uncomfortably. "Nothing's changed, Remi."

"This is career suicide," he said, shaking his head. "You know that, right?"

"My hands are tied," I said simply. "There's nothing I can do."

Remi studied me for a long moment. "Your call. Merry Christmas, man."

"Merry Christmas," I replied as he walked away.

I headed up the path to Keltie's front door and knocked. When she answered, the warm welcome I'd expected was nowhere to be seen. Her face was tight and her body language closed off.

"Luna," she called over her shoulder, her eyes never leaving mine. "Go upstairs and get Bunny. You don't want to forget him."

Once Luna's footsteps faded, Keltie crossed her arms. "I think Christmas might be too much, after all."

"What?" I took a step forward, confused by the sudden shift. "Luna was so excited at breakfast."

"I decided it would be better if we stayed home."

Something had changed in the short time since the diner. I replayed every moment of our breakfast, trying to identify what I might have done wrong.

"Keltie," I said softly. "What's going on? If I did something to upset you—"

"I'm just worried about Luna."

I shook my head. "Try again, darlin'. This isn't worry. You're not happy with me, and unless you tell me why, there's nothin' I can do to fix it. I'm not about to let Luna's Christmas be ruined because I'm a jackass."

She folded her arms, and her gaze flicked toward the street. "Who was that man you were talking to?"

"Remi? He's CB Rice's manager."

"I guess you know him well since you're in the band."

There was something in her tone I couldn't place—anger, certainly, but something deeper. Fear?

I sighed. "Yes, I was in the band, but I don't know him well."

"Was?"

"It's a long story," I said. "But they're heading out on a world tour, and I won't be going with them."

Her eyes scrunched.

"I have, err, family obligations that prevent me from being gone that long."

Before she could say anything else, Luna came bounding down the stairs, the well-loved stuffed rabbit she'd had at the hospital clutched in her arms.

"I'm ready!" she announced. "Is Santa waiting for us?"

I looked at Keltie, mouthing "Santa" with pleading eyes. Whatever had upset her, I didn't want Luna to miss out because of it.

Keltie's expression softened as she took in her daughter's excitement. "All right." She sighed. "We'll go. But if you get another fever, we won't be able to stay." I caught her pained expression when the smile left Luna's face.

"I understand," the little girl said, looking down at the floor.

"Maybe I should drive. You know, in case something comes up."

I shook my head. "If you need to come home, I'll give you a lift."

"If you're sure…"

"Positive."

We got Luna's booster seat out of Keltie's vehicle and were on our way to put it in my truck when I noticed her glancing in the direction Remi had gone. The odd expression I'd caught earlier resurfaced. There was a story there, but now wasn't the time for me to ask what it was. Knowing Remi, he'd frequented the Goat and was an asshole to her or her staff. That was the kind of guy he was.

Like my reasons for being unable to go out on tour, Keltie obviously had reasons for not liking a guy I didn't much care for myself.

I felt a tug on my sleeve. "Mr. Wheaton? Are we gonna get in? It's kinda cold out."

"Yeah, sorry, sweetheart." I opened the door, and after I attached the booster seat, she climbed into the cab.

When I turned to help Keltie in, she was standing close enough that if I leaned forward a little, I could kiss her. And why did that feel like the most natural thing in the world? Rather than resist, I brushed her cheek with my lips. "Merry Christmas, Keltie."

"Merry Christmas, Holt," she said with wide eyes when I stepped to the side to let her get in.

7

Keltie

My mind raced as I stared at the truck I was leaving parked in front of my house. The kiss Holt had placed on my cheek still burned there, but that wasn't what had unsettled me.

Remi Gilbert. In Crested Butte. Five years after he'd dismissed me from his life as if my unborn baby and I were nothing.

I'd never expected to see him here, of all places. The last I knew, he had apartments in both London and Manhattan, orchestrating CB Rice's rise to international fame from one of his penthouse offices. I hadn't kept tabs on him—actively avoided any news about him, in fact—but his sudden appearance in this small mountain town couldn't be a coincidence.

My stomach knotted. What if he saw Luna? Would he even recognize his own daughter? Would he care? The man who'd flatly stated, "*It* isn't mine," when I told him I was pregnant had no right to her now, but the fear of him somehow entering our lives sent ice through my veins.

"You okay?" Holt's words pulled me from my thoughts.

I nodded, unable to trust my voice. Luna was buckled safely in her seat, humming while clutching Bunny to her chest.

As we drove out of town, I caught Holt glancing at me, concern etched on his face. Something about him unnerved me in a completely different way than Remi did. He seemed to read me too easily, as if we'd known each other for years instead of weeks.

"Luna, have you ever been on a ranch before?" Holt asked, his eyes finding her in the rearview mirror.

"Nope!" she replied, bouncing in her seat. "Do you have horses?"

"We sure do. And cows, too."

"Can I see them?"

"Absolutely," Holt promised. "When the weather warms up, I'll show you everything—if it's okay with your mama."

His easy way with Luna only deepened my confusion. After Remi, I'd sworn off anyone connected to the music industry. In my experience, they were all players and narcissists who focused only on them-selves. But Holt seemed genuinely caring, almost protective of us both, which made no sense. We were practically strangers.

Yet I couldn't deny the pull between us—the way my body responded when he was near, the relief I'd felt when he appeared at the hospital. None of it made sense. Especially the comfort I'd felt when he held me in his arms after I'd broken down in the parking lot.

I took a deep breath, deciding not to spoil Christmas by overthinking everything. Luna deserved this day, this experience. She'd been through enough already without my paranoia casting a shadow over it.

I consciously relaxed my shoulders and loosened my grip on the door handle.

Holt smiled.

"What?" I asked.

"That's better," he replied, eyes back on the road.

Of course he'd noticed. The man didn't miss a thing.

The Roaring Fork Ranch sprawled across the valley, the main house rising from the snow like something from a movie. The large, rustic log structure with a wraparound porch gleamed with the Christmas lights strung along every eave. Smoke curled from multiple chimneys, and several vehicles were already parked in the circular drive.

"Wow," Luna whispered from her booster seat.

"Home sweet home," Holt said with an edge to his voice that made me wonder.

He parked beside a silver SUV and turned off the engine. "Ready?"

Luna was already unbuckling her seat belt. "I am!"

The front door swung open before we reached it, and Holt's sister, Flynn, stepped out. Her smile warm and welcoming despite the cold.

"I remember you from the other night," I replied, gazing into blue eyes like her brother's. "This is Luna."

Flynn knelt down to her level. "Hello, there! We're so excited you came to spend Christmas with us. There are some other kids inside, who can't wait to meet you."

Luna beamed, her shyness forgotten in the face of Flynn's warmth.

The interior of the ranch house was even more impressive than the exterior—soaring ceilings with exposed beams, a massive stone fireplace, and tasteful, comfortable furniture that looked both expensive and lived-in. A towering Christmas tree dominated one corner of the great room, surrounded by so many wrapped gifts that I wondered if they'd bought out every store in the state.

Sam and Juni emerged from the kitchen together.

"Keltie! You made it!" Sam hurried over, embracing me like we were old friends rather than newly discovered cousins.

Juni gave me a quick hug. "I'm so glad you could come. We've heard so much about Luna."

"You have?" I asked, surprised.

Sam's eyes twinkled. "Holt may have mentioned her once or twice."

I felt a blush creep up my neck and busied myself unwinding Luna's scarf.

TJ approached, carrying a toddler on her hip. "Great to see you again, Keltie. This little monster is Buckaroo."

The boy waved shyly at Luna, his chubby fingers wiggling. "Hi," he said, his face partially hidden against his mother's shoulder.

"Paxon and Rooker are excited to have another playmate," TJ said, nodding toward the twins. "They've been jabbering about 'new friend' all morning."

"Welcome to the madhouse," Irish, Flynn's husband, said with a grin from the living room, where he was supervising the twins.

Within minutes, Luna was on the floor with the other children, showing Buckaroo her beloved Bunny while the twins watched with fascination. Paxon—or maybe it was Rooker—reached out to touch Bunny's ear, and Luna gently showed him how to pet the stuffed animal "nice and soft."

"That didn't take long," Sam laughed, watching them interact.

"She doesn't get much time with other kids," I admitted. "I work a lot."

Flynn linked her arm through mine. "Well, she's in heaven now. Would you like some hot chocolate? I just made a fresh batch. You have the option of the adult version or the kid friendly one."

"Adult version, please."

As we moved toward the kitchen, I glanced at Luna, feeling the familiar pang of guilt that came with being a single parent and knowing she'd never have siblings of her own. As an only child myself, I'd always dreamed of having more than one, of giving my children the big family I never had. I hadn't planned on having Luna when I did—hadn't planned on doing it alone—but I wouldn't change it for anything. She was my entire world.

The kitchen was as impressive as the rest of the house—a chef's dream, with gleaming appliances and enough counter space to prepare a feast. Flynn ladled rich hot chocolate into mugs while Sam added whipped cream, along with a shot of butterscotch schnapps.

"Luna's adorable," Flynn said, handing me a mug. "She looks like you."

"That's what everyone says," I replied, though I knew if anyone saw her with Remi, they'd notice she also looked like him.

Through the open doorway, I could see Holt in the great room, down on all fours, giving the twins "horseback" rides while Luna and Buckaroo waited their turns, clapping and giggling. Something in my chest tightened while watching him. He was so at ease with the children, so naturally playful and gentle.

A man like that—a cowboy through and through, but also a gentleman who clearly cared deeply about family—was exactly the kind of man I'd once dreamed of marrying. The kind of man who'd make a wonderful father.

"He's good with kids, isn't he?" Sam's voice came from beside me, startling me from my thoughts.

I took a sip of chocolate to hide my embarrassment at being caught staring.

"Just so you know," Sam said quietly, leaning closer. "When you're not looking, he watches you the same way."

I nearly choked on my drink. "We barely know each other."

Sam shrugged. "Sometimes, that doesn't matter."

Before I could respond, Buck entered, stomping snow from his boots. "Sorry I'm late," he said. "Had to finish up some work."

"Buck!" Flynn exclaimed. "You promised no work on Christmas Eve."

He grinned, the family resemblance to Holt unmistakable. "Just a quick call. Had to make sure everything's set for tomorrow." He spotted me and waved. "Hey, Keltie. I'm Buck, the oldest and wisest of the Wheaton clan."

I remembered meeting all of them at the Goat but appreciated the reminder of each of their names.

"Don't believe a word he says," another man said, joining us. "I'm Cord. The one with actual wisdom."

I laughed as the brothers playfully shoved each other, their easy camaraderie making me smile.

"Is Porter coming tonight?" Flynn asked, her expression hopeful.

Buck shook his head. "Not looking likely. He and Cici are stuck in Parlin. The roads are getting bad."

Flynn's face fell, but she quickly recovered.

Dinner was a full Christmas Eve feast, with prime rib, ham, turkey, and every side dish imaginable. Luna sat between Buckaroo and one of the twins, all three of them in booster seats, while the other twin insisted on sitting on his father's lap.

"Flynn is an amazing cook," Holt whispered from beside me. "She's been running the ranch kitchen since she was sixteen."

I looked at the spread with newfound appreciation. "Everything looks delicious."

I found myself relaxing into the warmth of this family gathering in a way I hadn't expected. Luna was thriving, chattering happily with Buckaroo and occasionally looking over at me with a smile that made my heart swell.

"This is the bestest Christmas ever," she declared mid meal, chocolate smudged on her cheek.

Across the table, Flynn's eyes glistened with tears. Holt, seated beside me, straightened, his attention immediately on his sister.

"Flynn?" he asked softly. "You okay, sis?"

She dabbed at her eyes with her napkin. "I'm fine. It's just—this is the kind of Christmas I always dreamed we'd have someday."

Something passed between the siblings then—a shared understanding that spoke of old wounds. Cord reached over and squeezed Flynn's hand while Buck's expression darkened momentarily.

"Well, now, we do," Holt said, his voice gentle. "And it's only going to get better from here."

Flynn smiled, visibly pulling herself together. "The only thing that would make tonight better was if Porter was here too."

"He'll be here in spirit," Cord assured her. "And we'll talk to him later."

The mood lightened as Sam, Juni, and Juni's mom brought in dessert—an array of pies and cookies that had Luna's eyes growing wide with excitement.

"Remember the rules," I cautioned her. "One sweet tonight, one tomorrow."

Her lower lip jutted out in a familiar pout, but she said okay.

After dinner and the visit from "Santa," Buck gathered everyone for the reading of *The Night Before Christmas*. I was stunned by how engaged the three boys were. They couldn't be more than two, three at the most, yet they sat still and listened.

By the time he finished, all four kids were drowsy, fighting to keep their eyes open. Luna had crawled into my lap midway through the story, her head now heavy against my shoulder.

"I think someone's ready for bed," I whispered, stroking her hair.

"Let me help," Holt offered, standing and holding out his arms. "I can carry her to your room."

Too tired to object, Luna went willingly into his arms, her own wrapping around his neck as her eyes fluttered closed.

Flynn led us to a spacious suite with a bedroom and an adjoining sitting area that had a fireplace, sofa, and chairs.

"I thought you two would be most comfortable here," she explained. "The bathroom is through that door, and there are extra blankets in the chest if you need them."

"It's beautiful," I said, genuinely awed by the room's elegance. "Thank you for everything."

"It's our pleasure," she replied, squeezing my arm. "Merry Christmas, Keltie."

After she left, Holt gently laid Luna on the bed. I removed her shoes and covered her with the plush duvet, placing Bunny within easy reach.

"She's out cold," I whispered, tucking a curl behind her ear.

"Long day," Holt said. "Lots of excitement."

We returned to the sitting area, where Holt gestured toward the hearth. "Would you like a fire? Gets chilly up here at night."

"That would be nice."

He knelt in front of the fireplace, arranging kindling and logs like it was something he could do in his sleep. Within minutes, a warm glow spread throughout the room.

"Thank you," I said. "Today has been… unexpected, but wonderful."

"I'm glad you came," he replied, dusting his hands on his jeans as he stood. "I should probably let you sleep."

"Stay," I said, surprising myself with the invitation. "Just for a bit. Unless you're tired."

Something flickered in his eyes—surprise, pleasure, I couldn't tell. "I'd like that."

He settled beside me on the sofa, both of us quiet at first. The events from the last couple of days swirled in my mind—Luna's hospital visit, Remi's unexpected appearance, this beautiful Christmas Eve with the Wheatons. It was too much to process, yet sitting here with Holt made it all seem manageable.

I turned to find him watching me, those blue eyes intense in the firelight.

8

The light cast dancing shadows across Keltie's face, highlighting the delicate curve of her cheekbones and the thoughtful expression in her eyes. We sat in comfortable silence, the crackle of the logs the only sound beyond Luna's soft breathing from the next room.

I couldn't remember the last time I'd felt this content simply sitting with someone. No expectations. No pressure. The rock star life I'd lived for the past few years had been a blur of venues, hotels, and faces—rarely allowing for moments like this.

When she caught me watching her, a flush crept across her cheeks. "What?"

"Nothing," I said, though it was everything. The way her dark curls fell loose around her shoulders. The amber flecks in her eyes that caught the firelight. The strength I sensed beneath her vulnerability. Everything about her drew me in, in a way I couldn't explain.

Keltie pulled her legs up under her, getting comfortable on the sofa. "Earlier, at my house, you said something about family obligations keeping you from touring with CB Rice. I'm guessing there's a story there."

I rested against the sofa, stretching my legs out in front of me. "There is. Not a short one, either."

"I've got time," she said, a soft smile playing on her lips. "Unless you'd rather not talk about it."

I hesitated, weighing how much to share. The trust wasn't something the Wheatons discussed with outsiders. Even the ranch hands who'd worked for our family for generations didn't know the details. But looking at Keltie, I realized I didn't think of her as an outsider anymore. Something about her felt safe—like she belonged here.

"Have you heard much about our family's ranch?" I asked.

She shook her head.

"As you know, it's called the Roaring Fork. Been in my father's family since the eighteen hundreds. Anyway, after he died, we found out about something called the Roaring Fork Trust." I took a deep breath, wondering where to begin. "At first, we thought this thing was his doing—controlling bastard that he was. However, now, we aren't so sure."

Her head cocked, and I chuckled.

"I told you this was a long story."

"I'm still with you."

"Anyway, after he died, his lawyer called us in for the reading of the will. That's when we learned about the trust and its, err, *unusual* stipulations. The entire ranch—everything—was placed in a trust with specific conditions that we eventually learned each of the siblings had to meet. If we didn't, it would all be sold and given to charity."

Her brow furrowed. "What kind of conditions?"

"Weird ones. Buck had to live on the ranch for a year. He'd left right out of high school, swearing he'd never be back after the way our father treated him." I ran a hand through my hair, memories of those tense family dinners surfacing. "Our old man was a tough guy to live with. Hardest on Buck."

"It must have been difficult for him."

"Understatement of the century," I said, remembering the day Six-pack had delivered the news. "Buck was working for the CIA, living his own life. Had to drop everything and live on a ranch he didn't plan to see again."

I shifted, noticing how intently Keltie was listening.

"Our father had a way of making everyone around him feel small. For Buck, it was worse. Everything he did was wrong in our dad's eyes. When he left for college, Roscoe—that was our father's name—threatened to cut him off completely. Said if he turned his back on the ranch, he'd never own a square foot of it."

"That was harsh," Keltie murmured.

"Right? But then he met TJ, fell in love, and now, they've got Buckaroo. What seemed like a punishment ended up being the best thing for him." I smiled, thinking of how my brother had transformed from the tightly wound man he'd been to the contented husband and father he was now.

"TJ's a journalist, right?" Keltie asked.

"Award-winning investigative reporter. Anyway, how their relationship developed is their story to tell, but I've never seen my brother happier."

Keltie's expression softened. "And that's why Porter isn't here tonight? The trust?"

"Exactly. His stipulation required him to move to Morris Ranch, which is about thirty miles from here, for a year."

"Is that why you all seemed sad when Flynn mentioned him at dinner?"

"We miss him, but the irony is, going there was the best thing that could've happened to him. He reconnected with Cici Morris—they had a thing years ago. She owns the ranch now."

I paused, considering how much to share about my brother's struggles. "Porter was in a bad place before that… drinking too much, blaming himself for things that weren't his fault."

"What kind of things?" Keltie asked softly.

"My brother has a habit of shouldering blame that isn't his. Protecting others even when it costs him. There was an incident—a drunk-driving accident. He took the fall for someone else. Lost his reputation in the rodeo community. Turns out he'd already made a commitment to his sobriety by then."

Keltie's eyes widened. "Wow."

"Right? Well, anyway, the trust forcing him to Morris Ranch seemed like another punishment, but it became his salvation. Cici saw through him in a way none of us could."

"And now?"

"Sober over a year. Married to Cici—although that's kind of a secret. They're holding off for the big announcement and shindig until after his year is up.

Regardless, he and Cici are building something real there—a partnership between our ranches for rough-stock contracting. He found himself, I guess you could say."

Keltie tucked a curl behind her ear, her expression thoughtful. "What about Cord? Does he have a story too?"

"Cord's was the strangest. He had to go live in East Aurora, New York, for a year. None of us had even heard of the place. It turns out that's where our mother was from."

"Really? And none of you knew that?"

I shook my head, remembering the shock when we'd discovered our mother's hidden past. "Our mom died when Flynn was a toddler. I was seven. We didn't know much about her life before Colorado. She never talked about it, and our father shut down any questions."

The memory of my mother's face flashed before me—her gentle smile, the way she'd sing me to sleep. She'd kept so many secrets from us, yet I couldn't find it in me to be angry with her. Not anymore.

"Cord met Juni there and discovered all these connections to our mother's past. Even found out we had cousins we never knew existed. Sam is one of them."

She gasped. "Sam is your cousin?"

I scrubbed my face with my hand, wondering how much I should admit to. "But, uh, you and I aren't. I mean, we're on different sides of the family."

I could see her shoulders drop in relief.

"That's how I felt," I said.

Keltie raised her chin. "The way you read me, it's eerie sometimes."

She didn't know the half of it, but that was definitely not something I was going to bring up tonight or any time soon.

"Our mother kept a lot hidden that we're still unraveling."

I thought about the family tree Sam had shown us, the complex web of relationships that connected the Rookers, the Wheatons, and apparently, the Marquez family as well.

"There was a moment, when Cord first told us everything he'd discovered, that it felt like meeting our mother all over again. Learning she'd had all this history we knew nothing about." I swallowed, surprised by the emotion that still surfaced when I thought about it. "She told Cord something once, before she died. She said, 'I pray that someday, when you learn about the decisions I've made, you can understand why and forgive me.'"

"She knew you'd find out eventually," Keltie said softly.

"I think she did. I can't help but wish she'd been here to explain it herself."

Keltie reached across the space between us, her fingers brushing against mine. The touch sent warmth through me that had nothing to do with the fire.

"It's almost as if fate is directing you all to find your happiness," she said, her voice gentle.

I snorted. "It's not fate. It's a faceless, nameless trustee, who set the whole thing up to remain anonymous."

She must have heard the edge in my voice, because her expression turned more serious. "What do you mean by anonymous?"

"The trust is managed by an LLC we know nothing about. Six-pack—our family attorney—claims he doesn't know who's behind it. He gets instructions and delivers them to us."

"Six-pack?" Her mouth quirked up at the nickname.

"Yeah, we've known him since high school. He's as much of a jerk now as he was then."

"And he won't tell you who's pulling the strings?"

"Claims he doesn't know." I rolled my shoulders as the frustration of the past months bubbled up again.

Keltie moved her hand, resting it on my arm. "But your brothers all found happiness because of it, didn't they? Maybe it's not such a bad thing."

The trust had always felt like a manipulation, a final control tactic from beyond the grave. But she wasn't wrong. Each of my brothers had found something—someone—that had changed their lives.

"Maybe you're right," I conceded. "But I hate the way he or she is going about it."

"Sounds like you and your siblings might have control issues," she said with a smile.

"Ya think?" I chuckled. "It's the Wheaton family's specialty."

Her laugh was warm and genuine, drawing me in even further.

"So, what's your stipulation? What do you have to do?"

"Stay in Crested Butte for a year. Like my brothers had to adhere to, I can't leave town for more than forty-eight hours at a time. On top of that, I have to play music at local establishments at least three nights a week and donate half my earnings to the Miracles of Hope Children's Charity." I shrugged. "That's it."

"That doesn't sound so terrible," Keltie said.

"It wouldn't be, except it meant turning down the tour with CB Rice. That was my shot, you know? The kind musicians dream about. International venues, recording contract, the chance to finally make a name for myself beyond local bars."

"I understand," she said quietly.

"I never dreamed they'd ask me to join them, especially after they hit it big."

"How did it come about?"

"About four years ago, Ben Rice called me after seeing me play at the Goat. Our families have known each other for years. One thing led to another, and I became a permanent member. They've even recorded a couple of my songs. Now, it's all over. They'll replace me, and that will be that."

"What happens if you don't meet the requirements?" Keltie asked.

"We lose everything. Not only me. My brothers and sister too."

She winced. "That's harsh."

The weight of the day crashed over me. "The thing is, it's not only about us. The ranch supports families who have worked for us for decades."

"A lot of pressure," Keltie said softly.

"No more than running a bar and caring for a sick child on your own," I countered, immediately regretting bringing up Luna's illness when her expression tightened. "I'm sorry. I shouldn't have—"

"It's okay," she interrupted. "It's not like I can ignore it. The appointment is set for December 30."

I wanted to ask more—about what else the doctor had said—but her exhaustion was evident in the circles beneath her eyes and the slump of her shoulders.

"Anyway, it's getting late."

She covered her mouth when she yawned. "Thank you for telling me all this. I feel like I understand your family better now."

"There's more, but we've got time." The words slipped out before I could consider their implications—that I was assuming we'd have more nights like this, more conversations by the fire.

Keltie didn't seem to mind. She smiled, and the warmth of it reached her eyes. "I'd like that."

I stood, reluctant to leave but knowing I should. "Good night, Keltie. Merry Christmas."

"Merry Christmas, Holt," she replied with a sleepy smile that made my heart thud against my ribs.

I paused at the door, looking back at her silhouette against the firelight. Something about the image burned itself into my memory—Keltie curled on the sofa in the home where I'd grown up, as if she belonged there. As if she'd always belonged here.

The thought should have scared me. Instead, it felt right in a way I couldn't explain.

I closed the door to her suite quietly behind me, stepping into the dimly lit hallway and imagining Luna asleep in that big old bed. Her dark curls—so like her mother's—would be spread across the pillow. I squeezed my eyes closed when the same feeling that had hit me when I first met her washed over me again. Now, I knew there *was* something wrong. I also knew I'd do everything I could to help her and her mom.

As I silently made my way into the great room, where Buck and Cord were sitting by the fireplace, each with whiskey in hand, troubling emotions churned in my gut.

"Thought you'd left," Buck said, raising his glass in greeting.

"Was about to." I dropped into the armchair across from them. "Just saying good night to Keltie first."

Cord exchanged a look with Buck, a small smile playing on his lips. "She seems nice. Luna, too."

"They are," I said, feeling inexplicably uncomfortable under my brothers' scrutiny.

Buck pushed the bottle of whiskey toward me. "Everything okay? You seem thoughtful."

I grabbed an empty glass from the sideboard, poured two fingers, and swirled the hazy liquid before taking a sip. The familiar burn grounded me as I considered Buck's question. "Just thinking about something Keltie said. About how these codicils from the trust led each of you to find happiness."

Buck's eyebrows rose. "You told her about the trust?"

"Not everything."

"Huh." He stroked his beard. "She's not wrong, though. If it weren't for the trust, I doubt TJ and I would've ended up together."

"That's nothing," Cord added. "I never would've even met Juni."

I ran a hand over my face, exhaustion mingling with the uncomfortable realization that maybe there'd be more to it for me too. "Why Crested Butte, though? I'm already here."

"But you were about to leave," Buck pointed out. "Maybe that's the point."

"Maybe it's not about the place," Cord added. "Maybe it's about what—or who—you'd find if you stayed."

I set my glass down harder than I'd intended. "Don't start with that. Keltie and I barely know each other."

"And yet you invited her and Luna for Christmas," Cord said with a knowing smile. "Carried Luna to bed like you've been doing it for years."

"It's not like that," I protested, though something inside me wondered if it could be.

"Then, what is it like?" Buck asked. "Because I've seen the way you look at her, little brother. And I saw how you were with Luna today. That didn't come from nowhere."

I stared into my whiskey, not ready to voice the feelings swirling inside me. "She's going through a tough time. Luna's sick—maybe seriously. They needed something good for Christmas. Plus, it wasn't my idea to invite them. It was Sam's."

"You never know. Maybe by next Christmas, you and Keltie will be married too," said Cord.

I downed the rest of my whiskey in one swallow. "That's a serious stretch, man."

Cord laughed. "All I'm saying is it happened to me. And, honestly? I never dreamed marriage could be like this."

"Speaking of," Buck said, checking his watch, "I should head home. Santa has some assembling to do before morning."

"And I promised Juni I wouldn't be long," Cord added, standing. "You coming, Holt?"

I shook my head. "Think I'll crash in my old room tonight."

My brothers nodded, and I watched them go, their quiet conversation fading as they walked out the front door.

Buck and TJ had rehabbed the original homestead that sat closer to the ranch's main gate. Cord and Juni were building a place at the highest point of our property. When it was finished, the views from there would be unbelievable. For now, though, they were still living in a cabin near mine.

I remained by the fire a while longer, letting the embers burn down as I contemplated everything that had happened, including Six-pack delivering the news of my stipulation. The missed opportunity with CB Rice. The night at the Goat, when I'd met Luna. The hospital visit. And now, Christmas Eve with Keltie and her daughter, as if they'd always been part of our family celebrations.

When the fire had dimmed to glowing coals, I finally made my way down the hall. My old bedroom looked different now—Flynn had redecorated, replacing the old furniture with pieces that somehow managed to erase the memories of our father while preserving the character of the house.

A framed photo on the dresser caught my eye—the five of us Wheaton siblings, taken the last Christmas our mother was still alive. We'd been through so much in the years since.

And yet, here we were. Survivors. A family, despite everything.

I stripped down to my boxers and crawled under the covers, my mind still churning with thoughts of the trust, CB Rice, and most persistently, Keltie. Her warm eyes. Her resilient spirit. The fierce love she had for her daughter.

The house settled around me, creaking in the cold as it had since I was a child. I'd always found the sound comforting—a reminder that some things remained constant, even as life changed around them.

Just as sleep began to pull me under, a sound from the other room caught my attention. Soft, muffled sobbing.

I sat up, instantly alert—someone was crying. Not someone, Keltie.

For a long moment, I remained frozen on the edge of the bed, torn between respecting her privacy and the overwhelming urge to comfort her. Before I could talk myself out of it, I pulled on my jeans and T-shirt and moved to the door. The soft weeping continued, breaking something inside me with each gasping breath I heard.

I stood there, hand raised, heart hammering in my chest, trying to decide whether or not to knock.

9

Keltie

Luna called for me, her voice growing fainter as I ran through sterile corridors. Each turn revealed her briefly—small in a hospital bed that seemed to move farther away no matter how fast I ran.

"Mommy!" Her voice echoed. "Where are you?"

"I'm coming!" I tried to call, but my words died in my throat.

The corridor stretched before me as her cries faded to silence. For a moment, disorientation gripped me as I stared at the unfamiliar surroundings—the high wooden beams of the ceiling, the heavy curtains framing windows that looked out onto snow-covered mountains. Then reality hit me. The Wheatons' ranch. Christmas Eve.

My hand instinctively reached beside me for Luna, panic rising until my fingers brushed against her warm skin. She slept peacefully, her stuffed bunny clutched tightly to her. I touched her forehead. No fever, thank God.

My chest was still tight with lingering fear as I slumped against the pillows. Sleep wouldn't come easily, not with my mind racing and the remnants of the dream clinging to me like cobwebs.

I slipped from beneath the covers, trying not to disturb Luna. In the adjoining bathroom, I found a plush robe hanging on a hook and wrapped it around myself, grateful for its warmth. I tiptoed across the room, casting one more glance at my sleeping daughter before quietly closing the bedroom door behind me.

The sitting room where Holt and I had talked earlier still held the dying embers of our fire, and moonlight streamed through the windows. I added a small log from the neatly stacked pile beside the hearth and watched as the flames grew.

Curling up on the sofa, I hugged my knees to my chest and tried to quiet my mind. Luna's appointment in Denver looked over me like a shadow, the weight of the potential diagnoses and mounting medical bills crushing against my chest.

The tears started without warning—silent at first, then building to quiet sobs that shook my shoulders. I pressed my face against my knees, trying to muffle the sound. The days leading up to Christmas had always been Luna's and my time together. The two of us would decorate our small Albuquerque apartment with paper snowflakes we'd cut together and the tiny artificial tree that sat on our coffee table. Simple but happy.

This year should have been special too—our first Christmas in our new home. Instead, here we were, at the Wheaton ranch, surrounded by a family that wasn't ours while I tried to hold myself together for Luna's sake.

And yet, watching her with the other children earlier—that infectious joy as she played with Buckaroo and the twins—I couldn't deny she was happier here than she would've been in our quiet house. The Wheaton family had welcomed us with open arms, treating Luna like she'd always been part of their holiday tradition.

My thoughts drifted to Holt—his gentle patience with my daughter, the way he'd held me in the hospital parking lot, asking nothing but giving everything I needed at that moment. I barely knew him, yet I found myself wishing he were here now, his strong arms around me, telling me everything would be okay.

A movement in the doorway caught my eye, and I looked up through tear-blurred eyes. Holt stood there, hesitant, concern etched on his face. For a moment, I wondered if I'd conjured him from my thoughts—a figment of my imagination. I wiped my eyes and blinked hard, but he remained. He wore a T-shirt and jeans, his dark hair mussed from sleep.

"I heard…" he said, taking a tentative step forward.

"I'm sorry," I said, quickly wiping away my tears. "Did I wake you?"

"No, I was still up." He paused, uncertain. "I knocked, but you didn't answer. I wanted to make sure everything was okay."

I should have sent him away, maintained the distance I'd built around Luna and myself for years. Instead, I found myself telling him I was glad he was here.

The relief in his eyes as he crossed the room sent a fresh wave of emotion through me. He sat beside me on the sofa, close enough for me to feel his warmth but not touching me.

"Nightmare?" he asked quietly.

"About Luna. In a hospital. I couldn't reach her."

Holt's arm slipped around my shoulders, the gesture so natural that I easily leaned into him. "She's safe," he murmured. "You both are."

I rested my head against his shoulder, allowing myself to accept the comfort he offered. We sat in silence for several minutes. The only sounds were the crackling of the fire and my quiet sobs filling the room.

"I'm scared." I finally whispered the words I hadn't allowed myself to say to anyone else.

His arm tightened around me.

"What if she has…?" I couldn't bring myself to utter the word.

"Hey," he interrupted gently. "One step at a time, okay?"

I drew a shuddering breath. "I'm sorry. I shouldn't be leaning on you like this."

"Why not?"

"Because I'm supposed to be strong. Independent. That's who I've always been."

Holt was quiet for a moment. "Being strong doesn't mean carrying everything alone."

"Doesn't it?" I laughed bitterly. "That's exactly what it's meant since Luna was born. Her father walked away before she took her first breath."

"I won't walk away, Keltie," he said simply. "I'll be with you as much as you want me to be."

"Why would you do this for people who just came into your life?"

He shook his head. "It doesn't feel that way to me. It seems like, I don't know, more."

The words settled over me, resonating in ways I couldn't explain. "I know what you mean."

I told him how my father had helped after Luna was born, but moving to Crested Butte meant leaving that support system behind. How I'd struggled to balance single parenthood with running the Goat, even before Luna's health took a turn for the worse.

"When I first met her," Holt said quietly, "I felt something I can't explain. A closeness. Like I was supposed to be in her life. Like she'd need me."

I studied him. "What do you mean?"

"Like I said, I can't explain it. All I know is that I've had feelings like this since I was a kid. The first was when I knew my mother was sick before anyone admitted it."

"Is that what happened with Luna? You sensed something was wrong?"

His somber expression reminded me of the way Mrs. Lopez had described his reaction—how odd it had been.

"That's why you came to the hospital," I whispered.

"Partly," he said. "But also because I knew *you* needed me." Holt's hand found mine, our fingers intertwining.

My eyes were heavy with exhaustion, but I didn't want to move. Didn't want to break whatever spell had formed between us in the quiet darkness.

"Stay with me?" I murmured, the words barely audible.

Holt shifted, adjusting his position so I could rest my head more comfortably on his shoulder. The last thing I remembered before sleep claimed me was the gentle stroke of his hand through my hair and the steady rhythm of his heartbeat beneath my ear.

"Mommy! Mr. Wheaton! It's Christmas and Santa came! I know he did!"

Luna's excited voice pulled me from a deep sleep. Disorientation hit me as I blinked awake to find myself still on the sofa, Holt's arm around me, both of us covered with a blanket I didn't remember retrieving. Sunlight streamed through the windows, and Luna stood before us, bouncing with excitement, not at all confused by the sight of her mother curled up with a man she barely knew.

Heat rushed to my face as I extracted myself from Holt's embrace, realizing how this must look. But Holt transitioned smoothly, stretching as if waking up on the sofa with me was the most natural thing in the world.

"Merry Christmas, Luna." His voice was raspy. "Did you say something about presents?"

Luna shifted on her feet, her curls bouncing. "I'm sorry, Mommy, but I peeked. There's a HUGE pile under the tree."

"It's okay, Luna-bug. I'm sorry I wasn't next to you when you woke up."

"There's even stockings for *both* of us!"

"Somebody told me he also left you a big, fluffy robe and a pair of slippers in your bathroom. Why don't you go check?" Holt suggested with a wink.

Luna needed no further encouragement, racing from the room with Bunny trailing from her hand.

I pushed my hair from my face, mortification setting in. "Holt, I—"

"Don't overthink this," he said gently. "Neither of us planned to fall asleep here. It just happened."

"But Luna—"

"Doesn't think anything of it," he finished. "Kids that age don't overthink things the way adults do."

He was right, of course. Luna had been entirely focused on the Christmas morning, oblivious to any potential awkwardness.

"I should get dressed," I said, gesturing vaguely toward the bedroom. "Make myself presentable."

His eyes traveled over me. "You look perfect to me." Despite my disheveled state, I felt beautiful under his gaze. "But I know what you mean. I should probably change too. Meet you out there in fifteen? I doubt you can keep Luna waiting much longer than that."

I watched as he stood and stretched, his T-shirt riding up to reveal a strip of tanned skin above his jeans. I quickly averted my eyes, but not before he caught me looking. His knowing smile followed me as I hurried toward the bedroom.

In the bathroom mirror, I confronted my reflection—flushed cheeks, wild curls, eyes still puffy from last night's tears. I splashed cold water on my face and attempted to do something with my hair before changing into the outfit I'd packed—jeans and a green sweater that Luna insisted was my "Christmas color."

By the time I emerged, the bedroom door was wide open. I walked out to the room where the family was gathered and saw Luna was already on the floor with the other kids, gazing at all the gifts but not touching any. Like Holt had said were waiting for her, she was wearing a fuzzy robe and slippers, both covered with mystical creatures. Self-doubt washed over me as I prepared to face Holt again.

I saw Flynn first when she approached from the kitchen, coffee mug in hand. "Merry Christmas," she said warmly, offering the steaming cup. "Thought you might need this."

"Thank you," I replied, searching her face for any hint of judgment but finding only genuine welcome. "And thank you for yesterday. For everything."

"We're so glad you're here," she said simply, linking her arm through mine and guiding me toward the center of activity.

Across the room, Holt caught my gaze, a small reassuring smile playing on his lips. He'd changed into a fresh button-down shirt and jeans, his damp hair suggesting a hasty shower. His expression made my breath catch—a quiet intimacy, as if we shared a secret.

Flynn motioned to the dining room, where an elaborate breakfast spread awaited. "TJ and I might have gone a bit overboard," she admitted. "Buck always insists presents come after breakfast," Flynn explained. "Family tradition. Though, with the kids this excited, we'll probably rush through it."

The scene was a warm chaos as everyone piled into the room—the children's excited chatter, adults laughing, the rich aromas of coffee and cinnamon filling the air. Luna took a seat between Buckaroo and an empty chair she was clearly saving for me.

Her visible happiness brought a lump to my throat. This was the kind of Christmas I'd always wanted to give her—warmth, tradition, multiple generations gathered around a table.

As we ate, I became aware of a growing anxiety. In the excitement of being invited and the rush to pack, I'd only brought what I'd gotten for Luna. I had nothing to give the Wheatons, who had opened their home to us.

Before I could dwell on it further, Buck stood, clapping his hands. "All right, who's ready for presents?"

The children erupted in cheers, Luna's voice among the loudest. We moved en masse to the great room, where stockings hung from the mantle—including ones marked with Luna's name and mine like she'd said.

Buck and Cord both played Santa, distributing gifts with theatrical flair. Luna's eyes grew impossibly wider as a pile began to form in front of her—packages wrapped in colorful paper that she tore into with unbridled joy.

To my surprise, several appeared in front of me as well. "You shouldn't have," I protested softly to Flynn and Sam, who sat nearby.

"It's nothing," Flynn assured me. "Just a few things to make you feel welcome."

Tears threatened again, but these were different from last night's—born of gratitude rather than fear. I'd expected this Christmas to be difficult, spent in a strange town without the traditions Luna and I had built together with my dad and his friends who made up our hodgepodge family. Instead, we'd been welcomed with open arms, treated not as outsiders but as honored guests.

"Mommy! This one's for you!" Luna exclaimed, bringing a small box wrapped in silver paper over to me. "It says 'From Santa' on it!"

I glanced questioningly at Flynn, who shrugged, equally puzzled. Luna climbed into my lap, eager to help me unwrap it. I pulled off the paper, revealing a velvet jewelry box nestled inside.

"Open it!" Luna urged, bouncing against my knees.

When I lifted the lid, my gasp echoed through the room. Resting against the dark velvet lay a stunning pendant on a delicate gold chain. The setting was deep blue, like the night sky, with a gold and diamond river winding across it beneath a crescent moon of tiny diamonds.

My breath caught as I instinctively looked up, finding Holt watching me from across the room. His expression confirmed without words that this was from him.

"It's you and me, Mommy," Luna said, touching the pendant with reverent fingers. "The river and the moon."

The entire family fell silent, watching the moment unfold. I sat frozen, overwhelmed by the thoughtfulness and significance of the gift.

"Mr. Wheaton," Luna called out. "Can you help put it on my mommy?"

Holt crossed the room and took the necklace from the box. I turned, lifting my hair as he fastened the clasp. His touch was warm against my neck, lingering a moment longer than necessary.

"Thank you," I whispered, my voice catching.

I'd never seen a pair of eyes as warm as his were right now. "You're welcome."

If there weren't so many people focused on us, my daughter included, I'd hug him after easing her off my lap.

He smiled as if he could read my mind, then rejoined his brothers as conversations resumed around us. Luna returned to her gifts, exclaiming over a stuffed unicorn identical to those on her robe.

I touched the pendant at my throat, feeling the weight of it—both literal and symbolic. No man had ever given me jewelry before, let alone something so clearly meaningful.

After our conversation last night, when he said he'd had a premonition about Luna and me needing him, I couldn't help but wonder.

As the gift-opening continued, I watched Holt with his family—the easy way he teased his brothers, his gentle patience with the children. When he laughed, the sound rolled through me like music.

The festivities gradually shifted as the children began exploring their gifts and the adults gathered in smaller groups. I found myself momentarily alone, touching the pendant at my throat, still processing its significance.

"It suits you," Sam said, appearing beside me with two mugs of hot chocolate. She offered one to me. "I thought you might like the adult version again today," she added with a wink.

"Thanks," I said, accepting it gratefully. "So, are you actually related to the Wheatons?"

Sam tucked a strand of auburn hair behind her ear. "Through my grandmother Pilar—your aunt. It's complicated, but yes, I'm a distant cousin to them on their mother's side. My great-grandmother Cena was from the Rooker family, who were related to the Wheatons."

"Family trees make my head spin," I admitted.

"Mine too." She smiled. "It's still strange to me. It was just my mom and me when I was growing up. I never knew my dad. Then I find out I have this whole extended family I never knew about."

I studied her face, recognizing something of myself in her expression. "I know what you mean."

Sam glanced across the room to my daughter, who was showing her new stuffed animal to Buckaroo. "She's beautiful, Keltie. You've done an amazing job with her."

"I try," I said, my voice catching. "Some days are harder than others."

Sam touched my arm gently. "Holt mentioned she hasn't been well. If there's anything I can do…"

"Thank you," I said, surprised by how much the offer meant. "Actually, I'd love to hear more about your family—our family."

Sam led me to a window seat overlooking the snow-covered landscape. "I never met my grandmother Pilar—she died before I was born. My mom didn't talk about her much," Sam said. "My grandfather's mother forced her to leave when she was pregnant with my mom."

I gasped. "Forced her to leave?"

Sam's expression was somber. "Family drama from another era. I didn't know any of this until recently. It's why my mom and I struggled so much—she grew up without a dad, like I did."

The parallels to our situation weren't lost on me. "I worry about the same thing happening with Luna."

"She won't have the same struggles we did," Sam said with unexpected fierceness. "She has you, and now, she has all of us too." She gestured around the room. "They can be overwhelming sometimes, but they're loyal to a fault once they consider you one of them."

"It might be a little soon for that."

"You don't know the Wheatons." Sam's gaze moved to Holt, who was helping Buckaroo with a new toy. "I'd say at least one of them definitely does."

I felt heat rise in my cheeks. "It's not. I mean, we barely know each other." Again, I heard those words coming out of my mouth.

"As I said before, sometimes, that doesn't matter." Sam said with a knowing smile. "Beau and I were friends for years before everything changed in an instant." She twisted the engagement ring on her finger. "When you know, you know."

"I have Luna to consider. My business. Eventually, he'll resume his music career."

Sam's eyebrow raised. "Has he told you about the trust?"

"Yes, last night. How it's keeping him here instead of touring with CB Rice."

"You know what I think?" Her voice dropped. "I've known the Wheatons for less than a year, but I've never seen Holt look at anyone the way he looks at you."

Before I could respond, Luna came bounding over, breaking the moment. "Miss Sam! Can you help me name my unicorn? Mr. Wheaton says you're good at names."

Sam laughed, reaching out to touch one of Luna's curls. "I'm terrible at names, but I'd be happy to help."

As they discussed what to call my daughter's precious, new stuffed animal, my gaze drifted to Holt, who stood across the room. As if sensing my attention, he looked up, our eyes meeting over the holiday chaos. Something silent but that felt significant passed between us.

Later, as the children played with their new toys and the adults cleaned up the wrapping-paper chaos, I found him alone in the kitchen.

"This is too much," I said, touching the pendant at my throat. "I can't accept it."

"Might not be easy to return it to Santa. You know how he is about things like that." He smiled. "It's called 'River Under Moonlight,'" he said softly.

I felt emotion rise in my chest, and my words stuck in my throat.

"As soon as I saw it, I knew it was meant for you."

Without thinking, I rose on tiptoe and kissed his cheek, both of us surprised by the impulsive gesture. Before either of us could speak, Flynn entered the kitchen.

"There you are," she said brightly. "TJ's asking if anyone wants to go sledding before lunch."

"Sounds fun," Holt replied, his eyes never leaving mine. "What do you think, Keltie?"

"I should call my father first," I said. "Wish him Merry Christmas."

"Take all the time you need," said Flynn. "I'm thinking after lunch would be better anyway."

I slipped out onto the porch, wrapping myself in a thick wool coat I found hanging by the door. Snow fell gently from a pearl-gray sky, the landscape stretching, pristine and white, in every direction. The contrast between the quiet outside and the joyful chaos within struck me as I dialed.

"Merry Christmas, *mija*!" my father's voice boomed through the phone.

"Merry Christmas, Dad," I replied, smiling at his exuberance. "How's New Mexico?"

"Sunny and beautiful, as always. How's my Luna?"

"She's great—having the time of her life, actually. We're spending Christmas at a ranch outside town."

"A ranch?" His interest piqued. "Whose?"

"The Wheaton family. Remember I told you about meeting someone who knew Aunt Ursula at the bar? Well, turns out we have other connections."

There was a noticeable pause. "What kind of connections?"

"Sam Marquez is here—Aunt Pilar's granddaughter. And the photo of you and Ursula at the original Goat caused quite a stir when they saw it."

His voice turned careful. "Is that so?"

"Dad, is there something wrong?"

"Not at all. I just miss you and my granddaughter."

"We miss you too, Dad."

"So, tell me, are you enjoying yourselves?"

I sighed and smiled. "Yes, we are. It's a wonderful place. Luna's playing with the other children, and everyone's been incredibly kind."

"I'm glad," he said, genuine warmth in his voice. "I wish I could be there with you both."

"I thought you might drive up," I admitted. "You said you were considering it."

"I'm at my annual Christmas gathering with the poker buddies," he explained. "You know we've done this for decades. But I'll come visit soon, I promise. Once things slow down."

We said our goodbyes after a few more minutes, neither of us mentioning Luna's hospital visit. That conversation could wait for another day—today was for celebration, not worry.

10

The winter air bit at my cheeks as I approached the house, my boots crunching softly on the frost-covered path. The scent of pine from the surrounding woods mingled with the woodsmoke curling from the chimney. The home I grew up in stood warm and inviting against the crisp December sky.

The path I took after Buck and I finished making sure the sled run was ready to go was obscured from where Keltie stood on the screened-in porch, her slender figure silhouetted against the warm glow spilling from the windows behind her. She was talking on her phone, her free hand tucked into the pocket of her coat. I knew I shouldn't eavesdrop, but I couldn't help myself. Something about the way she held herself—slightly hunched, as if bearing an invisible weight—made me hesitate.

"Dad, is there something wrong?" I heard her say. There was a pause as she listened, and I watched her pace a small circle on the wooden planks of the porch. "We miss you too, Dad." There was another delay, then she added. "It's a wonderful place. Luna's playing with the other children, and everyone's been incredibly kind."

The conversation wound down, and I wondered if she'd already told him about Luna's hospital visit. I was about to step forward and reveal myself, already composing a casual greeting to mask my intrusion, when the front door opened with a familiar squeak and Flynn came out onto the porch. The sudden appearance of my sister froze me in place, and I remained hidden, watching as she approached Keltie, two steaming mugs in her hands. She offered one to Keltie, who accepted it with a grateful smile.

"Everything okay?" The concern in my sister's tone was unmistakable, and I felt a surge of gratitude for her natural empathy.

I inched forward and saw Keltie nod, then tuck her phone into her pocket. "Just wishing my dad a Merry Christmas. He's spending it in New Mexico with his poker buddies."

"I'm glad you and Luna could join us instead," Flynn said, resting against one of the outdoor chairs.

Keltie smiled, but it didn't reach her eyes. "We should probably think about leaving soon. We've imposed enough, and I feel bad about taking Holt away from his family on Christmas."

"Don't be ridiculous," Flynn said, her voice taking on that firm tone she used when she wouldn't hear of an argument. The same one I'd heard on the rare occasions when she stood up to our father. "I know I'm probably oversharing, but to be honest with you, life was hard for all of us after our mom died. I was too young to even know her. Anyway, our father was a mean *sonuvabitch*. Abusive, really. Every memory I have of Christmas is depressing. I don't remember many gifts, and there was even less laughter."

I held my breath, surprised by Flynn's candor. My sister rarely spoke of our past so openly, especially to someone she didn't know well. The memories Flynn's words conjured sent a chill through me that had nothing to do with the December air—the sound of breaking glass, the shouting that shook the walls, and huddling with Flynn in one of our rooms, trying to block out the noise.

"Remember what I said last night? This Christmas is exactly how I once dreamed they'd be," Flynn continued, her voice softening to a near-whisper that I had to strain to hear. The emotion in her words made my throat tighten. "And you being here with Luna? It's added more to our holiday celebration than you realize."

I stood near the side of the house, my chest tightening at my sister's words. She was right—this Christmas had been different. Fuller and so much brighter.

"And honestly," Flynn added, placing a hand on Keltie's arm, "it's been so nice to see a smile on my brother's face again. That's a credit to you and Luna, truly."

I felt a strange mix of emotions—grateful for Flynn's kindness, but worried she might overwhelm Keltie with her earnestness. Heat crept up my neck at the realization that Flynn had noticed the effect Keltie had on me. Was I that transparent?

While I wanted to join them, make sure Keltie was okay, if I appeared now, they'd know I'd been listening. I remained frozen in place, unsure what to do, the cold seeping through my boots as I shifted my weight.

"Why don't we go inside?" Flynn suggested. "It's freezing out here, and I think Irish made fresh hot chocolate. The real kind, with cocoa, not the powdered mix. And I think I saw him adding a splash of peppermint schnapps to the grown-up version."

Keltie laughed, the sound warm and genuine, melting some of the tension from her posture. "That sounds perfect," she replied, tucking a wayward curl behind her ear. "We'll stay a bit longer."

Relief washed over me—both that I could now go in without revealing I'd been eavesdropping and that Keltie had agreed to stay. I hadn't realized how much I wanted her to remain until that moment, how much her presence had begun to feel right, here among my family.

I was about to head around to the front door when Buck approached from behind, his boots crunching on the frozen ground.

"Hey," he said, keeping his voice low. He jerked his chin toward the main gates, visible in the distance down the long, winding driveway. "Ben Rice is on his way in."

I felt tension knot in my stomach. "He probably plans to convince me to come on tour with them." The thought of explaining the trust situation to yet another person exhausted me.

"I think he already knows why you can't," Buck replied, his breath forming small clouds between us in the cold air.

"How?" I asked, my gaze darting to the driveway, where the vehicle was quickly approaching.

"I had to tell Matt Rice about both Cord and Porter," Buck explained, rubbing his gloved hands together against the cold. "He's our partner in roughstock contracting. He needed to know."

"At least I won't have to explain everything." I squared my shoulders, bracing myself for the inevitable awkwardness.

Ben arrived a couple of minutes later with his wife, Liv. Their SUV rolled to a stop in the circular driveway, the engine purring before falling silent. After exiting the vehicle, he bounded over with his usual energy, all smiles as he clapped me on the back.

"Merry Christmas, Wheaton!" he exclaimed, his voice booming in the quiet of the winter afternoon. "Sorry to crash your family gathering. Liv insisted we drop by since we were in the area." His gregarious smile was as bright as ever, even as his eyes held a hint of concern.

"Ben, Liv," I greeted them, forcing cordiality into my voice despite the anxiety churning in my gut. "It's good to see you both, and merry Christmas."

Liv kissed my cheek after greeting Buck. "Hope you don't mind the intrusion," she said softly.

"Not at all. Come on in."

As we entered the house, the warmth enveloped us immediately, along with the mingled scents of pine from the Christmas tree, cinnamon from Flynn's baking, and the rich aroma of Irish's homemade hot chocolate. Ben's gaze swept the room, taking in the festive decorations, the scattered toys, and the family gathered in small groups, chatting. His eyes stopped abruptly when he spotted Keltie standing near the fire-place, cradling a mug between her hands. His face lit up with recognition, eyes widening in genuine surprise.

"Well, I'll be damned!" Ben exclaimed, crossing the room in long strides and pulling her into a bear hug before she could react. Her mug sloshed as she strug-gled to keep it from spilling. "Keltie Marquez! How the hell are you?"

I watched in confusion as Keltie stiffened in his embrace, her eyes meeting mine over Ben's shoulder. The color drained from her face, replaced by a deer-in-headlights expression that sent alarm bells ringing in my head.

"So, how do you two know each other?" My mind raced with the possibilities, none of them easing the sudden tightness in my chest.

Ben released Keltie, keeping one arm slung around her shoulders. She looked small beside his burly frame, and I could see the tension in her jaw and the tremble in her hands as she set her mug down on the mantel. "The Goat, of course. Plus, Keltie used to work for CB Rice. She was one of the best sound engineers we ever had." He turned to me, seemingly oblivious to Keltie's growing discomfort. Her shoulders hunched as if bracing for impact. "This was right before you joined up with us, Holt."

The revelation stunned me. Keltie had worked for CB Rice? Why hadn't she mentioned it? We'd spent enough time talking about how I couldn't join them on tour.

Ben turned to face her. "It's good to see you, girl. You left us so quickly I never even got to say goodbye. One day, you were there; the next—poof! Gone." He shook his head, still chuckling, though Keltie had gone pale, her brown eyes standing out starkly against her bloodless complexion.

Liv stepped forward, placing a gentle hand on her husband's arm. Her perceptive gaze flicked between Keltie's rigid posture and my own bewildered expression. "Ben, honey. Maybe we should talk about why we're here?"

She smiled apologetically at Keltie, seeming to sense her discomfort. The silent communication between the two women spoke volumes—a shared understanding of when men were being obtuse.

"Right," Ben agreed, turning to me. "Holt, can I have a private word with you?"

"Sure," I said, glancing at Keltie, who was already heading toward the hallway, her eyes avoiding mine. The distance she was placing between us left me cold.

"Excuse me," she murmured, her voice barely audible above the holiday music playing through speakers.

I led Ben toward the library, my mind whirling with questions about why Keltie hadn't mentioned knowing him, let alone working with the band. It nagged at me, making my skin prickle with unease.

Once we were alone, Ben's jovial demeanor changed.

"I know about the situation with the trust, Holt," he said, his voice gruff with sympathy. "Matt filled me in. It's a raw deal, man."

I sank into one of the armchairs, the aged leather stiff beneath my weight, and gestured for Ben to take the other. "It is what it is." The words tasted bitter on my tongue. "Nothing I can do to change it."

"Remi's being a dick about it," he continued, running a hand over his bald head. "Already talking about your replacement, acting like you're gone for good. But I want you to know something. CB Rice is *my* band. When you're ready to rejoin us, you'll be welcome. I'll make sure whoever fills in for you knows that's all there is to it—just filling in."

The offer stunned me, and warmth spread through my chest at this unexpected loyalty. "That's really nice of you, Ben." I swallowed hard.

He waved off my thanks. "You're family, Holt." Earnestness replaced his usual bravado. "There's something else. Those new songs of yours we were discussing? I still want to talk about recording a few.

But I respect if you want to keep others for your own album.”

“My own album?” I repeated. “That won’t be happening any time soon.” Without the money I’d make on tour, it would never become a reality.

“Why not? You’ve got the talent.” He grinned. “And you’re welcome to use our recording studio at the ranch anytime you want. State of the art, and it’s sitting there empty when we’re not using it.”

His offer left me speechless. “I don’t know what to say.”

“Say you’ll think about it,” Ben replied. “No rush. You’ve got a year, right?”

“Right,” I said, still somewhat dazed by the turn of events, by the door he was opening for me. “So, uh, does Remi know about the trust?” The thought of his reaction, if he did, made my stomach clench. He’d never been my biggest fan, and it would give him more ammunition to get rid of me.

Ben shook his head. “Not from me. Didn’t feel like it was my place to tell him. I’m not expecting you to tell him either, unless you want to.”

“Thanks, man,” I said, meaning it. “For everything.”

The conversation was at an end, but my mind kept drifting to Keltie, to the shock on her face at seeing Ben. I knew I shouldn't ask, but I couldn't help myself. "What happened with Keltie? Why'd she leave?"

Ben's expression darkened. He shook his head slowly. "I wish I knew. Remi just showed up one day and said Keltie was gone, that he had to fire her. Wouldn't elaborate about why." A grimace crossed his face. "It bothered me then, and I still think about it occasionally, wishing I'd handled it differently. I should've pushed for answers, but you know how Remi gets."

"I expected him to fire me more than once," I joked, trying to lighten the mood.

Ben chuckled, but there was little humor in it, more like resignation. "That's the thing. Remi really liked Keltie. In fact"—he glanced toward the door, lowering his voice to barely above a whisper, the sudden quiet making me lean forward to catch his words—"I probably shouldn't say anything, but I kind of got the impression the two were an item."

A cold weight settled in my stomach, and my grip on the armrest tightened until my knuckles whitened.

"Maybe it went south," Ben continued, oblivious to my inner turmoil, "and instead of being a stand-up guy,

Remi let one of our best sound engineers go. Wouldn't be the first time his personal life messed with the band."

I cleared my throat, trying to sound casual despite the jealousy burning in my gut. "If I do record some music," I said, forcing my tone to remain light, conversational, "would you recommend I ask Keltie to help produce it?"

"Absolutely," Ben replied without hesitation.

"When did this all go down?" I asked, dreading the answer even as I needed to hear it.

Ben thought for a moment. "Let's see… We were working on the *Firestarter* album. About five years ago."

The timeline formed in my head with sickening clarity. If Luna was four now, and Keltie had left the tour pregnant, could Remi be Luna's father? The little girl looked like her mother, with the same wild curls and expressive eyes, but now that I thought about it, there was something else that reminded me, uncomfortably, of Remi Gilbert.

I stood, needing to move, to breathe. "We should probably rejoin the others."

Ben rose as well, resting his hand on my shoulder. "Remember what I said, Holt. The door's open whenever you're ready."

When we came out of the library, Liv was waiting in the great room, silhouetted against the Christmas tree. "Ben, we should go. We have somewhere to be, remember?" Her pointed look suggested they'd discussed not staying too long.

Everyone exchanged goodbyes, the ritual of handshakes and hugs playing out against the backdrop of holiday decorations and the crackling fire. I noticed Keltie had returned, standing away from the group. Luna was behind her, playing with the twins. Her face was flushed with excitement, her curls even wilder than usual.

Ben hugged Keltie again, and when his gaze shifted in Luna's direction, his expression changed subtly—a flicker of recognition that he quickly masked. My heart hammered against my ribs as I watched him put the pieces together, grateful when he didn't say anything.

"I'll walk you out," I offered. Once outside, the cold air was a relief against my heated skin. Ben opened

Liv's door for her, but when he came around to where I stood, he hesitated.

"Not my business," he said in a low voice, "but whose little girl was that?"

I felt uncomfortable under his scrutiny, the weight of his unspoken suspicion hanging in the air between us. "She's Keltie's daughter."

"How old is she?" he asked, his tone casual, but his eyes sharp, missing nothing.

"She's exactly as old as you think she is," I replied, meeting his gaze steadily, unwilling to lie but unable to confirm what we both suspected.

"Fuck," he muttered, then climbed into the SUV, where Liv's curiosity was evident in the tilt of her head.

I remembered Keltie's reaction to seeing Remi on her street and made a quick decision. "Ben," I called before he could close the door, laying my hand on the cold metal of the frame, "I'd appreciate it if you didn't mention seeing Keltie to Remi."

Ben held up both hands, his expression solemn. "Hell no. I already butted my bald head in way too much as it is. This is between them—and you, apparently." He studied me for a moment. "Happy New Year, Holt. I look forward to you being on the road with us this time next year."

"Appreciate it, and same to you," I replied, stepping away as he pulled the door closed.

I watched their SUV disappear down the driveway, but I stood there a moment longer, gathering my thoughts, steeling myself to face Keltie and ask the questions that now burned like fire in my mind.

11

Keltie

I peered through the curtains, watching Holt and Ben Rice still talking by the SUV in the driveway. Their breath formed clouds in the cold air, their conversation clearly serious from the way they stood—faces close, shoulders tense. My stomach twisted with dread. What was Ben saying?

Without my own transportation, there was no escape from the confrontation I feared was coming.

I let the curtain fall into place and turned to find Luna playing with the twins on the rug near the Christmas tree, lost in a world of stuffed animals and imagination. She was so happy here, surrounded by warmth and acceptance. The thought of dragging her away because of my past mistakes felt cruel.

The front door opened, bringing a rush of cold air and the sound of boots stomping snow onto the mat. I steeled myself, my shoulders tensing as Holt walked in. When his eyes found mine across the room, I braced for the accusation, the confusion, the hurt.

Instead, his expression was the same as it had been all day—warm, tender, with that hint of something deeper that made my heart race despite everything. It made no sense. Had Ben not explained, after all?

"Who's ready to go sledding?" Holt called out, rubbing his gloved hands together. His enthusiasm seemed genuine, not forced.

A chorus of excited responses erupted from around the room. The twins squealed and clapped their hands while Buckaroo jumped up and down, tugging on TJ's sleeve.

"I wanna go! I wanna go!" Luna exclaimed, racing over to me. "Can we, Mommy? Please?"

Flynn appeared before I could respond, smiling down at my daughter. "Come with me, sweetie. I think I have a snowsuit that should fit you perfectly. We keep extras for when friends visit."

Luna looked up at me, her eyes wide with hope. "Mommy?"

"Go ahead," I relented, unable to deny her this simple joy despite my inner turmoil. "Just be careful, okay?"

As everyone scattered to change into the appropriate winter gear, I approached Holt, trying to keep my voice steady. "Luna and I should probably head home soon. I can call someone to come get us."

Holt's arm slipped around my shoulders, pulling me against his side with a casual intimacy that left me breathless. "A little unicorn told me that you told Flynn you'd stay longer." His voice was low, meant only for me. "You're not running away, are you?"

"I know we need to talk." I swallowed hard, looking up at him. "You must have questions."

Before I could say more, he pressed his lips to mine, silencing my words with a kiss so tender it made my knees weak. When he pulled away, his blue eyes held mine with unwavering certainty.

"Later," he said simply.

I stared at him, stunned by the fact that he'd kissed me when anyone could have walked in and seen us. Yet he'd done it anyway.

What exactly had Ben told him? My history with CB Rice? The timing of my departure coinciding with my pregnancy? A chill ran through me at the possibilities.

Flynn's voice broke through my thoughts as she returned with Luna, who was bundled head to toe in a pink-and-purple snowsuit, her cheeks already flushed with excitement.

"Look, Mommy! I'm a snow princess!" Luna twirled, nearly losing her balance in the bulky outfit.

"You sure are, baby," I said, forcing a smile despite the storm of emotions churning inside me.

Flynn held out a bundle of winter clothes. "I brought these for you, Keltie. They should fit. Can't have you miss out on all the fun."

"Thank you," I said, taking the offered items, a strange sense of inevitability settling over me.

"I guess I should put this stuff on," I said to Holt, clutching the winter gear in front of me like a shield.

He surprised me a second time when he cupped my cheek. "Listen, I get why you didn't say anything. I was confused at first, but I'm not anymore."

I felt sick. Did that mean he'd figured out the one thing I didn't want him to?

"Keltie, look at me."

I raised my chin and met his gaze.

"Remi Gilbert is an asshole. I know it, you probably know it, and even Ben knows it. Let's not waste the rest of what's been a pretty spectacular day, thinking about someone who isn't worth our time or energy."

"Okay," I murmured, biting my lip. "But you should know that Luna's never done this before. I'm not sure she should be out in the cold for too long, with everything…"

"Looking pretty stylish there, Luna," Holt said, walking over to her and tugging a knit cap over her curls.

Her giggles sounded like music to me. "It's so fluffy. I can hardly move my arms!"

"That's the idea." He winked. "The snow monsters can't get you if you're all puffy."

"Snow monsters?" she gasped, her eyes wide.

"Oh yeah," he said seriously. "But don't worry. They only eat grown-ups. Kids are completely safe."

When she rolled her eyes at him, I couldn't contain my smile.

Once we were outside, Holt pointed to the run Buck had set up on the slope that led from the main house down toward the horse barn. The path looked gentle enough, and he'd strategically placed hay bales to prevent any wayward sledders from careening off course.

"*Unca* Holt!" Buckaroo called, waving frantically from where he stood with TJ. "We go fast!"

"Hang on, buddy. I promised Luna the first run." Holt knelt down beside her, pointing to where Irish was getting the twins settled onto a sled.

"See? It's not too steep. And your mommy and I will be right there with you the whole time."

"Promise?" she asked, looking up at me, her small face so serious it nearly broke my heart.

"Promise." I held out my pinky finger, and she wrapped hers around it solemnly.

"First run's with all three of us," said Holt, grabbing one of the larger sleds. "That way, I can show you all my expert sledding techniques."

Luna giggled, and we followed him up to the top of the rise, where Cord was helping Juni position herself on another sled.

"Expert, huh?" Cord smirked. "Should I tell them about the time you sledded straight into the manure pile?"

"That was strategic," he countered, arranging the sled. "I was doing important scientific research."

"On what? How bad you'd smell?"

Luna laughed so hard she snorted, which only made everyone chuckle more.

Holt settled onto the sled and patted the space in front of him. "Hop on, Keltie and Luna. Your chariot awaits."

After I seated myself with my back against Holt's front, my daughter climbed on slowly, her small body tense with anticipation. Holt's arms were long enough to wrap one securely around both of us while he held the sled's rope with his other hand.

"Ready?" he asked.

"Yes!" Luna shouted with glee.

"Okay, on three. One… two… *three!*"

We pushed off and went sliding down the hill, gathering speed. Luna squealed with delight, her hands gripping my arm that was also around her middle. The cold air whipped past us, snow spraying up from the runners of the sled.

"Wee!" Luna cried, her voice carried away by the wind and our momentum.

At the bottom of the hill, we glided to a gentle stop, well short of the hay bales. Luna immediately twisted around to look at us, her face bright with joy.

"Can we go again?"

I glanced over my shoulder at Holt, whose smile was as big as hers.

"I'm in," he announced.

"How about I let you two go on your own this time?"

Luna clapped her hands. "Then, we'll go even faster!"

"Remember that Holt promised to take Buckaroo too," I reminded her.

Luna looked from me to him. "It's okay if you want to take him first, Mr. Holt," she said, blinking her eyes quickly as though she was fending off tears.

"Nope. It's you and me, kiddo. We'll go as many times as you want. Or, err, as many times as your mommy will let us."

The hillside transformed into a symphony of laughter and shouts over the course of the next hour. While Luna went on rides with nearly everyone, it was Holt she kept begging for "just one more." With every successful run, her body relaxed and her trust in him built.

The wind picked up as the afternoon wore on, bringing with it heavier snow. I'd gone on a couple of runs on my own, crashed both times, then called it a day. After that, I stood and watched my daughter, my initial worry giving way to enjoyment as I watched her uninhibited excitement.

"I think it's time to head in," TJ called after a particularly strong gust sent snow swirling around us. "Hot chocolate for everyone who's frozen!"

Luna pouted but didn't argue when I suggested we follow the others inside. I looked around for Holt and saw he was helping Cord gather the sleds.

"Your girl's got spirit," Buck commented, walking inside with us. "Way more energy than Buckaroo, and he's a handful on a slow day."

I ruffled Luna's hair when she pulled off her cap once we were inside. "I'll admit she's pretty special," I said, smiling for the millionth time in the last hour.

Buck grinned in my direction. "Holt thinks both of you are, seems like."

"Well, we think he's pretty awesome too, don't we, Luna-bug?"

"He's the *awesomest* ever," she said before looking in the direction of the boys, who were back to playing with Christmas toys.

"Go ahead," I said, giving her a gentle push.

I laughed when she raced off.

"I better get dinner started," Flynn said on her way into the kitchen.

"I'll help," offered Juni.

"Me too," said Sam.

"I think you should all relax and let me do it," I offered. "I haven't helped at all."

"Tell you what; you can make the salad."

"I'm in," I responded, walking over to the sink to wash my hands. When I turned around, I caught Flynn wiping away a tear. She was facing away from the others, so I doubt they'd noticed. "You okay?" I asked.

She rolled her eyes and laughed. "Oh, I'm fine. Everything makes me emotional these days."

I raised a brow, and she put one finger in front of her lips. "I'm still in my first trimester, so we aren't saying anything yet," she whispered.

"My lips are sealed," I whispered like she had.

"Oh, yeah? Keepin' secrets?" said Holt, who I hadn't heard walk up behind me. I immediately tensed as guilt flooded me at his implication. Then I felt his arm snake around my waist and his warm breath near my ear. "I'm teasing, Keltie. That was more for Flynn than for you."

I nodded once, but the guilt didn't dissipate. "I'm, uh, supposed to be making the salad."

"I'll help," he offered.

Flynn pointed a knife in his direction. "You can mash the potatoes."

"See how mean she gets when she's pregnant?" he whispered quietly enough that only his sister and I heard him.

Flynn shook her head. "I swear the man is clairvoyant."

Before I could say anything else, Luna appeared in the doorway, rubbing her eyes with one hand while clutching Bunny with the other.

"Mommy?" she called sleepily. "When are we going on the sleigh rides?"

Flynn smiled. "Soon, sweetheart."

Luna's face brightened, and her fatigue dissipated. "Can we eat *now*?"

"No, honey," I said quickly. "But if you help us, I bet we can eat sooner."

"Over here, unicorn gal," said Flynn, pulling a stool up to the counter for her. She grabbed dough from the refrigerator and plastic cookie cutters that she set in front of her. "These will be for dessert," she explained. "Christmas trees and stars."

As I watched Luna press the cutters into the dough, her tongue poking out in concentration, I realized that, for today at least, we belonged here—in this kitchen, in this home, with this family, and with the man currently smashing potatoes like his life depended on it.

Sometimes, family wasn't what you were born into, but what you found along the way. As Luna giggled at Flynn's stories about her brothers as children, I touched the pendant at my throat and let myself believe that, for right now, perhaps we'd found ours.

12

Holt

The family was gathered in the dining room, the warmth of the Christmas dinner preparations filling the house with delicious aromas and laughter. As we were carrying dishes into the dining room, Buck's phone rang. He glanced at the screen, raising a brow. "It's Kaleb Ackerman. I better take this."

He stepped away, his expression growing serious as he listened. After ending the call, he looked out the window. "There's a fast-moving blizzard heading our way and moving north. The sheriff says it's a bad one."

Flynn crossed to the window, pushing the curtain aside. "It's already coming down pretty hard."

I looked out to see thick flakes swirling in the darkness, the ranch lights illuminating their chaotic descent. The wind had picked up too, bending tree branches in sharp, erratic movements.

"We should head home," Keltie said immediately, concern flashing across her face. "Before the roads get too bad."

Luna, who'd been happily arranging her stuffed animal in an empty chair at the table, looked up with dismay. "But we're supposed to go on a sleigh ride!"

"We'll have to do that another night," Keltie told her.

I glanced between Luna and the window, hating the thought of their evening being cut short, but more than that, hating the idea of taking the two of them out on the road in the deteriorating conditions.

"That's part of the reason Kaleb called. He wanted to make sure none of us were headed into town."

"The Goat's supposed to reopen tomorrow," Keltie said more to herself than any of us.

"Why don't you call Miguel?" I suggested. "See how bad it looks from his place."

Keltie pulled out her phone. The call was brief, but the concern on her face worsened with each passing moment.

"That bad?" I asked when she hung up.

"He says it's coming down heavily in town too. Road crews are already having trouble keeping up, and the highway between here and the butte might close soon." She sighed, running a hand through her hair. "Miguel offered to open the Goat tomorrow if he can make it in. Said not to worry."

"Then, stay," Flynn urged, bringing the last dish to the table. "We've got tons of room."

Keltie's expression shifted from concern to alarm. "Luna's medication. I don't have it with me."

"Medication?" Flynn asked.

"For her fever." Keltie's voice tightened with distress. "It's at home. I can't believe I didn't think to bring it. What kind of mother forgets something that important?"

"The kind who's been through a lot lately," I said softly, touching her arm. "We'll figure it out."

As I spoke, a flash hit me—a vision so vivid that it might have been a memory. Luna thrashing in bed, her face flushed with fever, her breathing labored. The intensity of it made me blink hard, my hand tightening reflexively on Keltie's arm.

"Holt? What's wrong?" she asked, frowning at my expression.

I shook it off, trying to hide how much the premonition had unsettled me. "I'm fine. Let's check the weather report and see exactly what we're dealing with."

Buck was already pulling up the radar on his phone. "Storm's moving north, not south. Highway to Gunnison should still be passable."

I made a quick decision. "I'll drive to the hospital in Gunnison and get her medication."

"What? No," Keltie protested immediately. "It's Christmas, and the roads are dangerous."

I motioned for her to join me in the kitchen so her daughter wouldn't hear us. "Luna's health is more important," I countered, memories of her hospital stay fresh in my mind. "You said yourself how bad it could get if her fever spikes again."

Keltie bit her lip, torn between worry for her daughter and concern for my safety.

"Call the hospital," I urged. "See if Dr. Patel or another doctor on duty can have the medication ready. It'll be a quick trip."

After a moment's hesitation, she made the call. Dr. Patel happened to be there tonight and agreed to have the prescription ready for pickup.

"He says to ask for him at the emergency desk," she told me, covering the phone's microphone. "He'll meet you there."

When she hung up, she turned to me with a mixture of gratitude and anxiety. "The medication is prescription-strength Children's Motrin, the liquid kind. He's giving us extra because of the weather. It's for when her fever goes above 101.5."

"I've got it," I assured her, already grabbing my coat.

"I'm coming with you," Buck announced, reaching for his own jacket. "Better to have two of us on the road in this weather."

Flynn appeared with a backpack full of emergency supplies. "Take the Expedition. It has the best tires and all-wheel drive."

Keltie followed me to the door, her expression torn. "Holt, I don't know how to thank you."

"No need," I said, zipping up my coat.

A small voice interrupted us. "Mr. Holt?"

I turned to find Luna standing in the entryway. I crouched down to her level. "Hey there, Unicorn Girl."

"Where are you going?" she asked, her big brown eyes serious.

"Just into town to get something for your mom. I won't be gone long."

She considered this, then held out her most-prized possession. "Take Sparkles with you. She'll keep bad things away."

My heart squeezed at the gesture. "That's very considerate, but I think Sparkles should stay with you.

How about I promise to return quickly so we can finish her story?"

Luna nodded solemnly. "You have to. We still don't know if she finds her magic flower."

"That's right," I agreed, fighting a sudden tightness in my throat. "And I never leave a story unfinished."

This seemed to satisfy her, and she hugged me quickly before rejoining the other kids. The trust in that hug cemented my resolve.

Keltie's eyes were suspiciously bright when I straightened. "Magic flower?"

I shrugged. "Your daughter has a vivid imagination, and I'm happy to take our story in any direction she wants it to go."

"You're a good man, Holt." I turned to leave, but stopped when I felt her hand on my arm. "Be careful, okay?"

"Always." On impulse, I pressed a quick kiss to her forehead. "Save me some dessert."

The drive started deceptively easy, the Expedition's headlights cutting through the falling snow. I handled navigation while Buck focused on the slick road.

"It looks worse than I thought they'd be," I admitted.

"They aren't as bad as they would be if it was snowing as much as it was at home."

My mind drifted to another snowy night drive years ago—my father grimly silent behind the wheel, me in the passenger seat, racing to the pharmacy for my mother's pain medication. The memory sent a chill through me that had nothing to do with the temperature.

"What's going on in that head of yours?" Buck asked, breaking the silence.

I shrugged, not wanting to admit how worried I was about Luna.

He glanced over at me. "Something's bothering you. Has been since we left."

"Just thinking about everything that's happened," I said vaguely.

He nodded, then after a moment, added, "Everything happens for a reason, as they say." His eyes met mine for a split second. "Kinda like you and Keltie."

"Might be early to talk about us like it's fate, brother."

"I disagree. You're nuts about her; she's crazy about you. That shit only happens when it's meant to be."

I rolled my eyes. "I've been with other women I was crazy about. None of them were meant to be."

He sighed and loosened his grip on the wheel. "If you were honest with yourself, you'd admit this feels different. And Luna, hell, she's the icing on the cake."

While I wouldn't look over at him, I could feel his eyes on me.

"What?" he asked.

I shook my head.

"Out with it, Holt."

"The moment I shook her hand, I sensed something wrong." I spoke quietly enough that I wasn't sure if he could hear me above the sound of the windshield wipers keeping hypnotic time. "Then meeting Keltie, finding out about Remi… It's like puzzle pieces clicking into place."

"Remi?"

"Shit," I muttered. "Forget I said anything."

Buck shook his head. "Out with it. What about Remi?"

"I think he's Luna's father."

"Wow," he said under his breath. "How do you feel about that?"

"He isn't involved, if that's what you meant."

"It wasn't."

I considered the question for several seconds. "It doesn't change my feelings for either of them. If anything, it makes me admire Keltie more, raising Luna on her own." I paused, watching the snow swirl in our headlights. "You should've seen her face when she saw me talking to him. Pure panic. I think she's afraid he'll try to take Luna away."

My brother's eyes scrunched. "Would he?"

I shrugged. "It's doubtful, but you never know." I sighed. "You think I'm crazy, don't you? Getting involved in all this?"

"Not crazy. But definitely setting yourself up for potential heartbreak. Question is, can you walk away?"

The answer came without hesitation. "No. I don't think I could if I tried."

"Then, you've got your answer." Buck smiled. "The trust brought each of us exactly where we needed to be. Funny how that works."

He grew serious, eyes on the road. "You know, I've been thinking, what if Mom's behind all this? The trust, the codicils… It's like she's still watching over us."

Before I could respond, a vision slammed into me—a sickly baby in a hospital crib, tubes attached to its tiny body. The scene shifted, and I saw my mother in a hospital chair, the same baby in her arms. The images were so vivid that my vision blurred.

"Holt?" Buck's voice sounded distant. "You okay?"

I blinked, shaking myself out of it. "Yeah. Fine." I didn't share what I'd seen. It made no sense—my mother died years before Luna was born—yet somehow, it felt important.

"We should get this medicine back to the ranch," Buck said, refocusing on the hazardous drive.

We reached the hospital without further incident. Buck stayed with the Expedition while I went inside, grateful for the blast of warm air that greeted me. The emergency desk directed me to a small waiting area where Dr. Patel soon appeared, medication in hand.

"Thank you for coming out in this weather," he said, his expression kind but concerned. "How is Luna doing?"

"She's good. No fever at the moment," I assured him. "Just want to be prepared, with this storm."

"Smart. I don't think I'll be venturing home tonight."

"Where's home?" I asked before it dawned on me that doctors might not like sharing that kind of information.

"Just this side of Crested Butte. On the outskirts."

My mouth gaped. "The Roaring Fork's my family's place. Roads are fairly clear between here and there right now."

"Had I known that, I could've made a house call." We both chuckled. "Anyway, this should see you through. The instructions for the dosage are on the bottle, but Keltie knows the routine."

I climbed into the SUV and told Buck the medicine was secured.

On the drive home, Buck asked the question I'd been avoiding. "What happens when they go home?"

"What do you mean?"

"Come on, Holt. You've barely spent a moment away from them since they arrived. When life goes back to normal, what then?"

My hands clenched. "All I know is that I don't want to be apart from them."

"Just take it slow. They've both been through a lot."

Nearly two hours after leaving, we pulled into the ranch's driveway. The house was a welcome sight, glowing warmly against the storm.

Keltie met us at the door, the tension visibly leaving her shoulders. "Thank goodness. I was beginning to worry."

I handed her the medication. "One Children's Motrin, as ordered."

She took it, then surprised me by throwing her arms around my neck in a hug. "Thank you. I don't know what I would have done."

I held her close, breathing in the scent of her hair. "Anytime."

Buck tactfully disappeared into the kitchen, leaving us alone in the entryway.

"How's Luna?" I asked, reluctantly releasing her.

"Asleep. She tried to wait up for you, but couldn't keep her eyes open." Keltie's hand remained on my arm. "Are you hungry? I saved you a plate."

"Starving," I admitted, realizing I hadn't eaten since lunch.

After dinner, we found ourselves in the sitting room of the suite she shared with Luna, in front of the fire where we were the night before. Everyone else had gone to bed, leaving us in comfortable privacy.

We sat in silence for a while. Finally, Keltie turned to me, her expression serious.

"Holt, about CB Rice…"

"That's a conversation for another day," I interrupted gently. "It's been a long night."

Relief and maybe gratitude crossed her face as I reached for her, pulling her closer until she was nestled against my side.

"I'm glad you're both safe here," I murmured into her hair.

She tilted her face up to mine, and the invitation in her eyes was unmistakable. I dipped my head, capturing her lips in a kiss that started gentle but quickly deepened with unexpected heat. Her hands slid into my hair as mine wrapped around her waist, drawing her closer.

Hunger built between us as the attraction we both felt became something we could no longer ignore.

With effort, I rested my forehead against hers as we both caught our breath. "We should probably slow down."

Keltie's eyes remained closed. "Probably."

Neither of us moved, though, content to stay in each other's arms as the fire crackled and the storm continued outside. Whatever questions remained unanswered, whatever complications lay ahead, this moment felt genuine, yet totally unexpected. It was definitely a Christmas I'd never forget.

13

Keltie

Holt's fingers traced lazy patterns on my shoulder while outside, the storm continued to howl.

"I should probably check on Luna," I whispered, though I made no move to leave the warmth of his embrace.

His chest rose and fell with a deep breath. "Probably."

Another minute passed. Then another. The spell between us remained unbroken, as if moving would shatter whatever fragile thing we'd created.

Finally, he pressed a kiss to the top of my head and loosened his hold. "I'll let you get to sleep."

As we stood, I found myself unsteady, whether from exhaustion or emotion, I couldn't tell. Holt's hand found the small of my back, guiding me through the sitting room to the bedroom door behind which Luna slept peacefully.

"Thank you," I said softly. "For everything today."

His eyes, impossibly blue even in the dim light, held mine. "Sleep well, Keltie."

I watched him walk away before slipping into the bedroom, my heart hammering against my ribs like a teenager after her first kiss. Inside, Luna was curled around Bunny and her new unicorn, her dark curls fanned across the pillow. I touched her forehead—cool, thank goodness—and crawled beside her under the covers, my mind racing with thoughts of Holt, Remi, and everything we'd eventually have to talk about.

Morning arrived with a quiet that suggested the storm had passed. Sunlight spilled across the bed as I blinked awake, disoriented for a moment until I remembered where we were. Luna was already up, sitting cross-legged at the foot of the bed with her stuffed animals arranged in a semicircle.

"Good morning, Mommy," she said when she noticed me watching. "Sparkles and Bunny are having breakfast. Pancakes with extra syrup."

I pushed myself up, smiling at her imagination. "That sounds delicious. Will they share with me?"

"These are pretend pancakes," she explained seriously. "But Flynn said she's making real ones for everybody."

"Is she, now? And how do you know that?"

"I went to find her, and she was in the kitchen. She said to tell you breakfast is whenever we want it." Luna bounced on the mattress. "Can we have breakfast now? Please?"

I glanced at my phone—just after seven. "Let me get dressed first, okay? Then we can go find those pancakes."

As I collected our scattered belongings, Luna watched with growing dismay.

"Are we leaving?" Her lower lip trembled.

I sat beside her on the bed. "We need to go home today, sweetie. We've imposed on the Wheatons enough, and the Goat needs to open tonight."

"But…" Her voice quavered. "What about the twins? And Buckaroo? And Mr. Holt's story about Sparkles?"

"Why did you start calling him Mr. Holt instead of Mr. Wheaton?"

Luna sighed and cocked her head. "Because every man here is Mr. Wheaton, Mommy. How would they know who I was talking to?"

While every man here *wasn't* Mr. Wheaton, her reasoning still made sense.

"You're pretty smart, you know that?"

She grinned. "You tell me enough. But you didn't answer my question. When can we see everyone again?"

"It won't be long. I promise." I smoothed a wayward curl from her forehead. "And I'm sure Mr. Holt will finish that story another time."

Luna clutched Sparkles tighter. "Are the roads still bad?"

I moved to the window and opened the heavy curtains. Outside, the ranch was transformed into a winter wonderland—snow blanketing every surface, icicles hanging from the eaves, and the distant mountains crisp against the clear blue sky. But the driveway had been plowed, a dark ribbon cutting through the pristine white.

"Looks like someone's been busy clearing the roads," I told her. "We should be able to get home okay."

Luna's shoulders slumped in defeat, but she began gathering her toys. The resignation on her small face made my heart ache. This Christmas had been magical for her—for both of us—in ways I hadn't anticipated.

I hesitated, then zipped our bag closed. "Let's go have those pancakes, and then we'll figure out the rest, okay?"

Her smile returned instantly. "Okay!"

When we reached the kitchen, the Wheaton family was already gathered for breakfast. Flynn was making pancakes shaped like snowmen, which delighted Luna and the twins. Irish handed me a coffee—black, just as I liked it—and mentioned that Holt had told him my preference.

I kept glancing toward the doorway, trying to keep my curiosity about his whereabouts from being too obvious. When he finally appeared, his hair damp from a shower, my pulse jumped. His eyes found mine, and the slow smile spreading across his face sent warmth spiraling through me.

"Mornin'," he said, sliding into the empty chair beside me. His knee brushed mine under the table, and I wondered if the contact was accidental or deliberate.

"Morning," I replied, forgetting my coffee, my breakfast, and everyone else in the room.

"Mommy packed our bag," Luna announced at large, breaking whatever spell had momentarily entranced me. "We have to go home today."

A chorus of disappointed sounds erupted from around the table. Sam was the first to speak.

"So soon?" she protested.

"The Goat reopens tonight," I explained, feeling strangely defensive about our departure. "And we've already imposed enough—"

"You haven't imposed at all," Flynn interrupted firmly. "We've loved having you both here."

I looked out the window at the clear day, knowing we had to leave, but wishing we could stay.

"Just let me know when you're ready," Holt said, his voice casual, though something in his eyes wasn't. "There are things I need to take care of in town. Then I was thinking maybe we could go to the Secret Stash for lunch; that's if you're hungry by then."

Luna pushed her plate in my direction. "I'm full, Mommy. Do you want the rest?"

"You haven't had five bites."

She sighed at me like she had earlier. "You *know* Stash pizza is my weakness. Plus, I want to show Mr. Holt my room at home."

I nearly choked on my coffee. "Luna, I'm sure Mr. Holt did say he had things to take care of—"

"They can wait," he interjected, a smile tugging at his lips. "Got nothing but time for my favorite girls."

From across the table, Buck snorted into his coffee while TJ elbowed him discreetly. I felt my cheeks warm, aware that everyone was watching our exchange with barely concealed interest.

After breakfast, Luna went to play with the twins one last time while Flynn prepared several containers for us to take home.

"Leftovers," she explained, setting them in front of me. "And I packed the Christmas cookies Luna helped make yesterday. I thought she might want to show them off at home."

Tears pricked unexpectedly at my eyes. "That's so thoughtful. Thank you."

"And this," she added, placing a small wrapped package beside the containers, "is a little something from all of us. A memory of your time here."

"I feel terrible that I didn't bring anything for any of you," I protested, embarrassed by their generosity.

TJ smiled from across the table. "Your being here was gift enough. This place needed new energy, and you two brought it."

"Tell you what. Name the day and time, and I'll host all of you for dinner at the Goat."

"You don't have to do that—"

"Yes, she does," argued Irish, interrupting her. "Their prime rib is the best in town."

Flynn glared at him, and he kissed her cheek.

"Other than yours of course, sweetheart."

Goodbyes were lengthy and emotional. Sam hugged me tightly as we prepared to leave.

"Don't forget about our coffee," she whispered.

"I won't," I promised, surprised by how much I wanted to maintain this newfound connection. "And you don't forget about dinner at the Goat."

I expected tears from Luna as we finally headed out to Holt's truck, our bags and gifts loaded inside, but she seemed content knowing she'd see everyone again. Perhaps the presence of Holt beside us eased the transition, a piece of the Wheaton family coming with us.

The drive to town was quick with the cleared roads. Luna chattered excitedly the entire way, recounting Christmas highlights and begging to go sledding again with the twins and Buckaroo. Holt caught my eye when she asked, and I promised we'd see about doing it again when the snow was fresh.

When we pulled up to my house, Luna was out of her booster seat and climbing out of the truck before I'd even unbuckled my seat belt. Holt grabbed our bags and followed us up the walkway, snow crunching beneath our boots.

Inside, the house felt cold and still, as if it too had missed us during our absence. I turned up the thermostat while Luna eagerly grabbed Holt's hand.

"Come see my room," she insisted, tugging him toward the hallway. "I need to show you where Sparkles is going to live."

Holt glanced at me, eyebrows raised in question.

"Go ahead," I said, smiling at Luna's enthusiasm. "I'll put on a pot of coffee."

As they disappeared up the stairs, Luna's excited voice explaining the importance of proper unicorn housing, I busied myself in the kitchen. The familiar routine of measuring coffee grounds and filling the water reservoir calmed my nerves, which had inexplicably tangled at the thought of Holt in my home, seeing my life up close, the small, ordinary details I shared with no one but Luna.

The coffee had finished brewing when Holt walked into the kitchen, minus Luna.

"She's arranging all her new toys," he explained, leaning against the counter. "Told me she needed to get everything perfect before I could see the final result."

I smiled, pouring coffee into two mugs. "She's very particular about her space. Gets that from me, I'm afraid."

"Nothing wrong with knowing how you want things," he replied, accepting the mug I offered.

Our fingers brushed during the exchange, and for a moment, I was transported to the previous night—his arms around me, his lips on mine, the heat that had built between us before common sense prevailed.

"About last night," I began, then faltered, unsure what I wanted to say.

Holt took a sip of his coffee, those blue eyes watching me over the rim of his mug. "Last night was nice."

"It was," I agreed, feeling my cheeks warm. "But there are things you should know. Things I should have told you before…"

He set his mug down and moved closer. "I'm listening."

I took a deep breath, steeling myself for a conversation I'd avoided for years. "You figured out I worked for CB Rice as a sound engineer."

"Ben mentioned it."

"And you probably figured out that Luna's father is—"

"Remi Gilbert," he finished quietly. "Yeah, I put that together."

Relief and anxiety tangled in my chest at having it out in the open. "It happened during the European tour five years ago when I was twenty-two. I was young, flattered by his attention, and thought I was in love."

Holt remained silent, giving me space to continue.

"We were together for three months. When I told him I was pregnant, he denied the baby was his and had me replaced on the tour that same day."

"Jesus," Holt muttered, his jaw tightening. "I knew he was an asshole, but that's beyond—"

"I flew home to my dad's place in New Mexico and stayed with him until Luna was born," I continued, pushing past the old hurt. "I haven't seen Remi since, and as far as I know, he has no idea Luna exists."

"You saw him on your street the other day," Holt observed softly.

I closed my eyes briefly, the panic of that moment washing over me again. "I never thought he'd be here, in Crested Butte, of all places. God, what if he sees Luna? Puts two and two together?"

"That's not going to happen," Holt said with unexpected fierceness. "I won't let it."

"You can't promise that," I whispered, though his certainty was oddly comforting.

"I can." He took my hands in his, our coffee forgotten. "Keltie, I know we haven't known each other long, but I care about you, and I care about Luna. I'll do whatever it takes to keep you safe."

The intensity in his eyes made my breath catch. "Why? Why would you take this on?"

"Because from the moment I met Luna, I knew she was special. And from the moment I met you…" He paused, his thumbs tracing circles on my hands. "I've never felt for anyone what I feel for you."

My heart hammered in my chest, a mix of hope and fear making it difficult to think clearly. "Holt, there's something else. Luna's appointment in Denver—"

"Mommy!" Luna's voice interrupted as she bounded into the kitchen. "I finished setting up Sparkles' new home! Mr. Holt, you have to come see!"

Holt released my hands, though reluctance flashed across his face. "Lead the way, Unicorn Girl."

Luna grabbed his hand, pulling him toward the stairs, leaving me standing in the kitchen trying to stop my head from whirling after hearing him say he'd never felt for anyone what he felt for me. If I'd had the chance, I would've confessed the same thing.

When they returned to the kitchen, Luna was practically beaming with pride. "Mr. Holt says Sparkles has the best home he's ever seen!"

"High praise, indeed," I said, forcing a smile despite the seriousness of our interrupted conversation.

"When will we see you again?" Luna asked Holt, her question direct in the way only children can manage.

Holt crouched down to her level. "Well, I haven't forgotten our pizza date. Have you?"

"No, but…I promised Sparkles and Bunny that we could play a while first."

"I don't know about you, but I'm still full from breakfast, Luna-bug." While she hadn't eaten her pancakes, we both ate far more in the last two days than we usually did.

"Maybe we could have pizza for dinner, instead?" She looked at Holt with wide eyes.

"I think that could be arranged. I'm playing music at your mom's bar. And probably a few more times this week."

Luna turned to me with pleading eyes. "Mommy, we can have pizza with Mr. Holt tonight, then tomorrow, you could make him dinner."

I glanced at Holt, whose expression divulged nothing. "If Mr. Holt wants to come for dinner, he's welcome anytime."

"I'd like that," he said softly, his gaze holding mine.

Luna clapped her hands in delight. "Good! Because Sparkles already told me you were going to be our new best friend."

Holt chuckled, ruffling her curls. "Smart unicorn you've got there."

As he prepared to leave, I remembered something. "About tonight—you said you need to play three times a week at local establishments, right? For the trust?"

"That's right."

"You're already scheduled to play Thursdays and Saturdays. If there's another night you want to add, you have your pick," I offered.

Surprise and gratitude flashed across his face. He leaned close enough to feel the warmth of his breath on my neck. "Not sure I'll be able to stay away any night, Keltie."

My cheeks flushed. "You're always welcome."

His lips brushed my cheek. "Glad to hear it."

Luna insisted on one more hug before he left, wrapping her small arms around his neck tightly enough that it looked like she was strangling him. I walked him to the door, feeling awkward now that our time together was ending.

"Thank you for everything," I said. "Christmas, the rides, the medication run…all of it."

Holt's eyes searched mine. "See you later?"

"Yes," I promised. "And about the Goat tonight—what time will you be in?"

"Eight?" he suggested. "Unless that's too late."

"Eight is perfect. Luna will be with Mrs. Lopez tonight."

He hesitated at the threshold, clearly debating something. Then, with a quick glance to make sure Luna wasn't watching, he leaned forward. His kiss felt soft on my lips. "All night?"

It took me a minute to figure out what he meant. "Oh, Mrs. Lopez? Err, no, not all night, but…"

He winked. "See you soon, darlin'."

I stood at the door long after his truck disappeared down the street, my fingers absently touching the pendant at my throat. Relief at finally sharing my past with him mingled with the apprehension about what was developing between us. Everything was happening so quickly—the connection, the trust, the feelings I couldn't deny.

And looming over it all was Luna's appointment four days from now, in Denver.

14

Holt

Back at my cabin, I picked up the guitar and began playing a melody that seemed to capture Luna's bright spirit. The notes flowed, building into a tune that felt both new and somehow familiar, as if I'd known it all along but was only now remembering. I thought of her face when she told me the name she'd chosen for the unicorn Santa gave her—Sparkles. And the absolute conviction in her eyes when she'd explained that the stuffed animal could "keep bad things away." Children believed in magic because they hadn't yet learned not to.

Lyrics began taking shape in my mind. A song about a magical creature with healing powers—one who helped sick children feel better, who carried away their fears on rainbow wings. It was sentimental, maybe even a little cheesy, but I couldn't stop the words from coming.

"Sparkles, with a mane of silver light, watches over children through the darkest night…"

My phone rang, breaking the creative flow. I considered ignoring it, but the caller ID showed Ben Rice's name.

"Ben," I answered, setting the guitar aside. "What's up?"

"Holt! Glad I caught you." His voice boomed through the speaker. "Listen, I meant what I said yesterday, about the recording studio. How about you come by tomorrow? Check out what we've got, maybe lay down a few tracks?"

My interest was piqued, and I sat up straighter. "That's generous, Ben. I appreciate it."

"Nothing generous about it. Your songs are good—really good. Like I said, just because you can't tour, it doesn't mean we can't get some recording done. I've been thinking about what you said about staying local. What if we recorded an EP? Four or five songs, something to keep your name out there while you're stuck in CB."

The offer was tempting—more than tempting.

"I'd like that," I said, surprising myself with how much I meant it.

"Great! Come by around noon tomorrow. I'll show you around, introduce you to our sound engineer. Manny's good—not Keltie Marquez good—but solid."

"Thanks again, Ben."

"See you tomorrow, then. Noon sharp."

After hanging up, I grabbed my guitar again, but my mind kept circling to the night at the hospital.

As I continued playing, it happened again.

Another vision hit me—this one more intense than before. Luna was in a hospital bed surrounded by machines. Doctors were discussing treatment options while Keltie wept silently.

I gasped, the guitar sliding from my lap and hitting the floor with a discordant clang.

Before I could talk myself out of it, I grabbed my phone and dialed Gunnison Valley Hospital. When the operator answered, I asked to speak with Dr. Patel.

He came on the line seconds later. "How can I help you?"

"Doctor, it's Holt Wheaton," I said, trying to keep my voice steady. "We met yesterday when I picked up medication for Luna Marquez."

"Yes, of course. Is everything all right? Has Luna's fever worsened?"

"No, nothing like that," I assured him quickly. "Actually, I have questions about children with similar symptoms. Purely hypothetical."

There was a pause on the other end of the line. "I see," he said, his tone suggesting he understood my true purpose. "Well, hypothetically speaking, recurring fevers in children can have many causes. Most are benign—viral infections, growth phases, even stress."

"And the more serious causes?" I prompted when he didn't continue.

Dr. Patel sighed. "Without specifics, it's difficult to say. But persistent, unexplained fevers, especially when accompanied by other symptoms, like fatigue or unusual bruising, can sometimes indicate more concerning conditions."

"Like leukemia?" I asked bluntly, the word sitting like a stone in my stomach.

"That would be one possibility, yes. But I'd caution against jumping to conclusions without proper testing."

"Again, hypothetically speaking, what would the treatment look like for something like that? For a child?"

"Protocols vary depending on the specific diagnosis," he explained. "But many childhood cancers respond well these days. We've made significant advances in finding cures."

"And the costs?" I asked, thinking of Keltie working late nights at the Goat.

"Substantial," he admitted. "But there are resources. Insurance, of course, and organizations like the Miracles of Hope Children's Charity here in Crested Butte that specifically helps local families with medical expenses."

The mention of the charity—the very one named in my codicil—sent a chill down my spine. I thanked Dr. Patel for his time and hung up, my mind racing.

Was it possible? Could there be a connection between the trust's requirement that I donate to this specific charity and Luna's condition? It seemed far-fetched, yet the coincidence felt too specific to ignore.

By the time I needed to head to the Goat for my required performance, my head was pounding with worry and information overload from spending hours researching childhood illnesses.

I arrived early, needing to see Keltie, to reassure myself that everything was all right despite what my premonition had shown me.

The bar was quiet when I walked in, typical for the day after Christmas. A few regulars occupied tables near the windows, nursing beers and watching the last of the daylight fade behind the mountains. Keltie stood behind the bar, arranging glasses.

"You're early," she said, turning at the sound of the bell. Her smile when she saw me eased the tightness in my chest. She wore her usual flannel shirt and jeans, hair pulled into a messy ponytail, the pendant I'd given her visible at her throat.

"Couldn't stay away," I admitted, setting my guitar case on a nearby stool. "How's Luna?"

"Still over the moon about Christmas," Keltie replied, her eyes softening. "By now, I'm sure she's shown Mrs. Lopez all her gifts twenty times."

I chuckled, picturing Luna's enthusiasm.

"Thank you again, Holt. For everything."

I moved closer, lowering my voice. "No need to thank me. It was the best Christmas I've had in years."

"Same here."

The bar was empty enough for me to speak freely. "Ben Rice called. Invited me to check out his recording studio tomorrow."

Keltie's head shot up; surprise and pleasure crossed her face. "Holt, that's great!"

"I mean, it's nothing more than a tour," I cautioned, not wanting to oversell it. "Although he did mention recording an EP while I'm stuck here."

"Stuck here," she repeated.

"Poor choice of words," I said quickly. "Trust me, there are worse places to be required to stay."

Her smile warmed her eyes. "I'm glad you think so."

I motioned toward the small stage. "Mind if I play something new? Something I've been working on today?"

"The stage is all yours," she said, gesturing with a sweeping hand.

I retrieved my guitar and settled onto the stool, adjusting the microphone, though I didn't plan to sing the lyrics yet. They weren't quite finished, and this song felt different—meant for Luna's ears first, or at least for Keltie's, before anyone else heard it.

My fingers found the notes of the gentle tune without conscious thought. The melody was hopeful and sweet, with a chorus that lilted upward like a child's laughter. I kept my eyes on my hands, but I could feel Keltie watching me.

When I finished, I looked up to find her standing motionless, clutching a towel to her chest, her eyes suspiciously bright.

"That was beautiful," she said quietly.

"It's for Luna," I admitted, setting the guitar aside and approaching the bar. "A healing song about Sparkles."

Keltie's breath caught. "Healing?"

I shrugged, trying to sound casual. "Kids believe in magic. Sometimes, it helps."

She blinked rapidly as if fighting tears. "My mother used to sing old Scottish lullabies about rivers and stars."

"I didn't know you had Scottish heritage."

"On my mother's side, obviously," she confirmed. "Hence the name Keltie. She died when I was very young. About the same age you were when you lost your mother."

I reached across the bar, covering her hand with mine. "She'd be proud of you, you know. The way you're raising Luna."

"I hope so," she whispered, turning her hand to lace her fingers with mine. "There are days when I feel like I'm failing her completely."

"Not possible," I said firmly. "That little girl adores you. Anyone can see it."

She squeezed my hand before releasing it, taking a deep breath to compose herself. "Speaking of Luna, did you know she asked if you could teach her guitar?"

I grinned. "She might have mentioned it a time or twenty. I'd be happy to, if you're okay with it."

"More than okay," Keltie assured me. "She needs good influences in her life. Male ones, especially."

The implications of her words—that she saw me as potentially filling that role—weren't lost on me. A weight of responsibility settled alongside the pleasure her trust brought.

"About Ben's studio," I said, changing the subject. "He suggested I ask you to come with me when I start recording. Not that it's happening right away, but…" I trailed off, watching her reaction. "Maybe someday you'd like to get behind a mixing board again?"

A flicker of uncertainty crossed her face before she admitted, "I'd love that. Someday." Her emphasis on the last word made it clear that "someday" wasn't today or tomorrow. "It's been a long time, but I miss it. The technical challenge, the creativity of it."

"You were good at it," I said. "Ben made that clear."

She looked away. "That feels like another lifetime."

"It doesn't have to be," I offered gently.

Before she could respond, the door opened and a group of people who'd obviously spent the day on the slopes entered, laughing and stomping snow from their boots. Keltie's professional smile slid into place as she turned to greet them.

I walked over to the stage, using the interruption to get ready for my first set.

Over the next couple of hours, more customers filtered in, though the crowd remained thin compared to a typical night. I played my usual mix of covers and originals, watching Keltie work the bar the same way she always did.

Closing time came early, given the place emptied out quickly once nine o'clock rolled around. I packed my stuff and found Miguel wiping down tables while Keltie counted out the register.

"I can finish up if you want to head out," Miguel offered, glancing from her to me. "Not much left to do anyway."

Keltie hesitated. "If you're sure. It has been a long couple of days."

"Go," he insisted with a smile. "I got this."

I packed up my guitar, trying not to appear too eager at this development. "Walk you to your vehicle?" I asked casually.

"Actually, I didn't drive," she explained, pulling on her coat. "It was such a nice afternoon. But I wouldn't turn down a lift home."

The cold air hit us as we stepped outside, stars blazing overhead in the clear mountain sky. I opened the passenger door of my truck for her, then rounded to the driver's side, my heart beating faster than the short walk warranted.

"Luna's with Mrs. Lopez?" I asked as we drove the short distance to her house.

"Actually, the other way around. Mrs. Lopez puts her to sleep in her own bed, then walks next door once I'm home."

I pulled up in front of her house, unsure of the protocol here. Were we saying good night? Was I invited in? The uncertainty must have shown on my face because Keltie smiled.

"I need to settle things with Mrs. Lopez," she said. "Wait here?"

"You got it." I watched as she disappeared into the house. Shortly after that, I spotted the woman I saw the first night I met Luna walk out of this house and into her own. Taking that as my cue, I approached Keltie's front door, which opened before I could knock.

She stood in the soft light of the entryway, her hair, freed from its ponytail, cascaded over her shoulders in wild curls. The sight of her stole my breath.

"Hi," she said simply.

The moment the door closed behind me, something snapped between us. I pushed her against the wall of the entryway, one hand cupping her face as I bent to kiss her. She met me halfway, rising on her toes, her arms wrapping around my neck as our lips connected.

The kiss was different from the tender ones we'd shared before—this was heat and hunger and release after days of building tension. When I tried to break away, needing to catch my breath, her fingers wove in my hair, holding me close as she deepened our connection.

With a groan, I lifted her in my arms. Her legs wrapped around my waist as I carried her to the living room. I sat on the sofa, with her straddling my lap, our mouths never breaking contact. The weight of her against me, the softness of her body pressed to mine, was intoxicating.

My hands moved to her hips, then slid under her sweater to find the warm skin beneath. I paused, leaning away enough to see her eyes.

"Is this okay?" I asked, my voice heavy with desire.

In answer, Keltie took my hand and guided it upward to her breast. "More than okay," she whispered.

I groaned at the feel of her, soft and perfect in my palm.

"Holt." She gasped as I tweaked her nipple.

We moved together in the warm quiet of her living room, learning each other's bodies with increasingly urgent touches. The rest of the world fell away—the trust, the band, even my worries about Luna—until there was nothing but Keltie and me and the heat building between us.

"I want you so much, darlin'…"

Her eyes met mine. "But…"

I raised a brow, waiting for her to say what we both knew.

"It's too soon, and…"

"Luna," I finished for her.

When she tried to scoot off my lap, I tightened my arm around her waist. "Let me hold you a little while longer? *Please?*"

She smiled when the last word came out sounding a lot like her daughter. "Gladly," she said, kissing me again.

15

Keltie

"Earth to Keltie," Miguel said, snapping his fingers in front of my face. "You okay, boss? That's the second time you've poured vodka instead of tequila."

I blinked, and the bustling reality of the Goat came into focus. Two days after Christmas, and the bar was packed with tourists who'd flooded Crested Butte for the post-holiday ski season. Shortly after the lifts closed, every table was full and the air was thick with conversation and laughter.

"Sorry," I muttered, dumping the vodka and starting fresh.

Miguel's knowing grin told me he'd guessed exactly why I was distracted. "If you say so."

I glanced toward the small stage, where Holt was setting up for an early set. He looked up as if he'd sensed my attention, and the slow smile that spread across his face sent a jolt straight through me. He remembered too—how we'd explored each other's bodies with increasing urgency, how his hands and mouth had brought me so close to the edge that even now, hours later, I was practically trembling with need.

I forced myself to focus on the drink orders piling up from well-dressed out-of-towners with expensive ski gear, willing to leave big tips. Under normal circumstances, I'd be thrilled with the business, but my attention kept drifting between Holt and Luna, who sat near the bar, coloring intently in a new book. I hated that I'd had to bring her with me, but Mrs. Lopez wasn't available tonight, and I hadn't lined up any other sitters.

As afternoon turned to evening, I made my way over to check on Luna during a brief lull. Her coloring had slowed, and she looked up at me with heavy-lidded eyes.

"You tired, Luna-bug?" I asked, brushing a curl from her forehead. The warmth of her skin made me pause.

"A little," she admitted, leaning into my touch. "My tummy feels funny."

I pressed my palm more firmly against her forehead, confirming what I already suspected. She had a fever—not high, but definitely there. I glanced toward the bar, where three deep lines of customers waited for drinks.

"How about some apple juice?" I suggested, keeping my voice light.

Luna rested her head on her arms. "Yes, please."

I hurried behind the bar, grabbed a plastic cup with a lid, and filled it with juice. Miguel glanced at me, then toward Luna.

"She okay?" he asked, mixing two cocktails simultaneously.

"Low-grade fever," I said quietly. "Nothing serious, but I should probably get her home."

Before he could respond, a group of rowdy guys I recognized from ski patrol approached the bar, calling for a round of shots. I handed them off to my other bartender and rushed over to Luna with the juice and medication from Dr. Patel after I'd measured the dose carefully into a small cup.

"Here you go, sweetie. This will help you feel better."

Luna took the medicine without complaint, a sure sign she wasn't feeling well.

I glanced at the crowded bar, then at my daughter. The responsible choice was clear—I needed to take Luna home, but leaving now would mean Miguel would be shorthanded.

"Everything okay?" Holt asked, appearing next to me. His eyes moved from Luna's flushed face to the medicine cup in my hand.

"Another fever," I explained, keeping my voice steady despite the worry gnawing at me. With the Denver appointment looming, every spike in temperature felt more ominous.

Holt crouched beside Luna's chair. "Not feeling too great, huh, Unicorn Girl?"

Luna shook her head, then looked up at him with her enormous brown eyes. "Can you tell me more of Sparkles' story? The one about the magic flower?"

"I'd love to," he said gently. "But I think we should get you home and into your pajamas first. Stories are always better in pajamas. Don't you think?"

Luna nodded solemnly, as if this was a universal truth she'd always known.

Holt straightened and turned to me. "I'll take her to your place."

"I can't ask you to do that," I protested. "You're supposed to be playing tonight."

"I've already done my first set," he pointed out. "That counts for my trust requirements. And wouldn't Luna feel better climbing into bed?"

I hesitated, glancing around at the packed room. Losing Holt's music would disappoint the customers, but my daughter had to come first, even if I wasn't the one to put her there.

"Come on, Keltie. Let me do this."

"You'd need her car seat."

"I know where it is," Luna piped up, her voice small but determined. "And Mr. Holt makes the best soup, Mommy, and I'm hungry."

More guilt settled on my shoulders. She usually didn't like to eat when she wasn't feeling well, but I should've asked.

Holt's eyes met mine over Luna's head. "I'll take good care of her. You know I will."

And the thing was, I did know. Despite how short a time we'd known each other, I trusted him with my daughter in a way I'd never trusted anyone besides family.

"Okay," I relented, brushing Luna's cheek. "But call me if her fever goes up even a little or if anything seems off."

"We promise," he said, offering his pinky to Luna, who solemnly linked hers with his.

I helped Luna gather her things while Holt let Miguel know he was cutting his set short.

At the door, Luna hugged me tightly. "Bye, Mommy. Don't worry. Mr. Holt will tell me stories until I fall asleep."

"Will he, now?" I smiled at Holt. The man seemed heaven-sent.

Luna tugged at his hand. "You'll make me soup too, right?"

"Sure will. Campbell's finest," he teased. "Plus, I make a mean grilled cheese to go with it."

"The house key is under the ceramic frog," I told him. "Her pajamas are in the second drawer of her dresser. And call me if—"

"Anything changes," he finished. "We'll be fine, right, Luna?"

"Yes, Mommy." My daughter was already perking up at the prospect of soup and stories. As they walked out into the cold night, Luna's small hand tucked trustingly in Holt's much larger one, a warmth spread over me that was replaced by loud warning bells that things between us were moving too quickly.

I threw myself into work, trying to stay focused despite my mind constantly drifting to my daughter and the man who was taking care of her. Miguel shot me reassuring glances, stepping up his pace to compensate for my distraction.

"Keltie?"

I turned to find Sam and Beau weaving through the crowd toward me, a welcome distraction from my spiraling thoughts. Beau stood behind her as she slid onto the one empty barstool, unwinding a scarf from around her neck.

"It's packed in here!"

"Ski season can be crazy."

"Want help?" she asked, surprising me.

"Um…"

"I used to run a wine bar, but I'm also pretty good at pouring beer."

I glance over at the line waiting for drinks and the servers at their station, doing the same thing.

"I'd love that," I finally replied. "Aprons are on the hook in the hallway."

"Perfect. By the way, where's Holt tonight? I thought he was playing."

"Luna got a fever," I explained, the worry creeping into my voice despite my efforts. "He took her home so I could finish my shift."

Sam's eyebrows rose, but her smile widened. "That's, err, nice."

"I feel bad taking advantage of him," I said quickly, feeling my cheeks warm.

"Don't. He wouldn't do it if he didn't want to. Plus, no one has missed the way he looks at you. The dude's got it *bad*."

The hours passed quickly, given how busy we were. I checked my cell periodically, and each time, Holt had sent a new photo of Luna. The last one was of her snuggled with her bunny and unicorn, sound asleep.

"He's a pretty good babysitter," Sam said, looking over my shoulder. "So, how's she doing?"

I busied myself wiping down the bar, knowing Sam didn't mean tonight. "We have a doctor's appointment in Denver soon," I found myself saying. "For tests."

Sam's expression immediately sobered. "When is it?"

"December 30."

"I can come with you," she said without hesitation. "For support. I can drive so you can focus on Luna."

The offer caught me off guard. "I thought you were leaving for New York."

Sam glanced at Beau, who'd spent the evening engaged in conversation with people at the bar.

"My husband suggested we stay until after the new year, and I happily agreed. I miss Cord and Juni so much now that they've moved to Colorado full time."

"While I appreciate the offer, I don't want to take you away from your family."

Sam nudged me. "You're family too. So is Luna."

Family. The word resonated more deeply than I'd expected. "Thank you." My throat tightened. "That would actually help a lot."

By the time she and Beau left and Miguel flipped the sign to "closed," my feet ached and my mind was foggy with exhaustion.

"Go home," he urged, collecting empty glasses from the tables. "I'll finish up."

"You sure?" I asked, already untying my apron.

"Positive. There isn't much left to do besides set the alarm and lock the doors."

"I appreciate it."

"Of course," Miguel responded.

I grabbed my coat and keys and went out to the parking area behind the bar, stunned to see someone had cleaned the snow off my truck. Knowing Holt wouldn't have left Luna alone at the house, I decided it must've been Miguel. I made a mental note to give the guy a raise.

The drive home took less than five minutes, but it felt endless. When I finally pushed open my front door, the house was quiet and warm. I kicked off my boots in the entryway and padded up the stairs to Luna's room.

The door was cracked open, a soft nightlight casting a gentle glow on Luna, who was sleeping peacefully. Holt was sitting in the rocking chair, reading something on a tablet, and smiled while I glanced over at him.

"Hey," he whispered. "How was the rest of your shift?"

"Busy," I replied, following him into the hallway and closing the door behind us. "How did she do?"

"Good. Her fever broke about an hour after we got here. We had soup, read about twenty stories, and she fell asleep around nine." He gestured toward the kitchen. "There's a plate for you in the microwave. Grilled cheese and tomato soup. Not gourmet, but it's sustenance."

I blinked, oddly touched by the simple gesture. "You made me dinner?"

"And cleaned up afterwards," he added with a half smile. "Don't look so surprised. I'm actually pretty handy for a would-be rock star."

The normality of it all—Holt in my living room, dinner waiting for me, Luna sleeping soundly down the hall—it was something I could get used to if I ever allowed myself to be so stupid. It felt like we'd skipped dozens of steps, fast-forwarding to a domesticity I'd never experienced with anyone.

"Thank you," I said, the words inadequate for the gratitude welling up inside me. "For everything. Luna's never this comfortable with strangers."

"We're not strangers anymore," he pointed out gently. "Are we?"

"No," I admitted. "We're not."

I went to the kitchen and found the plate he'd mentioned, then warmed it in the microwave. When I joined him in the living room with my late dinner, Holt stood by the window, gazing out at the snow-covered street.

"You should eat that while it's hot," he said. "And I should probably head out."

"You don't have to go," I said before I could stop myself. "Unless you want to."

He studied me, then slowly moved closer, as if giving me the opportunity to change my mind. By the time he was beside me, I'd set my plate on the coffee table.

"I don't want to go, but I don't trust myself to stay without touching you again."

Heat bloomed in my chest, spreading outward until even my fingertips tingled with awareness. "I wouldn't mind if you did."

That was all the invitation he needed. He sunk down next to me on the sofa and found my mouth with a kiss that started gentle but quickly deepened with the pent-up need we shared. My hands slid under his shirt to find warm skin stretched over firm muscles.

I shifted, and he rested his body above mine. His hands were everywhere—in my hair, skimming down my sides, slipping beneath the hem of my shirt to trace the outline of my bra. When his thumb brushed across my nipple through the fabric, I gasped against his mouth.

"Do you know how much I want you?" he murmured against my throat.

I arched against him in response, seeking more contact, more friction. I opened my legs, and his hardness ground against me in a rhythm that made stars explode behind my eyelids. Forgetting myself, I cried out in pleasure.

"Luna," I gasped, knowing how sound carried up the stairwell.

"She's sound asleep," Holt replied, his breath hot against my ear. "But we don't have to do anything you're not ready for."

"It's not that I don't want to," I began, trying to organize my jumbled thoughts. "God knows I do."

"But, you have a little girl to consider. I get that, darlin'." I melted at the understanding in his eyes. "I'm not going anywhere, Keltie. Whatever happens with Luna, whatever comes next—I want to be here for it. For both of you."

"You say that now," I whispered, voicing the insecurity that always crept in. "But once your year in Crested Butte is up, you'll get back to your real life."

Holt shook his head, cupping my face in his hands. "*This* is my real life. Time on the road isn't."

I wanted to believe him. More than anything, I wanted to lean into what he was offering—support, companionship, maybe even love, eventually. But the fear of getting hurt again or Luna losing his presence in her life stopped me.

"I need time," I admitted.

"We can go as slow as you want," Holt said, brushing his thumb across my cheekbone. "I should go so you can sleep before Luna wakes up." He shifted off the sofa—off me—and I immediately missed his warmth.

I walked him to the door, our hands linked loosely. In the entryway, he turned to me one last time.

"Call me tomorrow? Let me know how Luna's feeling?"

"I will. And, Holt?" I hesitated, then continued, "Thank you for understanding."

His smile was warm enough to chase away the winter chill. "That's what friends do, right? Although," he added with a wink, "I'm hoping we're more than 'friends' by now."

After he left, I stood in the quiet house for a long moment, touching my fingers to lips still tender from his kisses. Going back to my abandoned dinner, I realized there was no denying the truth anymore: I was falling for him, faster and harder than I'd ever fallen for anyone.

16

Holt

I bolted upright at five in the morning, my shirt damp against my skin despite the winter cold permeating my cabin. The dream of my mother sobbing as she cradled a tiny, frail baby refused to fade. My father stood on the opposite side of a window, looking in at them with tears streaking down his cheeks. His unmistakable distress, when he was usually rigid with stern authority, jarred me. I'd never known him to show grief or such stark vulnerability, even after my mom died.

The sheets were twisted around my legs as I sat there, my pulse racing. These dreams were intensifying, gaining detail and clarity with each occurrence. What baby? My mother had died when Flynn was a toddler. There hadn't been another child after her.

I pulled the blanket up to my chin to ward off the cold. The fire had died during the night, and I'd forgotten to turn the heat up before I went to bed. Yet, instead of getting up, I remained motionless, the dream scene replaying in my thoughts.

After several minutes, I finally pushed myself to my feet, pulled on a T-shirt and sweats, then shuffled to the fireplace. My fingers trembled as I arranged kindling and struck a match. The tiny flame expanded through the dry pine until a proper fire radiated heat, pushing away the darkness.

But the unease inside me persisted.

I retrieved my Gibson from its stand, seeking the comfort I always found playing the guitar. My fingers moved across the strings, discovering that same melody I couldn't remember learning yet somehow recognized intimately. Its mournful sound was almost a lullaby with darker undertones.

For nearly two hours, I played variations of the haunting tune, attempting to dispel the disquiet the dream had created. As morning light spilled across the mountains, illuminating the snow-covered landscape outside my window, I set the guitar aside and pressed my palms against my face.

I needed a ride to clear my head.

After a quick shower, I pulled on jeans, boots, and my heaviest flannel before grabbing my coat on the way out. The crisp morning air bit at my cheeks as I trudged through the snow toward the barn.

Voices drifted from inside, where I found Cord and Bridger, our ranch manager. Their conversation halted as I pushed open the heavy wooden door.

"Mornin'," Cord said, glancing up from what looked like breeding records for our stock.

Bridger raised one hand in greeting, his steady green eyes landing on mine for a moment that felt too long. At six-foot-five, he was taller than both my brother and me, his imposing frame belying his quiet nature. In the three years he'd been managing the Roaring Fork, I'd never heard him waste a word. When Bridger spoke, people listened, mainly because they weren't sure when he might again.

"You look like shit," said Cord, frowning at the dark hollows beneath my eyes.

"Couldn't sleep," I muttered, moving past them to the tack room. "Thought I'd take Stang out for a ride. Either of you interested?"

Bridger and Cord exchanged a look, and Cord shrugged. "Why not? It's been a while since the three of us rode together."

Twenty minutes later, we were on our way out of the barn. The rhythmic crunch of hooves against packed snow and occasional equine snorts broke the winter stillness. We followed the trail winding toward the eastern ridge, where the vista extended for miles across the valley.

Stang picked his way carefully along the path, sure-footed despite the slippery conditions. Ahead of me, Cord rode his paint gelding, Midnight, with the easy confidence of someone born to the saddle. Bridger led the way on Thunder, a massive black stallion that matched his demeanor.

We rode in silence until we reached the ridge. When we stopped, Cord twisted in his saddle to look at me. "You gonna tell us what's eating at you, or are we supposed to guess?"

I sighed, my breath forming puffs in the frigid air. "Just got things on my mind."

"Things like a bar owner and her daughter?" Cord's voice held no judgment, only curiosity.

"Partly," I admitted, turning Stang to take in the vista spread out below us. From here, the distant ranch buildings looked like toys, and I could see smoke curl from the main house's chimneys. "But there's other stuff too."

Cord dismounted, letting Midnight's reins hang loose as the horse dropped his head to sniff at the ground. Bridger followed suit, his expression unreadable as always, although he appeared more interested in our conversation than he sometimes did.

I hesitated, considering how much to share. These were the two of the men I trusted most—along with Buck and Porter—yet what I needed to say sounded delusional even to me.

"I've been having these… dreams," I began awkwardly, getting off my horse too. "Or visions, I guess you could call them."

Cord's eyebrows rose. "What kind of visions?"

"About Mom." The words felt thick in my throat. "She's in a hospital, holding a baby. Last night, Dad was there too—standing outside the window, crying."

My brother's expression shifted to one of concern. "A baby? Flynn?"

I shook my head. "No, not Flynn. A smaller baby, sickly looking. Hooked up to machines."

Saying it aloud made it sound even more absurd. But the dream had felt real—more memory than fantasy.

"This isn't the first time I've had… feelings about things," I admitted, looking out over the valley rather than at my companions. "When Mom got sick, I knew. Before anyone told me, before the doctors even diagnosed her."

"You never mentioned that," Cord said quietly.

"How do you tell people something like that? 'Hey, by the way, I get these premonitions sometimes.'" I forced a laugh that sounded hollow even to my own ears. "Sounds crazy."

"Not necessarily." To my surprise, it was Bridger who spoke. "Native Americans believe there are people who are born with a spiritual sensitivity—the ability to see beyond what others can."

Cord and I both turned to look at him.

"My grandmother used to talk about it," he continued, his eyes on the distant mountains. "She said certain folks have different eyes for seeing."

"Thanks, man," I said, genuinely touched by his attempt to normalize what I was experiencing. "Still feels pretty messed up."

"So, what do you think these dreams about Mom and the baby mean?" Cord asked.

I removed my hat and ran a hand through my hair. After the night Keltie and I almost let things go too far, I'd given her space—not wanting to crowd her, to push for more than she was ready to give. But the separation was making me restless, worried. "I don't know. Maybe they're stress dreams. There's a *helluva* lot going on."

"I, err, don't know if you've heard, but Sam's going to Denver with Luna and Keltie tomorrow. For the appointment," said Cord.

"Seriously?" I said, unable to mask my hurt. "I was supposed to go with her."

Bridger cleared his throat softly. "Sometimes, when people are scared, they reach for what feels safe. A woman might understand another woman's fears better."

His insight caught me off guard again. For someone so quiet, he certainly had a lot to say today.

We mounted up and rode to the ranch in silence, my mind churning with the dreams, the trust, and most of all, Keltie and Luna. By the time we reached the barn, I'd made up my mind to drive over to Ben Rice's studio today. We'd postponed getting together since another storm was supposed to dump snow on us, but that didn't end up happening. Now, I needed a distraction, and recording an EP felt like the perfect escape.

Ben's studio was impressive—everything a musician could dream of. He played me a track from the new album, one I'd helped write but would never perform live, and my gut twisted with regret.

Ben watched my face carefully as the song played. When it ended, he said, "Your fingerprints are all over that track, Holt. No one plays it the same way you do."

"It sounds great," I said, meaning it despite the pang of what-might-have-been.

"It's ready for you to lay down your tracks," he said quietly. "Whenever you're into it."

"Seriously?" I said for the second time today, albeit in an entirely different way.

"Absolutely. We need you on this one."

Liv stepped farther into the room. "How are Keltie and Luna?" she asked, setting her coffee cup down. "Luna is such a sweet child."

The mention of the little girl's name brought an immediate smile to my face. "She is. Smart as a whip too."

"And quite attached to you, from what I could see," she added.

I couldn't deny it. "The feeling's mutual."

"For both mother and daughter?" Ben asked, his tone teasing, but his eyes serious.

Heat crept up my neck. "Yeah, I guess that's fair to say."

"Good." Liv's smile widened. "You deserve someone special, Holt. Both of you do."

"This is beyond generous, Ben."

"It's selfish, really," he countered. "I want to hear what you come up with. And, hey—if Keltie ever wants to get behind a mixing board again, you should encourage it."

I tensed, remembering how Keltie had reacted to Ben's recognition of her at Christmas. "I'll mention it," I said, hesitating. "But, as you know, it's been a while since she's done that work."

"Like riding a bike," Ben said with a wave of his hand. "That kind of talent doesn't go away."

The tour continued as Ben pointed out the features of the studio while Liv occasionally added her own insights. They were gracious hosts, yet I found my mind continually drifting to Keltie and Luna. Two days without seeing them felt like an eternity.

When I pulled up to my cabin later that afternoon, Cord was waiting on my porch, arms crossed against the cold.

"Six-pack's been asking questions," he said as I climbed out of my truck.

I frowned, unlocking my door and gesturing for him to follow me inside. "What kind of questions?"

"About whether you're fulfilling the stipulations. Playing three nights a week, donating half your earnings." Cord stomped snow from his boots before stepping into the warmth of my cabin. "I don't know if he's got someone breathing down his neck about it or if he's being his usual asshole self."

I hung my coat on the hook by the door, then moved to stoke the fire I'd banked earlier. "Did you have to deal with this shit?"

Cord shook his head, settling onto my sofa. "It was more complicated with me cuz of the accident."

"Right. Sorry, man."

"You didn't have a premonition about that, did you?"

"If I had dreamed you were ambushed out in a snowstorm and left for dead, I sure as hell would've warned you."

"Good to know." He chuckled, but then his expression grew more serious and he rested his elbows on his knees. "Now that you mention having these visions or whatever, I'm wondering if there's more to all this than we've realized."

The flames intensified, casting shadows across the cabin walls. "Like what?"

"Maybe Mom's trying to communicate with you."

I barked out a laugh. "From beyond the grave? Come on, Cord."

He shrugged, unperturbed by my skepticism. "Stranger things have happened. And you're the one having prophetic dreams."

I couldn't argue with that logic, annoying as it was. "Either way, I'll be more careful about documenting my performances. Make sure there's no question that I'm meeting the requirements."

"Good idea." Cord stood, heading for the door. "One more thing—Sam wanted to know if you're okay with her going to Denver tomorrow."

The reminder stung. "Why?"

Cord studied me. "Why what?"

"I guess you shared my reaction with her."

He picked up his hat and stuck it on his head. "Juni did."

I raised a brow. So Cord told Juni, Juni told Sam. Had Sam told Keltie? "Not really my call, is it?" I tried to keep the hurt out of my voice, but something must have shown in my expression.

"For what it's worth," Cord said, his hand on the doorknob, "I think Keltie would want you there if she thought she could ask."

With that cryptic statement, he left, the door closing quietly behind him.

I stood in my cabin, suddenly unable to remain apart from Keltie and Luna for another minute. Decision made, I grabbed my keys and headed out into the cold afternoon.

Keltie's house glowed warmly against the approaching dusk as I pulled into her driveway. I sat in my truck briefly, mustering my resolve before walking to the front door and knocking.

Her face when she opened the door was a mixture of surprise and—to my relief—genuine pleasure. "Holt! I wasn't expecting you."

"I probably should have called," I stammered. "Is this a bad time?"

"No, not at all. Come in." She moved aside, allowing me into the entryway. "Luna's watching a movie. She'll be thrilled to see you." Keltie glanced at where her daughter was stretched out on the sofa. "Or she would be if she hadn't fallen asleep."

I followed her into the dining room, noticing the scattered papers on the table.

"I've been trying to get organized for tomorrow," she explained. "Making sure I have everything we need for the appointment."

"Let me help," I offered, moving to sit in the chair beside her. "I'm pretty good at checklists."

She raised a brow. "You are?"

My cheeks flushed. "Organization is kind of my thing. People don't expect it because of the whole musician vibe, but I like having my ducks in a row, as they say."

Keltie handed me a notepad with a half-completed list. "Be my guest."

For the next twenty minutes, we worked together, creating a checklist of everything she might need—medical records, insurance information, comfort items for Luna, and snacks for the drive.

"This is really helpful," Keltie said when we finished. "Thank you."

I steeled myself for what I needed to say next. "Cord told me Sam's going with you tomorrow."

Keltie's expression clouded. "Yes, she offered when I mentioned the appointment the other night at the Goat. I hope that's okay."

"Of course," I said quickly, though the hurt lingered. "I understand why you'd want her there." I took a deep breath. "I want you to know I'd like to be there too. For both of you. But I understand if that's not what you want."

She frowned, setting the list aside. "What do you mean, 'not what I want'? Holt, I haven't heard from you in two days. I thought maybe you needed space after… the other night."

"I thought *you* needed space. I didn't want to crowd you, especially with everything happening with Luna."

A small laugh escaped her. "So, we've both been sitting around, waiting for the other person to call?"

"Seems that way," I admitted, reaching for her hand. "I'm sorry. I should have checked in. I missed you both."

Her fingers interlaced with mine. "We missed you too. Luna kept asking when 'Mr. Holt' was coming to see us."

Guilt washed over me. "I really am sorry."

"No, I understand. We're, uh, a lot." She shook her head. "I should have reached out too. I guess I was afraid you'd been scared off."

"You're not a lot in a bad way. I mean… Shit, Keltie, I'd be with you every minute if you'd let me." I squeezed her hand. "But if we're being this cautious about calling each other, we're gonna have communication problems. How about we agree to say what we're thinking? If one of us needs space, we tell the other person directly."

A small smile played at her lips. "I'd like that. And for the record, I would love if you came to Denver with us tomorrow."

Relief washed over me. "Then, it's settled."

"What should I do about Sam?" Keltie asked.

"The more support you have, the better," I assured her.

Her eyes shone with unshed tears. "Thank you. You don't know what this means to me."

Before I could respond, Luna got up from the sofa and her eyes lit up as soon as she saw me.

"Mr. Holt!" she exclaimed, running over and climbing up on my lap. "Where have you been? I've been waiting and waiting!"

"I'm sorry, Unicorn Girl," I said, guilt intensifying at the genuine hurt in her voice. "I had some grown-up things to take care of."

She frowned. "Grown-up things are boring. We missed you." She fixed me with a serious look. "Did you miss us too?"

"More than you know," I said honestly.

That seemed to appease her. "Good. Because I made something for you." She slid off my lap and ran up the stairs, returning a couple of minutes later with a drawing clutched in her small hands.

She held it out, and on it was a small girl with wild, dark curls riding on a mystical creature with a rainbow mane streaming behind them.

"See?" Luna said, pointing. "We're riding to the magic flower that makes people better."

My throat tightened as I examined the drawing. "It's beautiful, Luna. Thank you."

"I want you to have it," she said earnestly. "So you won't ever forget about me."

Her words had me close to tears. I glanced at Keltie, whose expression mirrored my own distress.

"I could never forget about you, Luna," I promised, gathering her into a gentle hug. "Not ever."

When I released her, she studied my face with solemn brown eyes that seemed too old for her years. "Pinky promise?"

I extended my little finger, linking it with hers. "Pinky promise."

Satisfied, Luna turned to her mother. "Mommy, can I have ice cream? Please?"

Keltie smiled, clearly relieved by the change of subject. "Just a small bowl. It's almost dinnertime."

As Luna skipped off to the kitchen, Keltie turned to me. "I know we're laying on the guilt pretty thick."

"I deserve it," I said ruefully. "I should have called. No matter what I thought you might need."

She gestured to the paperwork on the table. "I'm not used to having someone to share the load."

"You do now," I said firmly. "If you want me to be that person."

Her smile was answer enough.

From the kitchen came the sounds of the freezer door opening and drawers being pulled out in search of a spoon.

"She's got such spirit," I said, lowering my voice. "It's one of the things I love most about her."

Keltie's eyes warmed at my words. "She does. She's always been that way—determined, brave."

"She gets it from her mother," I pointed out, earning another smile.

A thought occurred to me, something I'd been considering since my visit to Ben's studio. "Keltie, what would you think about helping me produce my album? Not right away," I hastened to add, seeing her surprised expression.

"I—" she began, but was interrupted by a harsh coughing sound from the kitchen.

We both turned to see Luna standing in the doorway, one hand pressed to her chest, the other still holding a spoon. Her face was flushed, her breathing rapid.

"Luna?" Keltie was on her feet immediately, racing to her daughter. When she placed her hand on Luna's forehead, her face paled. "You're burning up."

I watched in dismay as Luna's legs weakened, her small body collapsing against her mother. Instantly, I moved to them, catching Luna as another deep, wracking cough shook her entire frame.

"We need to get her to the hospital," I said, scooping her into my arms. Her skin was hot to the touch, her breathing becoming more labored with each passing second.

Keltie raced for her purse and keys. "The emergency bag is by the door," she instructed, her voice tight with fear.

I carried Luna to my truck, holding her against my chest as Keltie grabbed the car seat. The little girl's eyes appeared unfocused, vacant.

"It's going to be okay, Luna," I said softly, helping Keltie secure her into the booster seat. "We're going to get you help."

As we accelerated toward Gunnison Valley Hospital, Luna's labored breathing filled the truck's cabin. I gripped the steering wheel fiercely. "I swear when she was sitting on my lap, she didn't feel warm at all."

"It comes out of nowhere sometimes," Keltie said from the backseat, where she sat holding her daughter's hand and murmuring reassurances that didn't reach her tear-filled eyes.

17

Keltie

The emergency room at Gunnison Valley Hospital held the same stark intensity I remembered from our previous visit. Luna lay, small and pale, on the gurney, her eyes glassy with fever as a nurse attached monitors to her chest. I stood frozen at her side, my hand clutching her too-warm fingers, while the medical staff moved around us.

"Her temperature's 104.2," a nurse announced, frowning at the thermometer. "We'll get IV fluids started right away. Doctor Patel has ordered blood work and broad-spectrum antibiotics."

Holt stood at the foot of the gurney, his face tight with worry. Every few moments, his eyes would meet mine across Luna's small form, silent reassurance passing between us.

The doctor arrived a few minutes later, scanning Luna's chart before examining her. "Her oxygen levels are good, but I don't like this fever pattern," he said, his brow furrowed as he listened to her chest.

Luna whimpered when he touched her abdomen, flinching away. "It hurts, Mommy."

"I know, baby," I whispered, brushing damp curls from her forehead. "The doctors are going to make it better."

When he signaled for me to join him, Holt took my place at Luna's side, distracting her with gentle questions about her stuffed animals.

"Her blood work from the other day remains concerning. With the addition of her struggling to breathe, combined with the recurring fevers and abdominal pain…" He paused, then put his hand on my shoulder. "I've contacted Children's Hospital. They're sending their flight team to transport Luna immediately."

My legs nearly gave out. "Flight team? As in helicopter?"

"Yes. Given the urgency of her symptoms and the specialized care she needs, it's the fastest way. They have a pediatric oncology team waiting."

My stomach twisted with the acceptance that I could no longer put this off. "How soon?" I managed.

"The flight team should arrive within the hour. We'll stabilize her here until then."

I returned to Luna's bedside, forcing myself to be calm and reassuring, even though I felt anything but. Holt looked up, reading the fear in my eyes instantly.

"Luna-bug, the nurses are going to give you medicine to help with the fever," I explained, keeping my voice steady. "Then we're going to take a special helicopter ride to another hospital in Denver."

Luna's eyes widened. "A real helicopter? Like on TV?"

"Just like on TV," I confirmed, grateful for her excitement rather than fear.

Holt stepped away, phone in hand. I could hear fragments of his conversation with Buck—something about leaving his truck at the hospital.

"The emergency bag," he said, his eyes meeting mine. "Yeah, I gotta run and get it." He paused. "Right. Thanks, man." Another pause. "Yeah, I know about the forty-eight hours. I'll figure it out."

The mention of the forty-eight-hour stipulation limitation sent a chill through me. With everything happening so fast, I hadn't considered what this meant for Holt. If he stayed with us in Denver beyond that time frame, what would he be risking?

Dr. Patel came in with a nurse who administered medication through Luna's IV. Within minutes, her eyelids grew heavy.

"This will help her rest during the transfer," he explained. "The flight team should be here at any moment."

Holt approached with our bag.

"Listen, I know you can't go with us—"

His eyes bored into mine. "You're not going without me. Understood?" When he pulled me into his arms, tears threatened, but I couldn't cry now. Luna needed me to be strong, and if Holt was with us, I could be.

The flight crew arrived and transferred Luna to their stretcher. After a brief discussion about accommodations, the lead paramedic confirmed there was room for both Holt and me.

The journey took under an hour, but it felt equally endless and brief. Luna slept through it while I tried to process how quickly our world had changed.

By the time we touched down on the hospital's helipad, the sun was setting over Denver. A team waited to receive us and whisked Luna directly to the pediatric oncology floor.

As they settled Luna into her room, I stepped into the hallway to call my father, my hands shaking as I dialed.

"Mija?" His voice answered, warm and familiar. "I was about to call you."

"Dad," I said, my voice breaking. "Luna's sick. Really sick. We're at Children's Hospital in Denver."

A beat of silence. "What happened?"

I explained everything—the emergency trip to Gunnison, the helicopter transfer, the oncology floor. "They haven't confirmed anything yet, but they're talking about cancer, Dad."

"I'm leaving now," he said without hesitation. "I'll drive straight through."

"Dad, it's at least a five-hour drive—"

"I'll be there as soon as I can," he insisted. "Hold on, *mija*. I'm coming."

When I returned to Luna's room, a doctor was introducing herself to Holt. "I'm Dr. Robbins, the attending oncologist," she said, extending her hand to me. "We need to run several tests, but based on the initial blood work, we want to do a bone marrow aspiration right away."

"What does that mean?" I asked.

She explained that she'd insert a needle near Luna's hip and, essentially, extract a sample of her bone marrow.

"Will it hurt her?" My eyes filled with tears that I quickly brushed away.

She glanced at her watch. "When did she last eat?"

"Maybe two hours ago? She had ice cream before her fever spiked."

"In that case, we'll proceed with local anesthetic instead of sedation. We don't want to wait." Dr. Robbins looked between Holt and me. "Both parents can be in the room with her, but you'll need to wear scrubs. Since we're not putting her under, it'll help if you keep her distracted. She won't feel pain from the procedure, but she might be scared."

I opened my mouth to correct her assumption about Holt, but stopped. The technicality didn't matter. What mattered was Luna having both of us with her.

"Let us know what we need to do," Holt said without hesitation.

As Dr. Robbins left to prepare, Holt turned to me. "You don't have to explain who I am or am not to her right now. This isn't about paperwork or biology."

Relief and gratitude washed over me. "Thank you."

In the procedure room, Luna lay on her side while Holt distracted her with stories about Sparkles and magical butterflies. His steady voice and animated storytelling kept her attention away from what the doctors were doing. The procedure was quick, but watching that needle slide into my daughter's hip was one of the most difficult things I'd ever endured. Without Holt there, I'm not sure I could have maintained my composure.

Once in her room, the exhaustion of the day finally caught up with my little girl. She fell asleep clutching Bunny. Thankfully, the antibiotics and fever reducers had brought her temperature down.

I watched her sleep, the weight of what might be coming pressing on my chest until I could barely breathe. A strangled sound escaped me—not quite a sob, but close.

Warm arms wrapped around me from behind, turning me gently until my face was pressed against Holt's chest. He led me outside the door, holding me tightly. Only then did I let go, tears soaking his shirt as I clung to him.

"What if—" I couldn't finish the thought.

"Shh," he murmured against my hair. "We'll handle each challenge as it comes."

I breathed in the scent of him, letting it anchor me in the moment.

"I don't know what I'd do if you weren't here," I whispered.

His arms tightened around me. "You'd be just as strong, just as brave."

We stayed that way until a nurse stepped around us on her way into the room to check Luna's vitals. After she had, she adjusted her IV and slipped out again.

It was close to eleven when my father arrived. I spotted him in the doorway of Luna's room. His eyes moved from her sleeping form to me, and in that moment, I was five years old again, running to him with a scraped knee.

"Papa," I whispered, crossing the room to fall into his arms.

"Oh, Keltie," he murmured, his voice heavy with emotion. He held me tightly before releasing me to approach Luna's bedside. The sight of his vibrant granddaughter pale against the hospital sheets seemed to age him a decade in seconds.

"She's been sleeping peacefully," I said softly. "Her fever's down."

My dad gently touched Luna's curls at the same time Holt rose from the chair in the corner.

My father turned and extended his hand. "Victor Marquez."

"Holt Wheaton. Good to meet you, though I wish it were under better circumstances."

"Abuelo?" Luna's sleepy voice interrupted the moment. Her eyes brightened when she spotted my father. "You came!"

Dad's face transformed into a smile. "Of course I did, *mi corazón*. Nothing could keep me away."

Luna smiled at both men. "Mr. Holt was telling me about unicorns talking to butterflies," she told her grandfather.

"Is that so?" Dad raised a brow at Holt, who shrugged with a sheepish smile.

"They had interesting conversations," Holt confirmed seriously. "These were very philosophical butterflies."

Luna giggled, the sound so normal, so precious, that tears pricked my eyes again.

The overnight hours passed, with nurses and doctors coming to check on my daughter. She remained remarkably resilient, perking up whenever Holt or my father entertained her, then dozing when the exhaustion overwhelmed her.

Around eight the next morning, the unit secretary appeared in the doorway. "Dr. Robbins would like to speak with Luna's parents."

My heart stuttered. The results.

Holt stood immediately, but hesitated, looking at my father.

"I'll stay with Luna," my dad offered. "She'll be more comfortable with me here."

Surprise flickered across Holt's face, followed by gratitude.

Dr. Robbins was waiting in a small consultation room, a folder in her hands. Her expression was guarded as we entered, but something in her eyes told me what was coming.

"Please, sit," she said, gesturing to the chairs across from her. "I have Luna's test results."

I gripped Holt's hand, his fingers interlacing with mine as we sat.

"The bone marrow aspiration confirms what we suspected from the blood work," Dr. Robbins continued. "Luna has acute lymphoblastic leukemia. I believe Dr. Patel told you it's also referred to as ALL."

I gasped and covered my mouth with my hands. *Leukemia. My baby had cancer.*

"I know this is devastating news," Dr. Robbins said gently. "But I want to emphasize that ALL has one of the highest childhood cancer survival rates. With proper care, successful remission rates are approximately ninety-eight percent."

"Care?" Holt asked, his voice steadier than I could have managed.

"We'll start chemotherapy as soon as possible. The protocol for ALL involves several phases. The first phase—induction—is the most intensive, aiming to achieve remission within the first month. For that, we'll keep her here at the hospital. Once we're sure she's handling it okay, you'll be able to take her home. After that, the subsequent rounds can be handled on an outpatient basis."

The clinical terms blended together as I struggled to process them.

"Will she lose her hair?" I asked, the question slipping out unbidden.

"Yes, it will cause hair loss. But children are remarkably resilient—often more so than we adults expect."

The doctor continued explaining the potential side effects and success rates, but I could barely focus. Holt's arm slipped around my shoulders, pulling me against his side when I started to tremble.

"I'll let the two of you talk," Dr. Robbins finally said. "I'll be right outside if you have any questions. The nurse will have an information packet waiting in Luna's room that explains everything in detail. We'll meet again later to discuss the next steps."

When the door closed behind her, I finally broke down. Holt held me, reminding me of the odds and assuring me that Luna would face this with her characteristic curiosity rather than fear.

Eventually, the storm passed, leaving me drained but calm enough to return to Luna's room. I needed to be strong for my daughter. She'd take her cues from me.

When we walked in, my father took one look at my face and knew. His eyes filled, but he blinked the tears away before turning to face Luna, who was happily drawing more pictures.

"Look what I made!" she exclaimed, holding up a picture. "It's Sparkles and me at the hospital. See the butterflies coming to visit?"

I swallowed hard, forcing a smile. "It's beautiful, baby."

"I'm going to hang it up so the doctors can see it," she announced.

A nurse appeared with tape, helping Luna place her artwork on the wall beside her bed. My father used the distraction to pull me into the hallway.

"How bad is it?" he asked quietly.

"The doctor says the survival rate of the type of cancer she has is high—ninety-eight percent."

"We will get through this, *mija*. All of us."

My father's gaze shifted to Holt, who was helping Luna with another drawing.

"He's a good man," Dad said simply.

"You've known him less than twenty-four hours," I pointed out.

"I know enough." His eyes met mine. "He looks at Luna the way I look at you."

Before I could respond, the elevator doors at the end of the hall opened, revealing Sam and Beau, who spotted us immediately. Sam hurried forward to wrap me in a hug.

"Buck called us last night." Her eyes searched mine. "How is she?"

"It's cancer."

Sam's hand flew to her mouth. Beside her, Beau's expression turned solemn.

"What can we do?" he asked.

"Being here is enough—"

"Keltie." Sam cut me off gently. "I've been making calls. There's an apartment building near the hospital that offers short-term rentals to families of patients. Beau and I made all the arrangements."

The unexpected gesture left me momentarily speechless. "Sam, I can't accept—"

"Please," she said quietly. "Let us help make this at least a little easier on you."

I felt the sincerity in her voice deep inside me. These people I'd only recently met were showing up when it counted most.

Beau cleared his throat. "I've also arranged for a private helicopter to be at your disposal with very little lead time. It can take Holt to CB when he needs to go, then fly him here afterward."

I blinked in surprise. "That's—you don't have to—"

"It's already done," Beau said simply. "Just let us know when."

We rejoined the others in Luna's room, where Sam immediately went to Luna's bedside while Beau approached Holt.

While the two men spoke quietly, I realized how long Holt had been here. With a sinking feeling, I remembered his conversation with Buck about the forty-eight-hour stipulation in the trust.

I moved to his side. "Holt, you have to go back to Crested Butte."

He looked down at me, fatigue evident in the shadows beneath his eyes. "I'll try to talk to the attorney, but it isn't only the time away I'm dealing with. I have to play a minimum of three nights a week."

"You need to leave now," I said, though the words hurt to speak.

"I can't—"

"You'll be back as soon as you can," Sam interjected. "Victor, Beau, and I will be here with Keltie and Luna."

Holt's jaw tightened, conflict clear in his eyes.

I led him into the hallway. "Look, I understand," I told him, meaning it. "But I won't let you risk the consequences of not adhering to the trust. Luna and I will be fine for a couple of days. We aren't alone."

"I can stay a few more hours."

I raised a brow.

"I'll still have time to get to CB. More if I take Beau up on his offer to fly me there."

When we walked into her room and saw Luna was asleep, Holt led me over to one of the recliners, pulled me onto his lap, then shifted the lever to flatten it. "Close your eyes," he whispered. "If Luna wakes up, I'll tell you."

When I felt Holt's hand on my arm and heard him say my name, I realized I'd fallen asleep.

"I gotta go, darlin'. You call me immediately if anything changes. Anything at all."

"I promise I will."

Beau stepped forward. "The helicopter is ready whenever you are."

Holt turned to Luna. "Hey, Unicorn Girl. I have to go to Crested Butte for a little while. But I'll be here again tomorrow, okay?"

Luna's lower lip trembled. "Promise?"

"Pinky promise," he said solemnly, linking his little finger with hers. "And while I'm gone, maybe you can draw more pictures for our story?"

She brightened at this mission. "I will! The best pictures ever!"

I followed Holt into the hallway, where he pulled me into a fierce embrace. His kiss held everything I needed—promise, comfort, determination, and something deeper neither of us was ready to name. "We'll be okay," I assured him as we parted.

I watched him walk away, Beau at his side, until the elevator doors closed between us. Only then did I allow myself to acknowledge the hollow feeling his absence left—the space that, in the span of a few short days, had become his alone to fill.

18

Holt

The helicopter flight from Denver passed in a blur of mountains and snow, my thoughts never leaving the hospital room where I'd left Keltie and Luna.

When we touched down, Cord was waiting for me at the edge of the tarmac. "Good to see you, brother," he said as I slid into the passenger seat of his truck. "Though I wish the circumstances were better."

I stared through the windshield at the road ahead. "Thanks for coming to get me."

As soon as we pulled onto the highway toward Crested Butte, I fished my phone from my pocket and dialed Keltie's number. I needed to hear her voice, to know if anything had changed in the hour since I'd left.

She answered on the second ring. "Holt?"

"Hey," I said softly. "Just landed. How's she doing?"

"The same," Keltie replied, her voice heavy with fatigue. "She's still sleeping."

"Has the doctor been in again?"

"No. Nothing's changed since you left." There was a pause. "I'm glad you called, though."

"I'll be back as soon as I can," I promised, meeting Cord's understanding glance.

"I know," she said quietly.

"Is there anything I can bring with me?"

"Just yourself," she answered. "That's all we need."

"How are you holding up?" I asked, pitching my voice lower.

Her pause said more than her words. "My dad's been great. And it's nice to have Sam and Beau here. But… never mind, I shouldn't say it."

"Not what we agreed on, darlin'. Whatever it is, say it."

"I know you just left, but I still wish you were here. I also know that isn't fair."

"I'll call again after I finish up at the Goat," I promised.

"Be safe," she said softly before hanging up.

When I put my phone away, Cord kept his eyes on the road, giving me a moment to collect myself.

"How is she?" he finally asked.

"It's confirmed—leukemia," I said, fighting to keep my voice steady. "The doctors are moving quickly with the treatment."

"God, man, I'm so sorry. Did they say how long she'll need to stay in Denver?"

"A month. They're focused on getting through the first phase of treatment."

My cell rang, startling me, but when I looked at the screen, I saw it was Buck.

"Hey, we're headed your way."

"Good. Flynn's got dinner ready at the main house. Everyone's here."

"Everyone?"

"Yeah. Porter, Cici, and Maverick drove over from Morris Ranch."

I didn't like the thought of everyone gathered, waiting for news. "Don't forget I have to play at the Goat tonight."

"Right. I'm sure Flynn can make you a plate to go, unless you'd rather eat there."

I'd rather not eat at all, to be honest. "I'll grab my truck and swing by. I won't be able to stay long, though."

"Understood, brother." The resignation in Buck's voice echoed my own.

Twenty minutes later, I parked in front of the main house, my exhaustion hitting me all at once. Before I could even reach the porch, Flynn swung the door open and raced over to me.

"How is she?" she asked, pulling me into a hug.

"Not great." My voice caught. "They've confirmed it's cancer."

Her arms tightened. "That poor little girl."

Inside, the scene was exactly as I'd imagined—my siblings and their partners were gathered in the great room, their faces turning toward me as I entered. No one was sitting around the dining table, though, and the casual way they lounged made it seem less like an ambush.

"Here." Buck handed me a shot of whiskey as I sank into one of the armchairs. "You look like you need it."

I accepted the drink, swallowing it before facing their questioning looks.

"I wish to fucking hell I was there instead of here."

Porter eased off the sofa and walked toward me. "Merry Christmas, Holt. Sorry I missed it. Guess I should say happy New Year, instead." When we embraced, he held on extra long, and I appreciated it.

"What can we do?" TJ asked, sitting beside Buck on the sofa, their fingers interlaced.

I shook my head. "I don't know. This is all new territory for me."

"For both of you," Flynn added gently.

My throat tightened, thinking of Keltie trying to process all this medical information alone, making decisions about her daughter's care. I'd texted her again before coming inside, but she hadn't responded yet.

"I need to be in Denver," I said.

"But first, you need to play tonight," said Porter. "And we all plan to be there."

I lowered my gaze. "You don't have to do that," I said, even though I'd love to have them there for support.

"We're goin'," said Buck, sounding a little too much like Roscoe. When his eyes met mine, we both chuckled. "Fuck, I sound exactly like the ol' bastard," he muttered.

"At least you don't look like him," Porter added.

"Ain't that the truth?" said Cord.

"What our brothers are dancing around," Flynn said, "is that we've figured out a way for you to be with Keltie and Luna while still satisfying the trust requirements."

"I talked to Beau. It isn't an issue to have the helicopter bring you here, touch down, then you leave again," said Cord.

"That'll be mighty expensive."

Cord's eyebrows flashed. "As Beau said, there's no better use of his money, and just so you aren't worried about it, the guy's a billionaire."

"Again, I appreciate it, but I can't let him do that."

Flynn stepped closer and put her hand on my arm. "Look at it this way. He isn't doing it for you. He's doing it for Keltie and Luna."

Their immediate willingness to help struck a chord in me, and I realized she was right. If it meant I could be there with them, I could damn well lower my pride and accept Beau's offer. "Thank you," I said, looking around the room. "All of you."

"When are you heading back to Denver?" Buck asked.

"The day after tomorrow, if I can arrange it."

"I'll take care of it," Cord offered.

After a quick bite to eat, I drove myself to the Goat. As soon as I walked in, Miguel spotted me and lifted his chin in greeting. I made my way through the crowd toward him, acknowledging familiar faces but avoiding conversations.

"Didn't expect to see you tonight," Miguel said as I approached. "We don't usually have music on New Year's Eve. We leave the shindigs to the resorts."

"Good night for me to play, then," I muttered. "How's business been?"

"Steady. We can handle things here. Don't worry about the bar." His expression turned serious. "How's Luna?"

"Holding up better than any of us. She's a tough kid."

"Good with me if you only do one set," he offered. "No offense, man, but you look like shit."

"I feel even worse."

After getting my mic and speakers set up, I glanced around the room. There were more familiar faces here than usual at this time of year. Locals tended to only come out once the skiers left. On the other hand, as Miguel said, the Goat wasn't hosting an event tonight, so most everyone figured it would be quiet here.

I didn't bother with my usual greeting. I simply began to play. I knew I'd need to mix in covers to keep the crowd happy, but I sure wasn't in the mood for it.

The bar quieted for a couple of minutes, but then conversations picked up again. I was happy not to have all eyes on me tonight. When I finished the first couple of originals, I transitioned into old favorites that required little thought, allowing me to go through the motions while my mind remained in Denver.

Between sets, several locals tossed money in the tip jar. Plus, Stacey from McGill's, Dave from the hardware store, Sheriff Kaleb, and Mrs. Winters from the elementary school all offered different kinds of help—watching the house, organizing fundraisers, and helping with the bar.

Their overwhelming support had me tearing up. "Thanks," I managed.

Stacey handed me a small box. "This is for Luna. Coloring books, small toys. Stuff to keep her occupied in the hospital."

"And this is for Keltie," Dave added, passing me an envelope. "From folks around town. It's not much, but it might help with expenses."

My throat tightened at their generosity. While Crested Butte was my home, had been all my life, Keltie was a newcomer. That everyone cared so much about her and her daughter spoke volumes about how much of an impact they'd made on our small town in a very short amount of time.

I ended up playing my usual two sets, mainly because of how overflowing the tip jar was. I knew every penny was meant to help Keltie, and I sure appreciated it. My family contributed quite a bit too, including more than one hundred-dollar bill tossed in with the usual ones and fives.

Back at my cabin, I called Keltie. Her voice was heavy with exhaustion, but she shared that Luna was resting peacefully. When she mentioned that a representative from Miracles of Hope Children's Charity would be visiting them, my attention sharpened immediately.

"That's the charity named in my codicil," I told her. "The one I have to donate to."

"I forgot about that," she said slowly.

"It's too strange to be a coincidence," I muttered. "There's something going on here that I don't understand yet."

We talked for a few more minutes, both of us exhausted but reluctant to disconnect. We whispered how much we missed each other and finally said good night.

After we hung up, I found myself too restless to sleep despite my exhaustion. Damn, if that charity—the very one named in my codicil—didn't keep popping up. Why? I pulled out my laptop and settled on the sofa to research more about the organization I was required to support.

Their website was professionally designed, with pages about their mission, programs, donation options, and a brief history. I clicked on the "About Us" section, scanning for any clues that could explain why my inheritance and that of my siblings would all go to them should I fail to fulfill my part of the trust's stipulations.

"Founded in 1993 by an anonymous donor," I read aloud, "specifically to help children with leukemia and their families in the Crested Butte area." That it mentioned the same disease Luna had fucking rattled me.

I pulled up the family tree, which Sam had updated and sent everyone. It was easier to check it than try to remember when we were all born. The year the charity was formed fell between Buck's and Porter's birthdays.

I dug deeper, looking for any mention of founding board members, but the site maintained their anonymity. The charity's logo caught my attention—a scarlet blanket adorned with scattered stars. Something about it tugged at my memory, but I couldn't place it.

After grabbing a beer from the fridge and lighting a fire in the hearth, I sat my ass on the sofa, knowing I should go to bed instead. My eyes wandered to the built-in bookcases on either side of it. I stood, walked over, and picked up the photo that was taken the Christmas before Mom died. We all had copies of it. I carried it into the kitchen and flipped on the light, studying my mother's face. Damn, I missed her.

Something else caught my eye that I'd never noticed before—the necklace she was wearing. I couldn't see it well enough to pick up any detail, so I used the magnifying app on my phone to zoom in more.

"Fuck," I practically yelled, almost dropping the picture and my cell. I grabbed the chair nearest to me and fell in it as much as sat. After blinking several times, I looked again, and sure enough, there it was. The same pendant I'd seen in the window of the consignment shop next door to the toy store. The one I gave Keltie for Christmas.

Rather than get another beer, I opened the cupboard and pulled out a bottle of whiskey, then grabbed a glass. I took them both and the photo over to the sofa.

I looked up at the beams above me. "What's goin' on, Mama? You visitin' me in my dreams? Tryin' to send me messages?" My eyes filled with tears that ran down my cheeks. "I wished you'd straight out tell me. I know this is all connected, but I can't figure out how or why."

After downing another shot, I grabbed my laptop again, scrolling back to the charity's website to examine the logo more carefully. The scarlet blanket with stars—why did it seem so familiar? And then it hit me. I jumped off the sofa and picked up another frame. The picture inside was of my mama holding me, wrapped in a scarlet blanket embroidered with tiny silver stars. I remembered her using it when Flynn was born too.

When my phone rang at nine the next morning, I was still on the sofa, where I'd dozed off—passed out might be a better way to describe it. The caller ID showed Six-pack's office.

"Wheaton," I answered curtly.

"Holt," Six-pack's voice came through, unusually hesitant. "I need you to come in tomorrow. There's something—"

"I have questions," I interrupted, the whiskey I'd consumed last night making my tongue feel thick and heavy. I cleared my throat. "About the trust and the Miracles of Hope charity."

He paused. "What about them?"

"What's the connection, Six-pack? And don't you try to tell me there isn't one," I said.

"I can't answer that, Holt."

"Hey, here's another one for you. The woman who owns the Goat—Keltie Marquez? Guess what her daughter's been diagnosed with. Got nothin'?" I spat without giving him time to respond. "Leukemia. I mean, hell, what are the odds? Oh, and the charity's logo? I had a baby blanket that looked a lot like it."

"Holt, I…"

"What, asshole? Spit it out. What games have you been playin' with my family? With our lives?"

"It isn't me."

"Then, tell me who the fuck it is." I was yelling now.

"I don't know. That's the God's honest truth."

"Cut the bullshit, Richard," I snapped, using his real name for the first time in years. "I'm sick to death of you giving us the runaround."

Another pause, longer this time. "When certain conditions are met, I'm given more information," he said carefully.

"What conditions?" I demanded.

"I can't say. But the trustee does have a message for you." His tone shifted, becoming more formal. "If you could come to my office tomorrow morning—"

"I'm needed in Denver," I cut him off.

"This is important, Holt."

"So are they," I retorted. "Either tell me over the phone, or I'll call you when I'm in Crested Butte again—within forty-eight hours, of course."

"But—" Six-pack began.

I hung up, my patience gone. The phone immediately rang again. I stared at Six-pack's name on the screen before sending it to voicemail.

Whatever the trustee wanted, it would have to wait. I had more important matters to attend to—a brave little girl fighting for her life and the woman I was falling in love with, who needed me by her side.

19

Keltie

The constant beep of Luna's heart monitor provided a steady backdrop to our new reality. I'd memorized every detail of her hospital room in the three days we'd been here—the faded blue curtains that never fully blocked the hall light, the squeaky hinge on the bathroom door, and the way the third ceiling tile from the window had a water stain shaped like Texas.

My father dozed in the recliner near Luna's bed, his head tilted at an angle that would guarantee neck pain when he woke. Sam had left to grab lunch for all of us, insisting we needed to eat something other than vending-machine snacks.

I stretched my stiff muscles and checked my phone. Holt had texted that he'd be here this afternoon. The empty space he'd left behind was startling in its intensity, considering how recently he'd entered our lives.

"Mommy?" Luna's voice was small but clear. I moved to her side in an instant.

"I'm here, baby. How are you feeling?"

"Tired," she replied, her eyes sleepy, but alert. "When can we go home?"

"Soon," I promised, the word intentionally vague. "The doctors are helping you get better."

My father stirred at the sound of our voices. "There's my *corazón*," he said, leaning forward to take Luna's hand. "Would you like to hear more stories about when your mama was little?"

A soft knock interrupted us, and Dr. Robbins entered with a nurse I hadn't met before, who motioned for me to join them.

"How are you doing?" the doctor asked.

"As well as can be expected."

"We'll be starting Luna's first chemotherapy session tomorrow morning," she said gently. "But before we discuss that further, there's someone here to meet you." She gestured to a woman waiting behind her. "This is Echo West from the Miracles of Hope Children's Charity."

The woman who stepped forward was slim, with an elegant bearing. Her long gray hair was pulled back, and her green eyes held a depth of compassion that felt genuine.

"Ms. Marquez," she said, extending her hand. "I'm so sorry about Luna's diagnosis. I'd like to talk with you about how our organization can help."

"Um, sure, thanks," I stammered, attempting to steady my voice. I stuck my head in the room. "Dad, do you mind staying with Luna while I speak with Ms. West?"

My father waved me off, already launching into another story.

"This way, and please call me Echo," the woman said, leading me to the same private room where Holt and I had met with Dr. Robbins the first time.

Once seated, with the door closed, she placed a folder on the table between us. "Miracles of Hope was created specifically to help families like yours," she explained. "Children who live in the Crested Butte area and have been diagnosed with certain kinds of blood cancers."

"That's... very specific," I commented, thinking of what Holt had mentioned about the charity being named in his trust.

"We've since branched out to help families facing other illnesses, but the organization was founded by a mother who lost her child to the disease. She wanted to ensure no family had to face a financial burden on top of an emotional one."

Something about Echo seemed familiar, though I couldn't place where from. Her features, the cadence of her speech—maybe she'd been into the Goat.

"Our organization will take care of most of Luna's medical costs that are above what insurance covers," she continued, sliding the paperwork toward me.

I stared at the papers, unable to process what she was saying. "Most of the costs?" I repeated, my voice barely audible.

"In my experience, we cover everything your insurance doesn't take care of, along with things like lodging, meals, and transportation," Echo clarified.

Tears welled in my eyes before I could stop them. The weight that had been crushing my chest since we'd arrived at the hospital lightened. I'd been calculating and recalculating our finances, wondering how I'd keep the Goat open while caring for Luna or how I'd pay for the medical care that could stretch into years.

"I don't know what to say," I whispered.

She smiled gently. "You don't need to say anything. This is exactly why we exist."

There was a knock at the door, and before I could stand to open it, Holt stuck his head inside. His appearance sent a wave of comfort through me so strong it nearly made me dizzy.

"Sorry to interrupt," he said, stepping into the room. "Dr. Robbins said you were in a meeting with the representative from the charity."

"It's fine," I said, gesturing for him to join us. "This is Echo West from the Miracles of Hope Children's Charity. Echo, this is Holt Wheaton."

Holt extended his hand. "Nice to meet you. Thank you for what you're doing for Keltie and Luna."

Echo shook his hand. "Do you have any connection to the Roaring Fork Ranch?"

"It's my family's place," Holt replied. "We've owned it for generations."

"My son King works there," Echo said, a mother's pride evident in her voice. "He's the ranch manager."

Holt's expression brightened with recognition. "Bridger? He's a great guy. And a hell of a musician too, or so I've heard. Err, but not from him."

"That's my son," Echo smiled. "He's always been more comfortable with horses than people."

"Well, he's respected by everyone at the ranch," Holt assured her. "Has been since he started three years ago."

There was a moment of silence before Echo looked at me. "Do you have any other questions about the assistance we provide?"

I glanced at the paperwork, still overwhelmed by their generosity. "No, I think you've covered everything. Thank you doesn't seem adequate, but it's all I can come up with at the moment."

"I have a question, if you don't mind," said Holt, leaning forward. "It might seem odd, but are you aware of any connection between your organization and our ranch, specifically?"

Echo's brow furrowed. "Nothing comes to mind. Why do you ask?"

Holt shrugged, his tone deliberately casual. "It's probably nothing. Just that the blanket in your logo—I used to have one exactly like it as a kid. Never seen another one."

Echo looked genuinely surprised. "I'm sorry. I don't know of any connection." She paused thoughtfully. "What I can tell you is that the charity's original name was Scarlett's Hope, if that means anything to you."

Holt shook his head.

"After the founder passed away," Echo continued, "the board decided to make the name more inclusive. We'd heard so often that we worked miracles for families that we chose Miracles of Hope."

"I see," Holt said, though I could tell from the set of his shoulders that there was more to his question than idle interest.

We finished reviewing the paperwork, and I signed where indicated. Echo promised to contact me the following day with more information about support groups for families.

After she left, Holt turned to me. "How are you holding up?"

"Better now," I admitted. "The financial help is… I can't even process it." I sighed. "Luna will receive the first round of drugs tomorrow, and that brings a whole new set of worries."

He took my hand, his thumb moving gently across my skin. His touch alone brought me so much comfort. "Come here," he said, pulling me over to his lap. "A little bird told me you needed a hug."

"I'd ask if it was Luna, but then you would've said unicorn instead of bird." We both smiled, and I snuggled closer to him. "I don't know how to thank you for your support, Holt."

"I'm here, Keltie, for you and Luna. Whatever you need."

"Speaking of my daughter, she asks about you at least once an hour."

"Then, I better go let her know I'm here." Before he released me, he brushed my lips with his. "I missed you so much."

"I missed you too."

We walked to Luna's room together. My father had fallen asleep again, and Luna was watching cartoons with the sound turned low.

"Mr. Holt!" Her face brightened. "Did you see my pictures?" She pointed to several drawings taped to the wall beside her.

"I did," he said, sitting on the edge of her bed and examining them. "These are amazing. Is this the mountain behind our ranch?"

"Sam gave me crayons. I'm drawing all the places I want to visit when I'm better."

"That's a great idea," Holt said, studying a particularly colorful creation. "And what's this one?"

"That's a recording studio," Luna explained, her voice growing animated. "Mommy told me she used to work in one, and that's where you make music. I want to see one someday."

As Holt and Luna discussed her artistic rendition of a mixing board—which looked more like a space-ship's control panel—Dr. Robbins stuck her head in the room.

"Keltie, if you have another moment," she said.

While I was reluctant to take Holt away from Luna, I needed his support. "Sweetheart, Mommy needs Mr. Holt's opinion about something, but we won't be too long, okay?"

Luna frowned, but it was quickly replaced with a smile. "I thought of somewhere else I want to go. I'll draw it while you're gone."

"I've never met anyone with her kind of resilience," Holt said once we were outside the room.

"Part of it is she's too young to truly understand what's going on. It's my fault for not explaining it better."

Dr. Robbins put her hand on my arm. "I will help when it comes time to broach specifics with your daughter. Ms. West also offered to be here again tomorrow if needed."

My eyes filled with tears. "Everyone has been so kind—"

Holt put his arm around my shoulders and pulled me close to him. He had no idea how much his strength did for me. How it gave me what I needed to keep going.

"We've already discussed Luna's treatment protocol," Dr. Robbins said as we settled into the consultation room. "But there's something important we need to address now." She rested her arms on the table. "In Luna's case, a bone marrow transplant might be beneficial."

My pulse faltered. "A transplant?"

"It's one of the most successful ways to win the battle against ALL," she explained. "We'd like to start testing for potential donors as soon as possible, so we have options if we decide to pursue that course."

"I'll get tested," I said immediately.

"Me too," said Holt.

"Parents are always considered at least half matches, which is good. But we prefer to find a full match if possible." She hesitated, then asked, "Is Luna's father available to be tested as well?"

I swallowed hard, avoiding Holt's gaze. "He's not in the picture," I said stiffly.

"I understand," she said gently. "But if there's any way to contact him, it could significantly increase Luna's chances of finding an ideal match."

I was unable to speak around the knot in my throat. The thought of contacting Remi—who had denied Luna was even his—made me physically ill.

"We'll get as many people tested as possible," Holt said, his hand finding mine. "Starting with Keltie and me."

The doctor left, saying she'd schedule the tests and let us know how soon they could take place. I rested against the chair when the magnitude of everything crashed over me.

"Hey," Holt said, reaching for my hand. "Talk to me."

"Remi didn't believe she was his," I whispered, staring at our clasped hands. "How am I supposed to ask him to get tested?"

"What if I talk to him?" Holt offered. "I can explain the situation, make it clear this isn't about parental rights or money."

I looked up at him, stunned by the offer. "You would do that?"

"I'd do anything for Luna," he said simply. "And for you."

The honesty in his voice made my throat ache. Before I could respond, he continued, "Actually, I have another idea. I'll call Ben."

"Ben Rice? Why?"

"Ben knows Remi better than I do. And he's got more leverage. Remi might ignore me, but he can't ignore his boss."

I considered this. "You'd tell Ben about Luna's paternity?"

Holt shook his head, then sighed. "Based on when you 'left' and Luna's age, he pretty much put it together. It's worth contacting him, Keltie. Luna needs as many potential donors as possible."

He was right, and when I accepted it, the relief that flooded me was immediate. "Thank you," I whispered.

Luna's nurse appeared in the doorway. "We're going to give your daughter something to help her sleep. She needs a lot of rest before tomorrow," she announced.

I took a deep breath and stood, Holt rising beside me. As we returned to Luna's bedside, he kept his hand at the small of my back.

My father woke as we entered, instantly alert to the change in atmosphere. Luna looked tiny in the hospital bed, her wide eyes taking in the array of medical equipment being wheeled into the room. "What's all this?" I asked as quietly as I could.

"For tomorrow," the nurse whispered.

"Mommy?" Her voice trembled. "What's happening?"

I sat on the edge of her bed, taking her small hand in mine. "Remember how the doctors said they needed to give you special medicine to make you better? They're going to give you the first part when you wake up in the morning."

She looked beyond me. "Are you leaving again, Mr. Holt?"

"I'm not going anywhere, Unicorn Girl," he promised, settling into the chair beside her bed.

Holt and I spent the night in the room with Luna, giving my father a much-needed break. By morning, the nurses began preparing for her first treatment. I gripped Holt's hand as the drugs that would hopefully save my daughter's life began flowing through her IV. Throughout it all, Holt continued his story of brave unicorn girls and magical healing flowers—his voice steady and reassuring when mine would have failed me.

When Luna finally drifted to sleep and the first round was complete, I remained seated at her bedside, knowing if I tried to stand, I'd probably pass out.

Holt dragged the other chair beside mine and sat down, offering me a cup of terrible hospital coffee.

"You should rest," he said quietly.

"I can't leave her," I replied, staring at Luna's pale face.

He rubbed my shoulders. "I know."

"You can go—"

"I'm not leaving your side, Keltie, so whatever you were about to say, don't bother."

Exhaustion pulled at me, but every time my eyes started to close, I jerked myself awake.

"Tell me about the first song you ever wrote," I said, desperate to stay awake, to keep watch over my daughter.

Holt smiled, understanding what I needed. "It was terrible. I was fourteen and thought I knew everything about heartbreak after Berta Thompson dumped me at the spring dance."

"Let me guess—lots of references to tears and rain?"

"And broken hearts and empty promises," he confirmed with a self-deprecating chuckle. "I played it for Flynn once, and she laughed so hard she almost choked on her cereal."

I smiled despite everything. "What was the first good song you wrote?"

He thought for a moment. "Probably 'Montana Sky.' I wrote it after a road trip with Cord and Porter when I was nineteen. It was the first time I felt like I'd captured something real."

"I'd like to hear it sometime," I said, my eyes heavy.

"You will," he promised.

We talked into the night, Holt telling stories about growing up on the ranch, about his brothers and sister, about his dreams for his music. I shared memories of my sound-engineering days, the bands I'd worked with before CB Rice, the thrill of crafting the perfect mix.

At some point, I moved to his lap and my head drooped against his shoulder. The last thing I remembered before sleep claimed me was the comforting weight of his arms.

I woke to new voices in the room. Luna was still asleep while Holt spoke with Dr. Robbins and a man I didn't recognize.

"This is Dr. Bigsby, our transplant specialist," Dr. Robbins explained when she noticed I was awake.

He stepped forward and shook my hand. "Hello, Ms. Marquez."

"Keltie, please." While I was able to speak a couple of words, my mind was reeling. Any hope I'd had of keeping Remi from knowing *my* daughter, was gone. I had no choice, though. Her survival was all that mattered. Not my pride, not how much of an asshole he was. Nothing trumped Luna's health. "How soon?" I managed to ask.

"Not immediately," Dr. Bigsby assured me. "We'll try to get her into remission with chemotherapy first. But I understand Dr. Robbins told you we'd like to start testing potential donors now, so we're prepared if the time comes."

"I'm ready whenever you are," I said firmly.

Dr. Robbins put her hand on my arm like she so often did. "I understand this is difficult, but I highly recommend we test Luna's biological father in the event you are not a full match."

"We'll make sure it happens," said Holt, who stood quietly beside me.

"The testing process is like any other blood draw. We can do yours this morning if you're ready," Dr. Bigsby suggested.

"We're ready," I confirmed, grateful for the doctor's professionalism.

After they left, I turned to Holt. "When do you have to leave?" I asked, too tired to count the hours since he'd arrived.

"About that…"

My eyes opened wide, and I gasped. Had he already been here over forty-eight hours?

He took my hands in his. "It's good news. Buck spoke with the attorney, who, I guess, spoke with the trustee, who agreed to allow me to remain in Denver as long as necessary."

"Holt, I don't want you to feel as though you have to—"

"Keltie, you and Luna mean the world to me, but I couldn't be the one responsible for my siblings losing their inheritance. Buck has it in writing if you want to see it." He winked.

"You're telling me the truth?"

His relaxed expression tightened. "I will always tell you the truth. That's a promise."

Before I could say more, Luna stirred, her eyes fluttering open. "Mommy? Mr. Holt?" Her voice was raspier than usual, an early sign of the drugs' effects.

"We're right here, baby," I assured her, leaning down to kiss her forehead.

"Can you hold me?"

Her pleading voice nearly shattered me. "Of course I can." I climbed beside her into the narrow hospital bed, careful not to disturb the IV line, and held my daughter as close as I could.

Holt kissed each of our foreheads. "I have to make a couple of phone calls, but I'm not leaving."

"Promise?" Luna whispered.

"I promise." He reached for her tiny hand and wrapped his pinky around hers.

20

Holt

I stepped into the hallway outside the room, determined to make the calls I needed without disturbing Keltie or Luna. After rounding a corner, I pulled my phone from my pocket. As I'd told Keltie, Ben Rice would have more sway over Remi Gilbert than I would. Most likely, the asshole wouldn't even take my call. I scrolled to Ben's number, but after several rings, his voicemail picked up.

"Ben, it's Holt. I need your help with something important involving Luna—Keltie's daughter. Call me as soon as you can. It's about Remi."

I hung up and stared at the phone for a moment. This shouldn't be so complicated. All we needed was for the guy to get tested. But given how he'd denied Luna was even his and abandoned Keltie when she was pregnant, I couldn't imagine him agreeing that easily.

The worst part was watching Keltie wrestle with the knowledge that she'd have to reach out to the man who'd hurt her so badly. I'd seen the flash of panic in her eyes that she'd quickly masked. It was the same expression she wore the day she'd seen me talking to him in the street in front of her house.

I needed a plan B if Ben couldn't help. I dialed Buck's number, grateful when he answered quickly.

"Everything okay?" Buck's voice came through clearly even though I could hear Buckaroo having a meltdown in the background.

"Sounds like you've got your hands full."

"Nah, TJ says sometimes we have to let him cry. No matter how much it rips our hearts out to do." I heard a door open and close, then silence. "How're you doin', Holt?"

"I'm okay. It's Keltie and Luna I'm worried about. She started treatments this morning," I said, keeping my voice low. "And this is the harder part; the doctors are recommending a bone marrow transplant. They want to test as many potential donors as possible, including her biological father."

"How's Keltie handling it?" Buck asked.

"Better than I would in her position." I leaned against the wall. "Buck, I can't walk away from them."

"And you don't have to," he assured me. "It's all taken care of with Six-pack. You have permission to stay in Denver as long as needed."

A nurse walked past, making quick eye contact before continuing down the hall. I lowered my voice further.

"Anyway, there's another reason I called. A couple, actually."

"What's up?" Buck asked.

"A woman from the Miracles of Hope charity—Echo West—was here, meeting with Keltie yesterday. Get this, she's Bridger's mother."

"Small world."

"Anyway, that's not the important part. I've been trying my damnedest to figure out why this charity is important enough that if one of us screws up, everything will go to them."

"And?"

"I'm not there yet, but she mentioned something that's been bothering me. The charity used to have a different name."

"Oh?" Buck's tone sharpened with interest.

"Scarlett's Hope," I said. "Named after the founder's daughter who died of leukemia. After the founder passed away, they changed it to Miracles of Hope."

The silence on the other end of the line stretched for several seconds.

"Scarlett," Buck finally said. "That's not a common name."

"You're right." I turned away from a passing doctor. "Could be nothing, but given everything with the trust and this charity specifically being named in my codicil…"

"You think we should find out who the founder was."

"Exactly. At least it might give us a clue as to who the trustee is."

"Makes sense. I'll call Decker Ashford and ask for his help."

"Worth a shot," I said. "After meeting Echo, learning about the charity's history… I'm convinced more than ever that it's a lead. Maybe ask Bridger what he knows."

"You got it." I could hear Buck moving around. "What else?"

"I tried calling Ben Rice, but couldn't reach him. It's urgent that I get in touch with him. Really urgent."

"You want me to head over to the Flying R and see if I can track him down?" Buck offered. "I've been meaning to talk to him anyway."

"About what?"

"Flynn suggested organizing a benefit concert to help with Luna's medical expenses. I figured if we could get Ben to support it, he might be able to bring in a few big names, even if CB Rice can't participate due to the tour."

A lump formed in my throat at the thought of my family rallying for Luna and Keltie. "That would be amazing," I managed.

"Flynn's thinking maybe have it at the amphitheater."

The idea of using music to help Luna's situation felt right. "I can't tell you how much this means to me, Buck. The family supporting my girls this way." I choked up again and brushed a tear away.

"Your girls," Buck repeated. "I like hearing you call them that."

"It's what they are, man. I love, err, care about them."

"You were right the first time."

"Hey, thanks for all this, Buck."

"Sure thing. I'm happy to do whatever I can to help."

After hanging up, I wandered toward the small visitor's lounge at the end of the hall. It was midafternoon, and thankfully, Luna had been handling her first treatment well so far, with just some drowsiness from the medication.

I hadn't set out to become so involved in their lives. When I first met Luna at the Goat, I'd felt that strange connection, that sense that something was wrong, but I never imagined being here, in a pediatric oncology ward, watching a four-year-old fight for her life.

The coffee tasted as bad as it looked. I dumped most of it in the trash and headed toward Luna's room, pausing at the nurses' station.

"Can you point me in the direction of the cafeteria?" I asked the nurse checking charts.

She smiled. "Second floor. Take a left off the elevator. The coffee there is actually drinkable, unlike the stuff in the lounge."

"Thanks," I said gratefully. "Can I bring anything back for the staff?"

She looked surprised by the offer. "We're fine, but that's kind of you. Luna's a special little girl. We're all pulling for her."

"She is that," I agreed.

I rode the elevator down to the cafeteria, which was busier than I expected. Hospital staff in various colored scrubs sat amongst visitors. I grabbed a tray, a turkey sandwich, a fruit cup, and a bottled water for Keltie, along with a decent-looking coffee. When I raised my head after inserting my credit card in the machine, I caught a man studying me from where he stood at another register, paying for his purchase. "Do I know you?" I asked.

"Don't think so," he said, holding out his hand for the change the cashier was giving him. He walked away but glanced over his shoulder. "Best of luck to you and your family."

"Huh," I muttered, although it wasn't that strange of a thing to say, considering we were in a children's hospital.

On my way out, I noticed a gift shop adjacent to the cafeteria. Through the window, I spotted a display of stuffed animals, including a unicorn that looked remarkably similar to Sparkles, except this one was pink.

I grabbed it, along with a soft blanket in Luna's favorite color, purple. The cashier wrapped everything in tissue paper and placed it in a gift bag.

"For your daughter?" she asked with a smile.

The question caught me off guard. "For a very special little girl," I answered, not bothering to correct her assumption.

Balancing the tray and gift bag, I made my way to Luna's room. Outside the door, I paused at the sound of Luna's voice, surprisingly animated, given she'd been sound asleep when I left.

"And then the unicorn flew all the way to the mountain with the magic flower," she was saying. "She wasn't scared at all, Mommy."

"That sounds very brave," Keltie replied, her voice gentle. "Just like a girl I know."

I knocked softly before pushing the door open with my knee. Luna's face brightened when she saw me.

"Mr. Holt! I was telling Mommy about the new story I thought of."

"Can't wait to hear it," I said, setting the tray and bag down. "But first, I brought something for your mom."

"You didn't have to do that," Keltie said, though the gratitude in her eyes conveyed otherwise.

"Figured you'd be hungry, and even if you weren't, you should eat something decent." I handed her the coffee first, which she accepted like it was liquid gold. "And I may have found something for a certain magical creature enthusiast."

Luna's eyes widened as I presented her with the gift bag. "Is it my birthday?"

"Who says presents are only for birthdays?" I winked at her, earning a giggle.

She tore into the tissue paper, gasping when she pulled out the pink stuffed animal. "Mommy, look!"

"What are you going to name her?" I asked, enjoying her excitement.

Luna cocked her head and tapped her cheek. "Shimmer," she decided. "Because she shimmers like the stars."

"Perfect name," Keltie said, meeting my eyes over Luna's head with a small smile that conveyed volumes.

A nurse came in to check her vitals and adjust her IV. Luna barely noticed, too busy introducing Shimmer to Bunny.

"How's our patient doing?" the woman asked, recording numbers from the machines.

"She's a rock star," Keltie said, her voice holding steady despite the worry I knew she carried.

"That's for sure," she agreed. "Oh, and Dr. Robbins said to tell you she'll be in shortly."

After she left, Keltie turned to me. "Did you reach Ben?"

"Left him a message," I said. "And I talked to Buck. He's going to track him down for us."

"Thank you," she said quietly. "I've been trying to figure out how to handle the, err, situation."

"Buck mentioned another idea too. Flynn's organizing a benefit concert for Luna."

"But the charity—"

"There are always costs that insurance and assistance don't cover," I said. "Besides, it gives everyone at home a way to help."

She blinked rapidly. "Everyone's been so kind."

"The Goat's a special place. So is the person who runs it."

A soft knock interrupted us as Dr. Robbins entered. "How's my favorite patient?" she asked with a warm smile.

"I got a new unicorn!" Luna exclaimed, holding up Shimmer alongside Sparkles.

"They're beautiful," Dr. Robbins said, checking the chart. "Just like your numbers. You're doing great, Luna."

As she and Keltie chatted, I helped Luna arrange her growing collection of stuffed animals on the bed.

"Mr. Holt," she whispered. "Can you add Shimmer to our story?"

"Absolutely," I promised. "I think they're going to have a lot of fun adventures together."

She smiled, her eyes heavy with medication-induced drowsiness. "Just like you and Mommy."

I was stunned silent. Out of the mouths of babes, as they say.

"Rest, sweet girl," I said, tucking the blanket around her. "We'll work on our story later."

Once the doctor left, Keltie sank into the chair beside Luna's bed, the emotional and physical toll of the day evident in the slump of her shoulders.

I took her hand and pulled her onto my lap instead. "Your little girl is quite a trooper. Like her mama."

Keltie gave a weary smile. "I don't feel like one right now."

"That's why I'm here," I told her. "To be strong when you need a break."

"And when do you get a break?"

I glanced at Luna, peaceful in sleep despite the tubes and monitors. "This isn't about me. This is about getting her better."

Keltie looked like she wanted to say more, but fatigue won out. She rested her head on my chest and let her eyes drift closed.

I sat in quiet vigilance, watching them both. Luna's face appeared peaceful while Keltie's expression, even in sleep, carried the worry she'd been hiding all day.

They deserved better than what life had handed them. They deserved someone who would stand by them through this fight and long beyond it. The certainty that I wanted to be that person surprised me with its clarity.

I loved them. Both of them.

21

Keltie

The night before we were scheduled to leave Children's Hospital, I stood at the window of the apartment Sam and Beau had arranged for us, watching the city lights shimmer against the dark sky. Two weeks had passed since we'd arrived—fourteen days that felt both endless and impossibly brief. The good news was we were able to return home earlier than anticipated since Luna had responded well enough that the doctors decided she didn't have to stay the full month.

Behind me, Holt was sprawled on the sofa, dozing while a mindless reality show played on the television. He'd finally agreed to take a break from the hospital room after my father insisted he do so since he'd be staying the night with Luna. The rotation had worked well—one of us was always with her while the others rested at the nearby apartment.

I'd just returned from checking on them, finding my daughter sleeping peacefully and my father settled in the recliner next to her bed, reading one of his

paperbacks. The doctors were pleased with her prog-
ress, and tomorrow, we'd finally be taking her home.

"Sleep, darlin'," Holt said, his voice thick with
fatigue. I turned to find him watching me, blue eyes
soft in the dim light. "Big day tomorrow."

"I know." I crossed the room and sank down beside
him. "I can't believe we're finally going home."

Holt got up, checked the locks, then turned out the
lights once I made my way down the hall to the first of
the two bedrooms. We paused outside the door.

"Thank you," I said, the words inadequate for everything he'd done.

"For what?" he asked, reaching out to tuck a curl
behind my ear.

"For being here. For everything."

He smiled, leaning down to press his lips to my
forehead. "I wouldn't be anywhere else."

We'd both agreed that separate bedrooms made sense
while we were here. Neither of us had discussed what
would happen once we were back in Crested Butte.
One day at a time had become our unspoken mantra.

Morning came quickly, and with it, the flurry of
activity that accompanied our discharge. I arrived at

Luna's room by seven, finding my father teaching her how to play Go Fish with a deck of cards he'd bought at the gift shop.

"Mommy!" She brightened when she saw me. "I'm winning!"

"That's because your *abuelo* lets you cheat," I said, kissing the top of her head.

The hair loss had started a week after her first treatment. She'd been surprisingly resilient about it, especially after Holt brought her a selection of colorful bandanas.

Dr. Robbins arrived with a tablet in hand, reviewing Luna's care instructions one final time. We stood near the doorway, looking over at my daughter.

"She did remarkably well with the first round," she began. "Better than we expected, though the next two weeks will tell us more about how her body is responding."

"What's next?" I asked.

"Dr. Patel in Gunnison will coordinate with me. We recommend Luna stay at the hospital there for the five days of her next round, so we can monitor how she tolerates the second cycle. After that, if all goes well, the time she'll have to stay will grow increasingly shorter."

"Do I get to ride in a helicopter again?" Luna asked.

"Not this time, Unicorn Girl," Holt said as he entered the room with coffee for all the adults. "We're driving home."

Luna considered this. "Can we stop for ice cream?"

"If your mom says it's okay." Holt glanced at me with raised eyebrows.

"We'll see," I replied, my standard answer when I was too tired to make decisions.

My father chuckled. "That's what my mother always said to me when I asked for something. It usually meant yes."

Dr. Robbins handed me a thick folder. "Everything is in here—medication schedules, signs to watch for, dietary recommendations, activity guidelines. Dr. Patel has all this information too, but I wanted you to have your own copy."

I thumbed through the folder, overwhelmed by the volume of information. "Thank you."

"And we should have the bone marrow compatibility results in another couple of weeks or so," she added. "From you, your father, and Holt."

The three of us had been tested the following day. A transplant wasn't guaranteed, but having the results would prepare us for any decision that might come later.

"Any word from Luna's father?" Dr. Robbins asked quietly, stepping farther away from where Luna was chattering with my dad about the stuffed animal hospital they planned to set up at home.

I shook my head, the familiar knot forming in my stomach. "Not yet."

Holt had spoken with Ben, who'd talked to Remi. The details of that conversation had been mostly kept from me, at my request. I knew it would be hurtful, and I was already carrying enough pain. What Holt had shared was that the band would be taking a break from the tour the same day Luna was scheduled to start her next round of chemo. With them returning to the States, there was hope Remi might agree to be tested then.

I wasn't holding my breath.

The drive to Crested Butte took four hours, including a stop for the promised ice cream. Luna dozed for most of the trip. As soon as we turned off Cottonwood

Pass and I saw the butte in the distance, I felt my shoulders relax. *Home.*

"I'm making chilaquiles tomorrow," my father said, touching Luna's cheek as we turned onto Elk Avenue—Crested Butte's version of Main Street. "With the extra queso fresco you like."

Luna clapped her hands. "With avocado too?"

"Is there any other way?"

She shook her head.

When our house came into view, I gasped. Someone had hung a hand-painted banner across the porch, its crooked letters spelling "Welcome Home Luna." Wind-whipped balloons were tied to the railing, and the walkway stood freshly shoveled.

"Wow," I murmured, taking in the sight.

Holt glanced over, a half smile forming on his lips. "I guess the town heard we were coming home today."

The surprises continued once we were inside. Our refrigerator had been stocked with labeled containers, someone had swept the pine floors, and the scent of cinnamon and nutmeg permeated the air. A wooden crate sat on the counter, overflowing with toys and games for Luna.

"My family, the crew from the Goat, and several other locals pitched in—including Mrs. Lopez of course," Holt explained.

I swallowed hard, trying to form words, but they stuck in my throat.

Holt and I followed Luna upstairs to her bedroom, which she inspected as though she'd been away for months instead of days. "It looks the same," she said, sitting on the edge of her bed.

I glanced over at Holt, who stood in the hallway, looking at something on his phone. "I should head to the ranch," he said, looking up at me.

A sudden unease hit me at the thought of him leaving. "I understand," I said, wishing he didn't have to go but knowing he'd already given us so much of his time.

When I stood to say goodbye, he opened his arms and I rested my forehead on his chest. "I didn't realize how tired I was."

"Sleep if you can. I'll let myself back in quietly when I return."

Before he left, he tucked Luna into her bed, promising that, when she woke up, they'd work on their stories again. While she didn't say, "Promise?" like she usually did, she lifted her hand and Holt wrapped his pinky around hers. He gave me a quick kiss goodbye, then went downstairs, where I heard him talking to my dad.

Since my room was right across the hall from Luna's, I left both doors open, then fell onto the bed. My dad was staying in the guest room on the first floor, and since he was familiar enough with my house, I didn't worry about him finding whatever he needed.

I'd drifted off, but my phone's vibration jolted me awake. Miguel's name lit up the screen.

"Hey," I said in a gravelly voice.

"You home yet?" he asked.

"We are, and all I can say is you're a godsend, Miguel. Thank you for making our homecoming so wonderful. How are things at the Goat?" While I'd checked in with him once a day while we were in Denver, our conversations didn't last more than a couple of minutes. Each time, he assured me everything was fine, and it had been enough for me. "I'll be by later, okay?"

"The Goat isn't going anywhere. Come in whenever you're ready."

After thanking him again and hanging up, I checked on Luna. She was sound asleep, like I soon hoped to be. Hearing my dad looking for stuff in the kitchen, I decided to check on him too. I found him gathering ingredients to make chilaquiles.

"Do you need me to run to the store?" I asked.

"No, *mija*. Holt said he'd pick up whatever I needed when he returns later."

"He's a good man," I said, resting against the counter.

My father's eyes met mine. "He loves you and Luna very much."

I raised a brow. "He cares about us. I wouldn't go so far as to call it love."

He pulled out a chair at the table. "Sit before you collapse on me."

I didn't argue. I wasn't sure I had the energy to walk up the stairs again.

"He feels the same as I did about your mother. I fell in love with Mary Grace the first time I saw her."

I opened my mouth to speak, but he held up a hand.

"There's nothing to argue about, Keltie. If you don't feel it yet, you soon will."

"I—" Before I could say more, I heard Luna calling for me. I kissed my father's cheek, then raced up the steps and sat beside her on the bed. "I'm here, sweetheart."

"Mommy, do you think Mr. Holt could be my daddy?"

I'd say her question surprised me, but it didn't. Given how close they were, I'd expected her to ask sooner.

"He's a very special friend to us, Luna-bug."

"But I want him to be more."

I stroked her cheek with my finger. "I know, but for now, let's accept he's an important part of our lives and take it one day at a time."

She sighed and turned to her side. "He said the same thing."

I stifled a gasp. "Sweetheart, did you ask him to be your daddy?"

Luna shook her head. "No."

I didn't say "good" out loud, but I sure felt relief she hadn't.

"But I asked him if he was going to marry you. Actually, when."

I stretched out beside her and gathered her in my arms. "One day at a time," I whispered.

That was where and how Holt found us later.

"Sorry I woke you," he whispered. "I wanted to let you know I'm headed over to the Goat."

"I'll go with you." I eased out from under Luna. "Mind if we run out for a few minutes?" I said to my father, who was unpacking the groceries Holt had delivered. "We won't be long."

He waved his hand without looking up. "Go. We're fine here."

When we arrived at the bar, it appeared empty from outside. Inside, the after-work crowd huddled at the bar while Miguel cleaned and stocked glasses. Faces turned when I entered, conversations halting mid sentence.

"Keltie." Miguel abandoned his towel, moving around the bar to hug me.

"How can I ever thank you?" I asked, surveying how amazing the place looked.

He shrugged. "You'd do it for any of us."

I walked through the familiar space, noting things I'd never paid attention to before—the way the light hit the shelves filled with bottles and the worn path in the hardwood from the entrance to the bathrooms. My space. My territory.

A large poster near the stage caught my eye. "Valentine's Day Benefit," it read in bold type across the top. Luna's name was underneath in smaller letters, followed by "Crested Butte's Fierce Fighter." Local band names filled the lower third, with "Headliner: TBA" prominent at the center.

I stood motionless, fingers hovering near the paper without touching it.

"Flynn's work," Miguel said, coming to stand beside Holt and me. "The amphitheater agreed to host. Restaurants are covering the food. Tickets go on sale tomorrow."

"This is—" Words failed me again as my fingertips traced Luna's name.

Holt wrapped his arm around my shoulders when Miguel went behind the bar. "I'll get set up to play tonight unless there's something else you need me to do."

"One thing," I responded.

"Name it."

I took his hand and let him to the office. "Easier to show you," I said, closing the door behind us once we were inside. As if he'd read my mind, his hands found my face, he cupped my jawline, and his mouth met mine hard.

My body responded instantly, my fingers weaving in his hair, pulling him closer. The sense of urgency I felt surprised me, but I couldn't let go of him. I looked into his eyes. "Stay with me tonight?"

"You know I will, Keltie."

"I mean in my bed."

"I wouldn't be anywhere else."

A sharp knock interrupted us, and Holt moved away reluctantly, opening the door to Miguel's apologetic face.

"Sorry. Something you need to see." He pointed toward a cluster of people hunched over a phone at the bar.

We followed, curious. A regular—Dave or Dan, I could never remember—held his cell up as we approached.

"Look at this."

The screen showed a social media post from Ben, saying CB Rice would be headlining Luna's benefit concert.

"Did you know?" I turned to Holt, searching his face.

He looked genuinely surprised. "No. He didn't mention anything."

"We'll sell out in an hour," Miguel predicted, scrolling through the comments that were posting faster than we could read them.

My brain struggled to process the information. CB Rice played arenas, not small-town benefits. Seconds later, the front door banged open. Stacey from McGill's burst in, clutching her phone like a winning lottery ticket.

"Have you seen?" Her words tumbled out. "Everyone's talking about it!"

"Just now," I managed.

"That's not all," she continued breathlessly. "Tickets went on sale four minutes ago. It's already sold out, and I heard Ben suggested adding a second night."

"Told you," said Miguel with a broad smile.

Holt's hand found the small of my back, steadying me.

"We're doing a raffle," Stacey added. "Hardware store's giving a generator. Ski resort donated season passes. We've got slope-side condos, other vacation packages, and gift certificates from everywhere from here to Salida. The list keeps growing."

My throat constricted. "Why would everyone—"

"Because we take care of our own," she said simply. "Gotta run. More calls to make!" She vanished as quickly as she'd appeared.

Holt squeezed my shoulder. "I need to get started," he said, but instead of heading straight to the stage, he guided me to a quieter corner near the office. "You okay?"

"Processing," I admitted. "It's a lot."

His thumb brushed my cheek, coming away damp. I hadn't realized I was crying.

When he finally moved toward the stage, I took a seat at the bar. Miguel slid water toward me without asking. The room quieted as Holt adjusted his microphone and tuned his guitar.

"Hey, everybody," he said, his voice filling the space. "For those who don't know, Luna came home today." He paused, fingers hovering over the strings.

"I wrote this song for her and her mama, but it seems fitting that I play it for the first time tonight."

I turned around to face him, barely breathing as he played the opening cords then started to sing. The song told of a unicorn with healing powers who got sick herself. It spoke of stars and invisible strength, of darkness that couldn't extinguish certain kinds of light. He'd transformed Luna's ordeal—the needles, the machines, the fear—into something a child could grasp without terror.

Tears came freely now as he sang the final verse, his eyes finding mine across the room. Through the worst moments of my life, Holt had remained steady. He'd made Luna laugh when nothing else could. He'd become part of our little family.

The music faded, and applause filled the silence. I sat motionless, aware that tomorrow would bring medication schedules, doctor follow-ups, and everything to do with illness management. But tonight, in this moment, I felt more than fear and uncertainty. I felt hope.

Holt's gaze held mine across the room, a question in his eyes I couldn't answer aloud yet. As he began his next song, I didn't look away. Somehow, I knew he understood.

I stayed another hour, letting the bar's familiar rhythms wash over me. Finally, gathering my resolve, I said good night to Miguel, waved to Holt, and headed home.

I found my father and Luna hidden in a blanket fort that took up half the living room. Flashlights illuminated their faces from below as they read from one of her books.

"Mommy!" Luna called. "Come sit in our fort!"

I crawled through the makeshift entrance, careful not to dislodge the chair supporting one corner.

"Quite an engineering feat," I said, settling beside them.

"We could sleep here tonight," Luna suggested, eyes bright.

My father shrugged. "My spine says no, but don't let that stop you two."

"We'll see," I hedged. The floor's appeal had diminished significantly after weeks of hospital chair sleeping. Not to mention, I had every intention of holding my body close to Holt's tonight, and not even my beloved daughter's pleading could get me to abandon that plan.

We spent the evening in that cloth cave, my father recounting embarrassing stories from my childhood that made Luna demand more. I had to wonder how many were actually true. Laughter filled our house again, something I'd feared might be a long time coming.

By the time Holt texted he was on his way over, I'd already carried my sleeping daughter up the stairs and put her to sleep in her bed.

"Hey," I said, opening the door to let him in.

My father stretched his arms over his head. "Calling it a night. These old bones weren't meant for floor sitting." He clasped Holt's shoulder as he passed. "Good night."

"Night," we echoed.

Alone finally, Holt eliminated the space between us. "About the song…"

"It was perfect," I said, reaching up to trace the line of his jaw. "She'll love hearing it."

His hands found my waist, drawing me closer. "I wrote it for both of you."

I rose on tiptoe, pressing my mouth to his. When we separated, I rested against him, listening to the rhythm of his heart.

"Let's go upstairs," I whispered.

"Holt, there's something I need to tell you."

While he looked like he was about to drift to sleep, his eyes opened wide.

"I, um, well, the thing is…" I stammered.

He put his fingertip on my lips. "Let me go first."

"Okay."

"I love you, Keltie."

My eyes filled with tears. "I love you, Holt."

22

Holt

Keltie's words washed over me, releasing the tension I'd been carrying for the last couple of weeks. I pulled her closer, burying my face in her wild curls as her arms tightened around me. The weight of everything I'd watched her go through—Luna's diagnosis, the treatments, the bone marrow search—seemed to lift, if only for this moment.

"Say it again," I whispered against her ear.

Her amber eyes met mine in the dim light of her bedroom. "I love you."

I claimed her mouth with mine, my hands sliding beneath her sweater to find the warm skin beneath. She moved against me with an urgency that matched my own, her fingers working the buttons of my shirt with trembling hands.

"Are you sure about this?" I asked, breaking the kiss long enough to search her face.

"More sure than I've been about anything in a long time," she replied.

Once we were both naked, I reached into my jeans pocket and pulled out the only condom I carried with me, hoping it would still work. When I opened the packet, then rolled it on, I breathed a sigh of relief.

"We need to pick up more of those," she said, breaking the tension in the most perfect way.

"Damn, I love you," I said, spreading her legs to rest between them. Holding myself with one arm, I took her perfect nipple in my mouth, sucking until she arched, then moving to the other.

"Holt?"

I shifted so my lips could brush hers. "Keltie?"

"It's, uh, been a long time since I've done this."

"Pretty sure it's like ridin' a bike, darlin'."

"That isn't what I meant."

I looked into her eyes. "If you aren't ready, we can stop right now."

Her eyebrows flashed. "*Not* ready? I'm beyond ready, Holt. In fact, if you could speed things up a bit, I'd be all for it."

I smiled, positioned myself at her entrance, then eased inside at the same time I circled her bundle of nerves with her wetness. She arched again, and her eyes drifted closed.

"You doin' okay?" I asked, barely holding on as well.

Her response, sinking her fingernails into the cheek of my ass and pushing me against her, was all the answer I needed. I thrust deeper, increasing our rhythm as she matched me stroke for stroke, and her hands moved to my shoulders.

"Holt?" she repeated.

"Come for me, Keltie." I thrust hard and fast until I felt her pussy clench and her wetness flood me. Only then did I let myself go.

For the next couple of hours, I traced every inch of her with my hands and mouth, memorizing the constellation of freckles across her shoulders and the places that made her breath catch. We were out of condoms, but that didn't mean we couldn't bring each other pleasure.

"I love you," she whispered again and again, each time we crested together. "I love you so much."

Dawn filtered through the curtains when I woke. Keltie's head was nestled against my shoulder, her breathing deep and even. I remained still, not wanting to disturb her after weeks of restless nights in hospital chairs. I watched her breathe, the gentle movement of her eyelashes against her skin.

Luna's voice drifted through the partially open door, followed by Victor's low reply. The smell of coffee and breakfast wafted up the stairwell. I eased carefully from beneath Keltie, pressing a kiss to her forehead before pulling on my jeans and shirt.

"And then they found a magic berry bush," Luna was saying as I descended the stairs. She sat at the kitchen table, a purple bandana covering her head, animatedly moving her hands as she described her latest story to her grandfather.

Victor looked up from the stovetop, where he was flipping what looked like French toast. "*Buenos días.* Coffee's fresh."

"Morning," I replied, gratefully accepting the mug he offered.

"Mr. Holt!" Luna beamed. "I'm telling *Abuelo* about the new story I dreamed!"

I sat beside her, ruffling her bandana gently. "I can't wait to hear it, Unicorn Girl."

Victor set a plate of French toast in front of Luna, who immediately doused it in syrup.

"Is Mommy still sleeping?" Luna asked between bites.

"She is. She needs the rest," I replied, sharing a knowing look with Victor.

"Did you sleep nice beside Mommy?" Luna asked, her innocent question nearly making me choke on my coffee.

Victor chuckled. "*Pequeña*, let Mr. Holt eat his breakfast before the interrogation, eh?"

"*Abuelo* says you make her happy," Luna whispered.

My heart squeezed in my chest. "She makes me happy too," I said, tapping her nose lightly.

Keltie appeared in the doorway, wrapped in a robe, her hair a wild tangle around her shoulders. My breath caught at the sight of her—sleep-rumpled and beautiful.

"Mommy!" Luna called. "We made French toast!"

"I see that," Keltie said, coming to kiss Luna's forehead before accepting the coffee mug Victor handed her. Her eyes met mine over the rim, and her cheeks pinkened.

"Morning," I murmured, fighting the urge to pull her onto my lap.

"Morning," she replied, her voice still husky with sleep.

Victor cleared his throat. "I thought I might take Luna to the park later, if she's feeling up to it."

"Can we, Mommy?" Luna asked, bouncing in her chair. "Dr. Robbins said I can play outside if I wear my mask."

Keltie hesitated, and her fingers tightened around her mug. "Let's see how you feel after breakfast," she said, her standard non-answer that made Luna sigh dramatically.

After we finished eating, I helped Victor with the dishes while Keltie took Luna upstairs to get dressed.

"She loves you," Victor said as he handed me a plate to dry.

"I love them both," I replied honestly.

"Good. They deserve that."

"I know," I said. "I'm not going anywhere, Victor."

He studied me, his weathered face solemn. "When Mary Grace died, I thought I'd never recover. Luna's mother—she was so young." He shook his head. "But I had to, for Keltie. Now, you understand, yes? What it means to be the rock someone leans on?"

"Yes," I said quietly. "I do."

"Bueno." He clapped me on the shoulder. "Then, we understand each other."

Later that morning, I offered to pick up Luna's prescription at the pharmacy. Elk Avenue had transformed overnight. Benefit concert posters hung on every shop window, telephone pole, and on the bulletin board outside the library. "Valentine's Day with CB Rice," they announced in bold letters. "Supporting Luna Marquez's Fight Against Leukemia."

The drug store was buzzing with chatter about the concert as I waited for Luna's medications to be filled.

"Did you hear they might add a second day?" the woman ahead of me asked her friend. "Sold out in under ten minutes!"

"My mother-in-law in Denver somehow scored tickets," the other replied. "She's driving all the way here for it. I warned her to make a reservation at one of the hotels now. I'm sure they're going to sell out too!"

I smiled to myself, still amazed by Ben's generosity and the town's response.

When I returned to Keltie's house, I found her curled on the sofa with a notebook, scribbling what looked like medication schedules and appointment times.

"Where are Luna and Victor?" I asked, setting down the bag of medications.

"Park," she replied, tucking a curl behind her ear. "Luna was bouncing off the walls, so I finally gave in and said she could go."

I sank down beside her, examining her list. "That's a lot to keep track of."

"Miguel's been incredible about scheduling everyone's shifts around me being away," she said, letting out a deep sigh. "But it's still a juggling act."

"Maybe you could use another juggler?" I suggested, taking her hand. "I meant what I said last night, Keltie. I love you. I love Luna. I'll do whatever I can to help. Whatever needs to be done."

"How are you at bartending?" she asked.

I raised a brow. "I grew up in a ski town. How do you think?"

She smirked. "But do you know how to do more than pour beer?"

I took the pen from her hand and pulled her onto my lap. "Come here, and I'll show you what all I can do."

Keltie melted against me, her body fitting perfectly against mine. Her lips found my jaw, then my mouth in a deep kiss.

"How long will they be at the park?" I murmured against her neck.

"Long enough," she replied with a smile.

We made love on the sofa, sunlight spilling across our tangled limbs, her soft cries muffled against my shoulder. Afterward, we held each other, my fingers tracing lazy patterns on her bare skin.

"I've been thinking," I said after a while. "I want to record Luna's song at Ben's studio."

"That would be amazing," she replied.

"I might work on other tracks too," I continued. "I was thinking of asking Bridger to come along. The guy's got serious talent, though he'd never admit it."

Keltie grew quiet, her fingers stilling on my chest.

"What is it?" I asked, tilting her chin so I could see her expression.

"Nothing," she said quickly, then bit her lip. "It's, um, been a long time since I've been in a studio."

Understanding dawned. "Would you want to come with me? See the setup?"

Her eyes lit up. "You wouldn't mind?"

"Are you kidding? I'd love it." I pulled her closer and nuzzled her neck.

"Could Luna and Dad come too?" she asked. "They could drive separately in case Luna gets tired."

"Absolutely," I replied, kissing her softly. "Ben said to give Liv a heads up when I planned to come by. I'll call her now."

"This place is amazing." Keltie's eyes were wide as she took in the mixing board.

Luna clutched my hand, her purple bandana a bright spot of color against the studio's muted tones. Her gaze darted nervously when Liv walked into the studio, holding the hand of her and Ben's five-year-old daughter, Caden.

"Everything all right, Unicorn Girl?" I asked, crouching to her level.

She shrugged. "It's fine."

"Do you want to play with Caden?" I asked quietly.

Luna shook her head.

I'd worried this might happen—that she'd feel self-conscious about her hair loss, despite the brightly colored bandana. "You don't have to do anything you don't want to."

She rolled her eyes in a perfect imitation of her mother. "*Of course* I want to play, but I don't want to miss hearing my song."

I laughed, relieved. "Tell you what—once I'm warmed up and your mom's ready, you and I will lay down the first tracks together. Okay? You can sit right next to me."

Her face lit up. "Really?"

"Really," I confirmed.

"If I knew the words, I'd sing along, but I haven't heard them yet." That statement sounded more like her *abuelo* than her mother.

"It's our story, Luna. You know *all* the words."

"So it's okay if I sing?"

"Sing, giggle, squeal—whatever you're feeling." I glanced over at Keltie, who gave me a thumbs-up.

Bridger arrived a few minutes later.

"Thanks for coming," I said, clasping his hand. "Keltie, Luna, this is Bridger—King West. He works at the ranch."

"We met your mother in Denver," Keltie said, extending her hand. "She's been incredibly helpful."

Bridger's expression softened. "Mom mentioned meeting you."

"Echo told us the charity was originally called Scarlett's Hope," I added, studying his reaction.

Other than a quick flicker in his eyes. There wasn't one. The guy probably won every hand of poker he ever played.

"Luna, would you like to play with Caden's horses? She's been excited about meeting you all morning," said Liv.

Luna looked torn, glancing between me and the little girl arranging stuffed animals on a blanket nearby.

"We'll start recording soon," I assured her. "But there might be boring grown-up talk first."

"Okay." Luna's eyes brightened. "But you'll call me when it's time for my song?"

"Promise," I said, linking my pinky with hers.

Just as Luna joined Caden, Ben walked in.

"Hey, I thought you were on tour," I said, walking over to shake his hand.

"I come home every chance I get. We're off tonight, so I'll fly out in the morning. Perks of having my own plane."

"Did the rest of the band return with you?" I asked, noting how Keltie's shoulders had tightened.

"Nope. Just me. They and the crew can do the heavy lifting. I'm getting too old for that shit." He looked over to watch Keltie's fingers trail over the equipment, muscle memory evident in the way she adjusted dials without thinking.

"Still remember how to use this?" Ben asked.

"Still? I never used this stuff. Crazy how things change in five years."

"You'll pick it up in no time. I mean, you're engineering this session, right?"

Keltie laughed. "I was going to until you showed up," she teased. "Now, I might be too nervous."

Ben shook his head. "From what I remember, you've got a hell of an ear."

I watched Keltie's expression change—her uncertainty fading as she took her place at the mixing board, checking levels and adjusting settings.

"Let's test the mics," she said, all business now. "Holt, can you give me a sound check?"

I grabbed my guitar and headed into the recording booth, unable to suppress my smile at her commanding tone. This was a side of Keltie I hadn't seen before. Sure, she was in control at the bar, but this was different. She belonged here. I hoped soon she'd realize it too.

For the next two hours, we worked on Luna's song. Keltie's suggestions subtly improved the arrangement, her technical expertise apparent in every adjustment she made. Luna sat beside me for the first recording, her face a picture of wonder. Keltie captured every reaction, every soft gasp, delighted giggle, and when she got close enough to the mic to sing along.

By midafternoon, Luna's energy was visibly waning despite her determination to stay involved. Victor caught my eye, motioning to his granddaughter's drooping shoulders.

"Luna-bug," he said gently. "Perhaps we should head home so you can rest before dinner?"

To my surprise, Luna didn't argue. "Okay," she said, yawning. "But Mr. Holt, can I hear the song when it's finished?"

"You'll be the first person who gets to," I promised.

After they left, we continued recording, with Bridger adding subtle harmonies that enhanced the track beautifully. His deep baritone complemented my voice in ways I hadn't anticipated, adding depth to the chorus.

"That's it," Keltie said through the intercom after our third take. "That's the one."

She spent another hour working her magic on the soundboard, and when she played the final version, I choked up. Luna's song, now professionally recorded, with her reactions woven throughout, transforming it into something both polished and personal.

"It's perfect," I said, squeezing Keltie's shoulder. "You're amazing."

She blushed, ducking her head. "It's your song. I just helped capture it."

Ben insisted on playing it through the studio's main speakers. "This is fantastic, Holt. We gotta get more of your stuff recorded. You're a damn good songwriter."

My phone buzzed with Buck's name on the screen. "Excuse me a minute," I said, stepping into the hall-way to take the call.

"How's it going?" my oldest brother asked.

"Great. We're at Ben's studio, recording Luna's song."

"I won't keep you, but I wanted you to know that Decker's been digging into Miracles of Hope," Buck continued. "Not much luck so far. It was definitely set up anonymously, with multiple layers of legal protection."

"Just like the trust," I muttered.

"Took the words right outta my mouth. Anyway, I wanted you to know I heard from him, and he said he'd keep digging. I'll keep you posted."

After hanging up, I found Bridger and Keltie deep in conversation about mixing techniques. Ben had disappeared, presumably to check on his daughter.

"Got what we need?" I asked, placing my hand on the small of Keltie's back.

"I think so. Bridger was showing me a new compression technique."

The guy inclined his head in acknowledgment. "Your girlfriend's got serious skills."

"Don't I know it," I replied, unable to keep the pride from my voice.

We wrapped up the session, thanking Ben and Liv for their hospitality before heading to our vehicles. Bridger's truck was parked next to mine, and as he unlocked it, I took a chance.

"Hey, uh, when you heard the name Scarlett, it seemed to mean something to you," I said casually.

His hand paused on the door handle, shoulders tensing. "Nope," he muttered before climbing inside the cab.

"He's lying," said Keltie when I turned around and saw her standing right behind me.

"I think so too. I'll keep pestering him until he talks."

Keltie shook her head and laughed. "Good luck with that."

The ride to her place was quiet, both of us processing the day. Keltie reached over, her hand finding mine on the console between us.

"Thank you," she said softly. "For today. For everything."

I squeezed her fingers. "No need to thank me."

"I know, but…" She paused. "Being in the studio again, doing what I love—it meant more than I can say."

I lifted her hand to my lips. "You were brilliant. Watching you work was incredible."

Victor and Luna were waiting when we arrived, Luna clutching a new stuffed horse that must have been a gift from Caden.

"Did you finish my song?" she asked immediately.

"We did," I confirmed, lifting her into my arms. "And it's amazing, thanks to your mom."

Luna beamed. "Can I hear it?"

"Tomorrow," Keltie said firmly. "After dinner and a good night's sleep."

Luna pouted but didn't argue, another sign of how tired she truly was.

After we'd eaten and Luna got ready for bed, Victor retired to the guest room, leaving Keltie and me alone in the living room. The moment the doors closed, she was in my arms, her mouth finding mine with urgent hunger.

"Let's go to bed, cowgirl," I said, lifting her into my arms and carrying her up the stairs. Once in the room, we shed our clothes between desperate kisses. As soon as we were both naked, she pushed me down and straddled me.

"Keltie, God," I groaned when she ripped open a condom, rolled it on me, then lowered herself onto my hardness. "Fuck, you feel good."

I reached up and palmed her breasts, tweaking her nipples between my fingers. She picked up her pace, grinding her body on mine until I was as deep as I could go. Then she'd ease all the way up, only to do it all over again.

"You're driving me wild, darlin'." My teeth clenched. "I'm not gonna last."

"I don't want you to."

I gripped her waist, holding her still as an orgasm shot through my body.

"Holt," she cried out, clenching me so hard as she came with me.

"Stay tonight?" she murmured against my chest.

"Try to make me leave," I replied, stroking her hair.

When we eventually slipped beneath her sheets, she curled against me, her breathing slowly evening out as sleep claimed her.

"*Holt?* Holt, wake up."

Keltie's voice broke through the nightmare, her hand cool against my face. I jerked awake, heart pounding and sweat cooling on my skin.

"You were having a bad dream," she said, her brow furrowed.

I pulled her close, burying my face in her hair as the remnants of it clung to me. A hospital room. My mother. The tiny, sick baby in her arms.

"I dreamed about my mom again," I whispered. "She was holding an infant who was very sick. But this time"—I swallowed hard—"she called the baby Scarlett."

Keltie's eyes widened in the darkness. "Scarlett's Hope," she whispered.

I nodded as her words sent a chill through me.

23

Keltie

The morning of Luna's second round of chemotherapy arrived too quickly. She sat at the kitchen table, eyes downcast beneath her purple bandana, arranging Bunny, Shimmer, and Sparkles in a protective line beside her.

The front door opened, and Holt's familiar footsteps sounded in the hallway. He appeared in the kitchen doorway, snow dusting his shoulders and his cheeks reddened from the cold.

"There's my favorite unicorn girl," he said, hanging his jacket by the door. He crossed to Luna and crouched beside her chair. "Ready for our big adventure today?"

Luna shook her head, tears spilling down her cheeks. "I don't want to go! The medicine hurts and makes me throw up and… and…" Her words dissolved into sobs that rattled her small frame.

Holt gathered her in his arms, holding her against his chest while she cried. Over her head, his eyes met mine, reflecting the same ache I felt.

"Let's work on our story," he was saying. "Remember how, in the last part, Sparkles was feeling sick after she drank from the magic pond?"

I moved toward the doorway, my father following quietly behind me.

I heard Luna's sniffling response. "She said it tasted like old socks."

"That's right. And remember how she felt afterward? All wobbly and sad?"

"She cried," Luna said softly. "And Shimmer came to help her."

"Exactly. She told Sparkles something very important. Do you remember what it was?"

A pause, then Luna's voice, steadier now. "That it's okay to cry. And it's okay to be upset."

"That's right," Holt confirmed. "The important thing is that when you feel upset or scared, you lean on the people who love you and let them help make you feel better."

Luna's voice dropped to a whisper I could barely hear. "Do you love me, Mr. Holt?"

My breathing stopped. Her question carried a weight that made the room grow still. I waited, motionless, for his answer.

"Yes, Luna," Holt replied without hesitation. "I love you very much."

"I love you too." The certainty in her voice brought fresh tears to my eyes.

My father squeezed my shoulder, drawing me away from the doorway. "That man loves both of you," he said quietly. "You know this, yes?"

Words failed me, my throat too tight to speak.

"It scares you," my father observed, his eyes gentle.

"Everything scares me right now, Dad."

"That's normal, *mija*." His weathered hand patted mine. "But don't let fear of one pain make you miss out on something wonderful."

Within the hour, we were on our way to Gunnison Valley Hospital. Luna sat quietly between her stuffed animals in the backseat, her small hand clutching mine.

When we arrived at the hospital, Dr. Patel was waiting for us. He greeted my daughter with a warm smile and a high five. "Hello there, Miss Luna. Ready for round two?"

Luna took a deep breath. "I'm scared, but I'm being brave."

"You know what?" he said, leaning closer. "The best people I know still get scared sometimes."

"Even Mr. Holt?" Luna glanced up at him.

Holt crouched down to her level. "Especially me."

The nurse led us to a room similar to one Luna had been in on a previous stay. She immediately went to the windowsill, where she arranged her stuffed animals, carefully positioning Sparkles and Shimmer beside Bunny.

"They're keeping watch," she explained seriously.

Dr. Patel walked in with another doctor, and they explained that they would be inserting Luna's IV shortly. I sat beside her on the bed, feeling her small body tense.

"Can I do something first?" Luna asked Dr. Patel.

"Of course."

Luna held out her arms, and I gathered her close, breathing in her sweetness. Then she reached for Holt, who wrapped his strong arms around both of us, creating a circle of warmth and love.

"We're ready," Luna said finally, her voice small but determined.

I stood, allowing the medical team to do their jobs, but kept hold of Luna's hand. Holt positioned himself on her other side, pulling a chair close to the bed.

"Tell me more about the Cloud Kingdom," Luna asked as the nurse prepared her IV.

Holt launched into an elaborate tale about mystical creatures who could jump between puffy white clouds, his voice steady and calm as the medication began flowing through Luna's veins. His stories had become our anchor—a bridge between the harsh reality of treatment and a world where anything was possible.

Hours later, after Luna had fallen asleep, the three of us—my father, Holt, and I—stood in the hallway outside her room. The treatment was complete, and now came the waiting, managing side effects, and the long hours of hospital life.

"I've arranged for a place for us to stay," Holt said. "It's right across the street. Two bedrooms, full kitchen."

"That must have been expensive," I protested. "I could have—"

"Let me do this, Keltie," he said softly. "Please."

My father cleared his throat. "I think I'll go check it out. Maybe rest a bit."

I smiled at him. "Thanks, Dad."

After he left with the keys Holt provided, exhaustion washed over me. "What if it's worse than last time?"

Holt took my hand and kissed it. "We'll help her through it."

I looked through the window into Luna's room, watching her chest rise and fall with each breath. "You helped her be brave today."

"So did you, Keltie."

I turned to face him fully, taking in the fatigue etched around his eyes and the worry lines on his forehead. "You should go rest too. You've been up since dawn."

Holt shook his head. "I'm staying right here with both of you."

"But—"

"No buts. I meant what I said to Luna. When it comes to the hard stuff, you lean on the people who love you." His hand came up to cup my cheek. "And I love you both. So much."

A nurse appeared in the hallway. "Ms. Marquez? Luna's awake."

Holt and I walked into the room together. Luna's eyes were drowsy, but alert.

"Hey, Luna-bug," I said, sitting beside her on the bed. "How are you doing?"

"Okay." She looked past me to Holt. "Is *Abuelo* still here?"

"He's resting at the place where we're staying," Holt explained. "It's right across the street, so he can return anytime you want."

Luna's expression turned serious. "Are you staying with me tonight, Mommy?"

"Of course I am. I'm not going anywhere."

Her gaze moved to Holt. "Will you stay too?"

"You can count on it," he promised, pulling his chair closer to her bed.

Luna's small hand reached out, grasping his larger one. "Good. Because I need both of you."

These seven words hung in the air, crystallizing something I'd been feeling but couldn't articulate—we had become a family.

Her eyes began to drift closed again, but her hands still held ours, creating a physical link between the three of us that mirrored the emotional one growing stronger each day.

"Sleep, baby," I whispered. "We'll be here when you wake up."

"Promise?" she murmured, already half asleep.

"Promise," Holt and I said in unison.

24

Holt

Luna's tiny face contorted with pain as the nurse adjusted her IV line. Her skin had taken on a grayish hue beneath the fever flush, and dark circles shadowed her eyes. This round of chemo hit her harder than the first. While I'd expected it to be rough, watching her little body fight against the medication meant to save her tore me apart in ways I hadn't anticipated.

For hours, I watched the chemicals drip into her veins, silently praying they would kill the cancer cells without destroying her spirit. Each time she clutched her stomach, I wanted to rip the lines out and take her and Keltie somewhere far away from the pain and anguish they were facing. Nothing in my life—not my father's abuse, not the trust's manipulation, not even losing my shot with CB Rice—had prepared me for the helplessness of watching someone I loved suffer while I could do nothing to stop it.

Keltie hadn't left Luna's side since the treatment began, her own face etched with exhaustion and worry. Victor stood at the foot of the bed, arms crossed, the same anguish I felt mirrored on his face.

The hospital room seemed too small, too sterile, the beeping machines a constant reminder of what was at stake.

I rested my hand on Keltie's shoulder. "Can I get you anything?"

She shook her head. "No, I'm fine. Thanks." The dark circles under her eyes told a different story, but I knew better than to push.

Luna's whimper broke the silence, and Keltie stroked her daughter's forehead. Her tenderness made my chest ache.

"It hurts, Mommy," Luna whispered, her eyes fluttering open, their usual brightness dimmed.

"I know, baby," Keltie murmured, her voice steady despite the fear I knew was churning inside her. "The medicine is working, but sometimes, it makes you feel worse before you feel better. Remember how the doctors talked about that?"

"Yes." Luna's small hand clutched Bunny against her chest. The stuffed animal looked almost as worn as she did.

"Remember what happened with Sparkles," I said, kneeling beside her so we were at eye level. The hospital bed made her look even smaller, more vulnerable. "And remember what happened next in the story?"

Luna's lips curved in a small smile despite her discomfort. Faint as it was, it felt like a victory. "Shimmer brought her special berries that made her feel stronger."

"That's right," I said, relieved to see that spark of imagination still alive in her eyes. I reached out to touch her cheek. Her skin felt hot beneath my fingers.

Luna's eyelids drooped. "Will you finish the story later?"

"I promise, Unicorn Girl."

My phone vibrated in my pocket, and I stepped away from the bed to check it. Ben's name flashed on the screen with a text that made my blood run cold.

At hospital with Remi. He wants to talk with Keltie before agreeing to test. Where are you?

My jaw clenched. Of course that asshole would have conditions. Even to potentially save the life of his own child, he couldn't do the right thing.

I glanced at Keltie, who had climbed onto the bed to hold Luna as another wave of nausea hit. Her focus was entirely on comforting her daughter, whispering reassurances as Luna trembled. There was no way I'd tell her Remi was here now. She needed to focus on her daughter, who was struggling enough already. And truthfully, I wasn't sure I could stop myself from dragging Remi out by his designer collar if he upset Keltie while Luna was this sick.

"I'm going to step out and look for Dr. Patel," I said, steeling the anger in my voice.

Keltie nodded without looking up. Victor caught my eye from across the room, his gaze sharp and questioning. The older man had an uncanny ability to sense when something was off. I gave a slight shake of my head, hoping he'd understand now wasn't the time.

"I won't be long," I promised.

In the hallway, I texted Ben to say I was on my way down, then headed toward the elevator. My mind raced through what to say to Remi. I'd never liked the guy from the moment I joined the band, but now, knowing what he'd done to Keltie—abandoning her when she was pregnant, calling her a liar—the thought of facing him made my blood boil.

As the manager, he usually stayed behind the scenes, but when he did appear, his arrogance filled the room. He'd been dismissive toward me until the moment Ben announced I was joining the band. Then his attitude had shifted to surface-level friendliness that never reached his eyes.

When the elevator doors slid open, Ben and Remi stood several feet away. The contrast between them struck me immediately—Ben's concerned expression versus Remi's irritated scowl, as if being asked to help save a child's life was an inconvenience to his busy schedule. Ben had thrown on jeans and a flannel shirt, looking rushed but composed. Remi wore designer clothes and sunglasses pushed up on his head, his entire appearance screaming self-importance.

"Holt," Ben said, stepping forward to shake my hand, his grip firm and grounding. His eyes held genuine concern. "How's Luna?"

"Not great," I replied, keeping my voice low. "This round is hitting her hard. She's really sick. The nausea's been terrible, and her fever keeps spiking."

"I'm sorry to hear that. Liv sends her best. She wanted to come, but she's with Caden at the doctor—just a cold, nothing serious."

Remi stood behind Ben, arms crossed over his chest, shifting his weight impatiently. "So where's Keltie? I need to talk to her."

The tone in his voice raised my hackles. I took a deep breath, reminding myself we were in a hospital and Luna needed him to cooperate. "She's with Luna, who's very ill. She's not leaving her daughter's side."

Remi's mouth tightened. "I didn't drive all the way here to be put off. I need to speak with her directly."

I squared my shoulders. "I said no, Remi, and I meant it."

"I'm not doing any bloody test without talking to her first," he declared, his chin jutting out. "I have conditions."

"Conditions?" Ben echoed, turning to face him. The disbelief in his voice matched my own. "You have *conditions* for potentially saving a child's life?"

Remi's expression hardened. "I've been blindsided enough by this situation. Before I agree to a test, I need to know for sure the kid is even mine."

Ben's eyes opened as wide as mine did. "What are you suggesting?" he asked.

"A paternity test. I need proof that kid is mine. For all I know, she screwed every guy in the band."

Remi's casual cruelty, his blatant disrespect for Keltie and Luna—at that moment, I saw red. Ben took a step forward, fury etched across his face too, but my fist connected with Remi's jaw first. The impact sent him stumbling backward, his hand flying to his face.

The sensation of knuckles meeting bone shot up my arm, a burst of pain that I barely registered through the surge of adrenaline.

A woman nearby shrieked, and several heads turned in our direction. Remi straightened, looking ready to lunge at me, a trickle of blood at the corner of his mouth. His eyes burned with anger, but Ben grabbed his arm.

"You fucking hit me!" Remi shouted, drawing more attention.

Hospital security approached fast, led by a guy I recognized from high school. He'd grown into his lanky frame, now filling out the security uniform with broad shoulders.

"What's going on here?" he asked, his eyes widening as he recognized Ben. "Holy shit, you're Ben Rice!"

Ben cleared his throat. "Sorry about the disturbance. My friend here"—he nodded toward me—"had a justified reaction to some extremely inappropriate comments about a sick child."

The guard's eyes shifted from Ben to me. "Wait. Are you Holt Wheaton? Damn, man, I hardly recognized you. Heard you were playing with CB Rice now. My wife and I have tickets to your Valentine's show."

I flexed my stinging hand, feeling the skin pull tight across my knuckles. "Thanks for the support."

The guy, whose name I still couldn't remember, looked at Remi, who was holding his jaw, murder in his eyes. "Want me to escort this one out?"

"No," Ben said firmly. "We need him—unfortunately. He's here to take a bone marrow test for a child who needs a transplant."

The guy's expression changed immediately, understanding dawning. "Luna Marquez? My daughter's in her class at school and talks about her all the time. Tell her they all miss her. She's a great kid."

A rush of warmth filled my chest at the mention of the sweetest, most precious little girl I'd ever met. She'd touched so many lives in her short time in Crested Butte.

Ben stepped closer to Remi, his voice low and cold, but carrying enough that I could hear every word. "You have two choices. Take the test right now, or I fire you on the spot. And I'll make damn sure everyone in the industry knows exactly why. You'll never work with another band again."

Remi's face paled beneath his well-crafted stubble. "You wouldn't."

"Try me," Ben replied, his posture rigid with anger. "After what you said about her mother? I absolutely would. Don't forget who brought CB Rice to national attention. The contacts are mine, Remi. The relationships are mine. Cross me on this, and you'll quickly find out how thoroughly I can end your career."

The standoff lasted several seconds as tension crackled between them. I'd never seen Ben like this—using his influence as a weapon. This was a side of him that explained how he'd risen to the top of a cutthroat industry.

Finally, Remi's shoulders slumped. "Fine. Where do I go for the fucking test?"

I pointed down the hall. "Lab's that way."

"I'll walk with you," said Ben.

"Your hand okay?" the guard asked.

"Yeah, I'll be all right. Sorry, but I don't remember your name."

"Pete, and don't worry about it. You've got a lot on your mind right now." He motioned to my hand. "You gonna be able to play guitar?"

I flexed my fingers, wincing as pain radiated through my knuckles. "Not right at the moment, but soon enough. I gotta tell you, it was worth it."

"That felt good to watch. The guy seems like a huge asshole," Pete muttered.

Seconds later, Ben was back. "I told the woman administering the test to make sure it hurt like hell."

"It's the same as any blood draw."

Ben chuckled. "I know, but seeing Remi panic was worth it."

Pete excused himself, and we moved to a quieter corner of the hallway, away from curious onlookers. Ben ran a hand over his face.

"Did you mean what you said about firing him?" I asked.

"Oh yeah," he replied without hesitation. "But not until we get the test results. If he's a match and they need him for the transplant, I want to maintain some leverage."

I clasped his shoulder, feeling a new respect for the man I'd known all my life. "I can't thank you enough for this. For bringing him here, for standing up for Luna and Keltie."

Ben's expression darkened, guilt flickering across his features. "Don't thank me. I should have done more when Keltie left the tour. She was the best sound engineer we ever had—truly gifted. Then she was gone, and Remi never gave an explanation as to why." He shook his head. "I knew something wasn't right, but I didn't do a damn thing about it."

"You're helping now," I said, recognizing the weight of regret in his eyes. "That's what matters."

"Yeah, well, it's the least I can do."

After ten minutes, Remi emerged from the lab, looking every bit as surly as before. The security guard followed behind him, keeping a watchful eye. After

Remi stalked past us without a word, Ben said a quick goodbye, then followed him out.

I returned to Luna's room, my hand throbbing in time with my heartbeat. Despite the pain, a sense of grim satisfaction settled over me. The punch had been worth it—more than worth it—for the things Remi had said about Keltie. Lost in thought, I almost missed the elevator doors opening as I approached. Keltie stepped out, her face creased with worry.

"Holt? I was looking for you." Her eyes drifted past me, widening as she caught sight of Ben and Remi right outside the entrance. "Is that—"

"Yeah," I admitted. "Ben brought Remi in. He took the test."

Her gaze dropped to my right hand, which I'd been absentmindedly flexing. "What happened?"

"Let's say I had to knock sense into him."

Keltie's eyes widened, and for a moment, I thought she might be upset. Then a small, fierce smile touched her lips. "Good."

I laughed softly, relieved she understood. "I promise I'll tell you everything later. How's Luna?"

Her smile faded, shoulders slumping with the weight of worry. "Not great. She's asking for you. Dad's with her, but she keeps saying she needs you to finish the story."

"Let's not keep her waiting, then."

We got on the elevator, and as the doors closed, Keltie wrapped her arms around my waist. I held her close, feeling her exhale shakily against my chest, her body fitting against mine as if it belonged there.

"Thank you," she whispered. "For looking out for us."

I pressed my lips to the top of her head, breathing her in. "Always, darlin'. Always."

"I only wish I would've seen you hit him."

Seconds ago, I didn't think I could laugh, but I did.

25

Keltie

Crested Butte had transformed into a place I barely recognized on Valentine's Day. Elk Avenue bustled with activity as vendors set up booths selling hot chocolate, handmade jewelry, and festival food. Storefronts displayed red and pink hearts alongside concert posters, and people streamed toward the amphitheater from every direction.

I guided Luna through the crowd, her small hand warm in mine. The scale of what friends, family, and even strangers had created for my daughter overwhelmed me. Flynn's modest fundraiser idea had grown into something massive—hotels were booked solid, and people had flown in from across the state.

"Mommy, look!" Luna tugged at my hand, pointing toward a booth where Echo West was arranging pamphlets about the Miracles of Hope Children's Charity. "It's Miss Echo!"

Echo looked up, her face brightening. "There's my favorite brave girl!" She came around the table and knelt to Luna's level. "How are you feeling today, sweetheart?" It warmed my heart that, after our first meeting, she stopped in at the hospital periodically to see how we were doing and also to check on my daughter.

"Good!" Luna declared, twirling to show off her special outfit—a purple dress with silver stars that Sam had brought with her from New York specifically for today. It matched her favorite bandana perfectly.

"You look absolutely beautiful," Echo said, her eyes meeting mine with silent understanding. We both knew how rare these good days were, how fleeting Luna's energy could be.

"Miss Echo, can I help give out the flyers?" Luna asked, already reaching for the colorful brochures.

Echo glanced at me for permission.

"Just for a few minutes, Luna-bug," I agreed. "Then we need to find our seats."

"How's she really doing?" Echo asked quietly, her eyes never leaving Luna.

"Better than last week," I admitted. "The doctors are amazed at how well she's responding. Her numbers are improving, though we've got a long road ahead."

"Understood," said Echo. "When do you get the father's bone marrow test results?"

My throat tightened. "Soon, I hope."

"There you are!"

I turned to see Sam hurrying toward us, her cheeks flushed from the cold. Beau followed her, carrying what looked like an enormous gift bag.

"Sam!" I exclaimed, embracing her. "Luna *loves* her dress!"

She smiled. "We have something else to go with it."

Before she could continue, Luna spotted them and squealed. "Miss Sam! Mr. Beau!" She abandoned her post at the charity booth and launched herself at Sam, who caught her in a hug.

"Hello, beautiful girl," Sam said, kissing the top of Luna's bandana. "I brought you something special." She glanced at Beau, who extended the gift bag toward Luna.

Her eyes widened as she peered inside. "A unicorn cape!" She pulled out a shimmering purple cloth. "Can I wear it now, Mommy? *Please?*"

I laughed, unable to deny her anything that brought such joy to her face. "Of course."

Sam helped her fasten the cape around her shoulders. "There. Now, you're officially the most magical person at the entire concert."

Luna twirled again, the cape fluttering around her. "I love it!" She wrapped her arms around Sam's waist. "Thank you, thank you, thank you!"

"You're welcome, sweetheart," said Sam. Her gaze met mine over Luna's head, and I recognized the emotion there—the same fierce love I felt for my daughter had somehow extended to this found family we'd created.

Beau checked his watch. "We should head to our seats. The first act starts in fifteen minutes."

Luna stood by my side, her cape billowing dramatically with each step. "Can we get ice cream, Mommy?"

"After the first set," I promised. "Let's go sit down first."

We said goodbye to Echo, who would be joining us later, and made our way toward the amphitheater. The special seating area near the stage had been reserved for Luna and our family—a term that had expanded far beyond blood relations in recent months.

My father was already there, chatting with Flynn and TJ. He stood when he spotted us, his arms outstretched for Luna.

"*Abuelo*, look at my cape!" Luna ran to him, twirling once more.

"Magnificent!" he declared, lifting her into his arms.

"You're silly." Luna giggled, patting his cheeks.

I settled into my seat beside my father, scanning the growing crowd. The amphitheater was filling quickly, a sea of faces—some familiar, others strangers, who'd come for the music but were now part of Luna's extended support network whether they realized it or not.

I looked up and saw Bridger—or King, as Echo called him—walk onto the stage, guitar in hand. The crowd cheered as he adjusted the microphone.

I'd grown to appreciate the man's quiet strength over the past weeks. While Holt had been my rock through Luna's treatments, Bridger had stepped in to fill his shifts at the Goat whenever Holt needed to be with us in Gunnison or Denver. He'd never complained, never asked for anything in return.

"Evening, folks," he said, his deep voice carrying across the amphitheater. "Thank you all for coming out to support Luna Marquez and her brave fight."

The crowd erupted in cheers and applause. Luna stood and waved from her seat.

Bridger spotted her and smiled. "There's our guest of honor. This first song is for you, Luna."

He played a total of four songs, each with its own haunting quality. When he finished the last one, he acknowledged the audience with a single wave before walking offstage. His understated exit commanded a different kind of respect than flashy performers typically received.

"He's good," my father commented, applauding. "Reminds me of the musicians who sang at coffeehouses in New Mexico when I was younger."

"He is," I said, searching the side of the stage for any sign of Holt. He was scheduled to play next, and my heart rate picked up at the thought of seeing him perform. Despite having heard him countless times at the Goat, there was something different about tonight— something electric in the air that had nothing to do with the Valentine's Day hearts decorating the venue.

Luna tugged at my sleeve. "When is Mr. Holt coming out?"

"Very soon, baby," I promised, squeezing her hand. "Are you enjoying the concert?"

Her smile was wide. "It's the best day ever!"

My eyes burned at her declaration. After everything she'd endured—the needles, the medications, the endless tests—she still found delight in the music and the crowd. Every moment of joy she experienced felt like a gift.

Holt stepped on stage, wearing dark jeans and a crisp, white button-down shirt with the sleeves rolled up. His dark hair looked freshly trimmed, and instead of his typical array of jewelry, he wore only a single silver pendant against the white fabric. The crowd's reaction was deafening. While Bridger had earned respectful appreciation, Holt received full-throated adoration. He grinned at the response, his confidence on stage a stark contrast to Bridger's quiet intensity.

"Good afternoon, Crested Butte!" he called into the microphone. His eyes scanned the crowd until they found our section, lingering on Luna and me. "Before I start, I want to thank everyone who made this benefit possible. Especially my sister, Flynn, who organized everything, and Ben Rice, who's headlining tonight."

More cheers erupted, along with several wolf whistles.

"Most importantly," Holt continued, his voice softening, "I want to thank Luna Marquez for being the bravest person I know."

Luna beamed, waving both arms. "Hi, Mr. Holt!"

The audience laughed, charmed by her enthusiasm.

"Hey, Unicorn Girl," he replied, his smile soft. "I'm going to play a couple of songs I wrote recently," he announced to the crowd. "This first one is called 'River Under Moonlight,' inspired by someone very special."

My hand flew to the pendant at my throat—the river and moon design he'd given me for Christmas. As he began to play, I recognized the melody we'd recorded at Ben's studio, but he'd added new verses, new depths to the arrangement.

His voice filled the amphitheater, rich and raw with emotion as he sang about finding unexpected love, about a river finding its course beneath a guiding moon. The metaphor wasn't subtle, but it was genuine, and I found myself blinking away tears as he sang.

When he finished, the crowd's response was immediate and overwhelming. Holt acknowledged it before launching into his next song—the one he'd written for Luna about Sparkles and Shimmer. Though the subject matter was whimsical, there was nothing childish about the arrangement. Instead, he'd transformed it into a powerful ballad about courage in the face of fear, about magic found in the darkest places.

I looked down at Luna, mouthing the words, her hand clutching mine as she listened, enraptured.

Holt played a third song—one I hadn't heard before—about finding family in unexpected places. By the final chorus, I was no longer trying to keep myself from crying. My tears flowed freely down my cheeks as I listened to this man, this incredible human being, put our journey into music.

When the song ended, Holt took a deep breath. "For my final number tonight, I want to share something brand new. I wrote this specifically for this benefit." He adjusted his position on the stool, his eyes finding mine in the wings. "Keltie, this one's for you."

The first notes were gentle, almost hesitant. Then his voice joined the melody, singing about a man who'd spent his life searching, never realizing what he was looking for until he found a woman with wild curls and fire in her eyes.

The lyrics told our story—meeting at the Goat, the Christmas at the ranch, the hospital vigils, and the moments of joy we'd stolen between the fear. Each verse built on the last, creating a narrative of two people finding each other amid chaos and uncertainty.

As he approached what I assumed was the final chorus, Holt stood, stepping away from the microphone.

To my shock, he set down his guitar and walked to the edge of the stage, extending his hand toward me.

"Join me?" he asked, voice carrying despite the lack of amplification.

My legs moved of their own accord, carrying me onto the stage. The lights were blinding, the crowd a blur beyond them. All I could see clearly was Holt, his blue eyes intense as he took my hands in his.

A movement at the opposite side of the stage caught my attention. My father appeared and led Luna by the hand. Her unicorn cape fluttered behind her as she hurried toward us, her face alight with excitement.

Holt knelt down when she approached. "Can I ask you something important?" he said, his voice carrying enough for those in the front rows to hear.

"Yes," said Luna solemnly.

"Would it be okay with you if I asked your mommy to marry me?"

The amphitheater fell silent. I could hear my own heartbeat thundering in my ears as I stared down at them, unable to process what was happening.

Luna's response was immediate and enthusiastic. "Yes, yes, yes!" She jumped up and down, her cape billowing. "I've been waiting forever!"

Laughter rippled through the crowd, breaking the tension. Holt smiled at Luna, then turned to me. Still kneeling, he reached into his pocket and pulled out a small box.

"Keltie," he said, his voice clear and steady despite the emotion in his eyes. "I never believed in love at first sight until I met you. I never thought I could love someone else's child as my own until I met Luna. You two have changed my life in ways I never imagined possible."

He opened the box, revealing a ring that caught the stage lights—a delicate band with a center diamond surrounded by smaller stones.

"I know this might seem fast," he continued, "but when you know, you know. And I know, with absolute certainty, that I want to spend the rest of my life with you both. Will you marry me?"

I stared at this man kneeling before me, this man who had appeared in our lives at the exact moment we needed him.

"Yes," I whispered, then found my voice. "Yes!"

Holt slid the ring onto my finger, then stood and pulled me into his arms. When his lips met mine, the cheers from the crowd faded into background noise.

All I could feel was him, solid and real, promising a future I hadn't dared imagine.

When we broke apart, Luna squeezed between us, her arms wrapping around our legs. Holt lifted her up, and the three of us stood there for a moment—a family, despite all the odds stacked against us.

Through my tears, I spotted Miguel near the front row, wiping his eyes unashamedly. My father stood at the edge of the stage, his smile wider than I'd seen in years. Sam and Beau were on their feet, along with Flynn, TJ, Buck, and the rest of the Wheaton clan.

Holt cleared his throat, obviously emotional. "Thank you, everyone. CB Rice will be taking the stage in twenty minutes."

The stage manager gestured for us to exit, and we made our way off to the side, still wrapped in our bubble of joy. Luna bounced between us, unable to contain her excitement.

"I knew it!" she exclaimed. "I told *Abuelo* you were going to be my daddy now!"

Holt laughed, ruffling her bandana. "Is that right, Unicorn Girl?"

"She did," my father confirmed, joining us. "Congratulations, *mija*." He embraced me tightly, then turned to Holt. "Welcome to the family, son."

"Thank you, sir." Holt's voice was thick with emotion. "I promise to take care of them both."

"I know you will," my father replied. "Now, I believe there's a little girl who was promised ice cream after the performance."

Luna's face lit up. "Ice cream! Can we go now, please?"

Holt glanced at me, eyebrows raised in question.

"You two go ahead," I said. "I'll let Sam and the others know and catch up with you."

"You sure?" Holt asked.

"I'll only be a minute," I said, still floating on the happiness of the moment. "Get Luna her treat before she combusts from excitement."

He laughed, then leaned in to kiss me quickly. "Don't be long, fiancée."

The word sent a thrill through me. "I won't, fiancé."

As they headed toward the exit, Luna chattering animatedly about what flavor she wanted, I turned to make my way to our seats. It was more crowded now, in anticipation of CB Rice's set.

I spotted Sam and was about to call out to her when a figure stepped directly into my path. The smile on my face froze as I stared straight into Remi Gilbert's eyes.

He looked different than I remembered—in a polished, manufactured way, with too-perfect hair and tacky designer clothes. Had he always been that swarmy? His eyes were cold as they swept over me, lingering on the ring now adorning my left hand.

"Quite the performance up there," he said, his voice dripping with sarcasm.

I lifted my chin, refusing to show how much his presence rattled me. "Excuse me, I need to get back to my family."

He shifted, blocking my path. "That's what I want to talk about, actually. *Family.*" His gaze hardened. "Just tell me one thing, Keltie. Have you been lying this whole time about who Luna's father is?"

Confusion replaced my unease. "What are you talking about?"

"Is it Holt?" he demanded. "Is that what this whole scheme has been about? Getting me to pay for another man's kid?"

I stared at him, genuinely bewildered by the accusation. "Luna is your daughter, Remi. I've never claimed otherwise."

"Then, why is Wheaton acting like her father? Why the big proposal with the kid right there?" His voice rose, drawing glances from people nearby. "If she's mine, then why are you letting another man claim her?"

"Holt loves Luna," I said, anger beginning to replace my shock. "Which is more than I can say for you. You've never even acknowledged her existence until now."

"I'm still not convinced this isn't all bullshit. This whole benefit thing, the sob story about cancer—how convenient that it lines up with Wheaton being stuck in town because of a mysterious family obligation."

My hand connected with his cheek before I even realized I'd moved. The sharp crack of the slap echoed in the open area, silencing conversations around us.

"How dare you," I hissed, shaking with fury. "How dare you suggest I would lie about my daughter being sick. You think I want this? You think I enjoy watching my four-year-old fight for her life?"

Remi's hand went to his cheek, his eyes narrowing dangerously. "You'll regret that," he said quietly. "More than you know."

"Get away from her," came a deep voice from behind me. Bridger appeared at my side, his imposing presence immediately changing the dynamic. *"Now."*

Remi hesitated, clearly weighing his options until Cord, Beau, and Porter all stepped forward. With a final glare at me, he turned around. He stalked away but glanced over his shoulder. "This isn't over, Keltie. Not by a long shot."

Beau's hand on my elbow steadied me as I began to shake.

"Come on. Let's find Holt."

As we navigated through the crowd, Remi's words replayed in my mind. The accusations, the sneering tone, the threat—"You'll regret that." Why, on one of the happiest days of my life, did he have to try to ruin it?

26

Holt

The sight of Keltie rushing through the crowd toward us stopped me. Her face was pale, her movements jerky and uncoordinated—something was wrong.

"Keltie?" I stepped forward, placing my hands on her shoulders. Luna looked up from her cone, oblivious to the tension radiating from her mother.

"I'm fine," Keltie said, her voice tight. Her gaze darted over her shoulder toward the amphitheater. "Really."

Victor's eyes narrowed as he studied his daughter. Like me, he knew something was off.

"What happened?" I asked, keeping my voice low, so Luna wouldn't hear.

Keltie shook her head almost imperceptibly. "I'll tell you later."

I wanted to press her, to demand answers now, but the way her fingers shook as she brushed the hair from her face told me this wasn't the moment.

"Mommy, get this kind," Luna suggested, chocolate ice cream smeared across her mouth. "It's the best."

Keltie's smile didn't reach her eyes. "Can I have a taste of yours?"

Luna pushed her cone toward Keltie, who pretended to take a bite. The action seemed to ground her, and color returned to her cheeks.

"Ben's set is about to start," I said, checking my watch.

"I can't wait!" Luna exclaimed, hopping with the boundless energy only a child could muster during an illness remission.

Victor took her sticky hand in his. "Let's go find our seats, *pequeña*."

As we walked toward the amphitheater, I placed my hand on Keltie's back, leaning close to her ear. "You sure you're okay?"

Her body was tense under my touch. "Just stay close?"

"Always," I promised, weaving our fingers together.

The crowd roared as CB Rice took the stage. Ben stepped up to the microphone, his trademark charisma filling the venue. "How's everybody doing, Crested Butte?" The response was deafening.

He grinned and launched into one of the band's biggest hits. The music swept through the amphitheater, guitars and drums creating a rhythm that pulsed through the air like a living thing. Three songs in, even Luna was on her feet, clapping and swaying beneath the bright afternoon sun. Keltie remained subdued, though her shoulders gradually relaxed as the music continued.

By the fifth song, Luna's energy began to fade. Her eyes grew heavy, and she crawled into Victor's lap, her unicorn cape tangled around her legs.

"She's tired," Keltie whispered, a mother's concern replacing whatever had troubled her earlier.

Victor stroked Luna's hair. "I'll take her home," he said. "She's had an exciting day."

"I should come too," Keltie began, already reaching for her purse.

"Stay," Victor insisted. "The show's almost over. You deserve this night, *mija*. Come home when it's finished."

Keltie hesitated, torn between her daughter and the first real break she'd had in months.

"I've got this," Victor assured her, gathering Luna into his arms. She didn't stir, her exhaustion complete after the emotional day. "You two enjoy the rest of the show."

After they left, Keltie moved closer to me as Ben introduced the next song, one of their newer releases that had been climbing the charts. The crowd sang along, voices rising into the clear blue sky.

"Thank you all for being here tonight," Ben said after the song ended. "We've got a special guest I'd like to invite up on stage with us." His eyes found mine in the throng of people. "Holt Wheaton, get your ass up here!"

The crowd erupted, and Keltie's face broke into a genuine smile for the first time since whatever had happened earlier. She rose to her tiptoe and kissed me quickly. "Go. Show them what else you've got." My eyes met Beau's and Sam's, who were seated with us. When they both nodded, I kissed Keltie, then hurried toward the stage.

When I walked over to Ben, he clasped my hand and pulled me into a quick embrace before steering me toward a guitar tech, who handed me my Gibson.

"We're going to play a little something different," Ben announced. "This is a song written by our friend

Holt here, a song that'll be featured on our next album. It's called 'Breaking Circles.'"

I stepped up to the microphone beside him, adjusting the strap across my shoulder. The weight of the guitar steadied me as I played the opening riff. When Ben came in with the vocals, the crowd fell silent, absorbed in the new song. By the chorus, they were swaying, caught up in the melody.

For those few minutes, everything else disappeared—the trust, Luna's illness, Keltie's fear—all of it faded as the music took over. The final chord rang out, vibrating through my fingers, and for a brief moment, everything was silent before the audience erupted.

Ben clapped me on the shoulder. "Ladies and gentlemen, Holt Wheaton!"

I gave a small bow, searching the crowd for Keltie. She stood near the front, clapping and smiling.

"Before we play our last couple of songs," Ben continued, "I'd like to invite Echo West from Miracles of Hope to the stage."

Echo emerged from the wings, and the crowd quieted as she approached the microphone.

"Thank you all for coming today," she began, her voice warm. "The Miracles of Hope Children's Charity began with a vision to support families facing the devastating diagnosis of childhood cancer. Our founder envisioned a world where no family would face that journey alone, where financial burdens would never stand in the way of a child's care." She paused, her gaze sweeping the crowd. "Today, you're making that vision a reality for Luna Marquez and for every child who will be diagnosed in the future."

Echo spoke of the charity's work, of children who'd won their battles, of brave families who'd faced unimaginable challenges. Throughout it all, her passion for the cause shone through. I found myself wondering again about the organization's mysterious founder, about the connection to my family and the trust that continued to guide our lives.

Ben put one arm around Echo's shoulders. "Ladies and gentlemen, thanks to all of you, I'm thrilled and honored to announce that today's show has raised over three hundred thousand dollars!"

A roar swept through the crowd. Echo's hand flew to her mouth in surprise.

"The first portion of these funds will ensure Luna's medical expenses are fully covered," Ben continued.

"The remainder will support Miracles of Hope in their mission to help other children and their families."

After Echo left the stage, the band played their final songs, closing with their biggest hit. The crowd sang every word, hands swaying in unison under the bright February sun. As the last notes faded, there was a sense of community, a shared experience none of us would soon forget.

Backstage, Keltie flew into my arms. "That was incredible," she said against my neck.

I held her in my arms, dancing to the encore the crowd refused to leave without. Her tears dampened my shirt, but I understood them. I felt like crying myself with both joy and sadness.

When Ben finally said farewell, I turned to tell Keltie I wanted to help them pack up and was almost floored by the dark shadows under her eyes.

"You should head home, darlin'," I told her. "Give Luna a giant hug from me and tell her I'll be there soon."

"You sure?"

"Positive. Go be with our girl."

She smiled at the phrase "our girl," her eyes softening. "Don't be long." With a quick kiss, she disappeared into the thinning crowd. I watched until she met up with Beau and Sam.

I helped the crew break down their gear, working with the band's techs. As I was coiling the cable, Bridger appeared beside me.

"You sounded good up there," he said, his usual economy of words intact.

"Thanks, man."

He shifted his weight, a sign of discomfort I'd rarely seen from him. "I need you to come out to the Roaring Fork with me. While it's still daylight."

I glanced at my watch. It was midafternoon, with plenty of daylight remaining. "Can it wait? I promised Keltie—"

"It can't." The urgency in his voice caught me off guard.

"What's this about, Bridger?"

He shook his head. "It's better if you see for yourself."

In the months I'd known him, Bridger had never been anything but straightforward. His request was unusual, which told me how serious this was.

"All right," I agreed, setting down the cables. "Let me tell Ben I'm heading out."

Twenty minutes later, we drove through the gates of the Roaring Fork Ranch. Bridger directed me past the main house, beyond the stables and corrals, past all the cabins, to a part of the property I rarely, if ever, set foot on.

"Over there," he said, pointing to a grove of pine trees sheltering a small meadow.

As I pulled to a stop, I saw more vehicles arriving—Buck's truck, then Cord's, followed by Porter's and finally Flynn's SUV with Irish in the passenger seat. My siblings climbed out, their faces reflecting the same confusion I felt.

"What's going on?" Buck asked, approaching my truck as I stepped out.

"I'm not sure yet," I admitted.

Bridger gestured for us to follow him. "This way. Stay on the path."

We moved in silence through the trees, the tall pines filtering the late-afternoon sunlight that dappled the ground.

The clearing opened before us, and in its center was a small tombstone, weathered by time yet clearly maintained. We gathered around it, speechless as we read the inscription carved into the granite.

Scarlett Blanche Wheaton
Born March 15, 1993
Died December 18, 1993
Forever Our Angel

Buck was the first to break the silence, his voice rough with emotion. "She was our sister," he said, kneeling down to run his fingers over the words carved into the stone.

He was right. This was our sister—born between Buck and Porter, who lived less than a year. I knew without it being said aloud that she'd died of leukemia.

As I touched the cold stone with trembling fingers like Buck had, tears ran down my cheeks. This discovery explained so much—the connection between our family, the mysterious trust, and the charity with its scarlet blanket logo. Everything connected to this tiny grave and the sister none of us ever knew about. As I stood to leave, the haunting melody I'd played at the Goat, to one both Keltie and I seemed to know but not where from, echoed in my mind. Had it been something my mother sang to all of us?

27

Keltie

I was pulling ingredients from the refrigerator when I heard the doorbell ring. The sharp sound cut through the quiet house, startling me. We weren't expecting anyone—Holt had texted that he'd been delayed by something with his family but would be here as soon as he could. Either way, he would've walked in.

"I'll get it," my father called from the living room, where he'd been reading the newspaper while Luna colored at the coffee table.

I heard the front door open, followed by my father's voice, low and unwelcoming. "Can I help you?"

"I'm here to see Keltie." The voice that responded sent ice through my veins. *Remi.*

"She's not available," my father replied firmly. "You should leave."

I hurried toward the entryway and watched Remi shove past my father. His expression was hard and determined, so different from the charming facade he'd once used to win me over.

"Keltie," he said when he spotted me. "We need to talk."

My father moved to block him. "I told you to leave."

"Dad, it's okay," I said, though it was anything but. "What do you want, Remi?"

He opened his mouth to respond, but his gaze shifted past me, into the living room, where Luna sat cross-legged on the floor, crayons scattered around her, completely oblivious to the tension unfolding mere feet away.

The color drained from his face. He stared at Luna, his eyes widening with recognition. I saw it happen—the exact moment he realized she was his daughter. His lips parted, but no sound emerged.

Luna looked up then, her crayon pausing mid stroke as she noticed the stranger in our entryway. Her innocent gaze swept over him with mild curiosity before returning to her coloring book.

Sam and Beau came out of the kitchen, where they'd been helping me throw a casual dinner together. Beau's expression darkened when he spotted Remi.

"What are you doing here?" Beau demanded, stepping forward.

Sam put a restraining hand on his arm and motioned to Luna, who looked up again at the harshness of Beau's voice. He took a deep breath. "If you don't leave right now, I'm calling the sheriff."

Remi seemed not to hear him, his attention still fixed on Luna. I moved between them, blocking his view.

"You need to go," I said quietly. "This isn't the time or place."

Something flickered in his eyes—shock, recognition, maybe even a hint of emotion I'd never seen from him before. I almost felt sorry for him. Almost.

"She's…" he began, his voice barely above a whisper.

"Not now," I interrupted. "Luna is very tired from the concert today. Call me tomorrow, and we can set up a time to talk."

Remi stepped away slowly, still looking dazed. Without another word, he turned and walked out the door. My father closed it firmly behind him.

"Are you okay?" Sam asked, coming to my side.

"Yes," I said, though my legs felt weak. "I never expected him to show up like that."

"He realized, didn't he?" Sam's voice was gentle.

"Yes," I whispered, trying to keep my voice steady so Luna wouldn't notice my distress. "The look on his face… I've never seen him like that."

"Do you think he'll cause problems?" Beau asked, his tone suggesting he was already planning how to handle any trouble Remi might create.

"I don't know," I admitted. "I never thought he'd want anything to do with her. He made that pretty clear five years ago."

Luna called from the living room, "Mommy, look what I drew!"

I plastered on a smile and went to her, crouching beside the coffee table. "That's beautiful, Luna-bug. Is that for your story?"

"This is Shimmer. She's at a concert with her friends."

"I love it," I said, touching her cheek with my fingertip. "Are you hungry?"

She shook her head, then changed her mind when she saw the apple slices and peanut butter I'd set beside her.

As Luna nibbled, Sam pulled me aside. "Holt called while you were with Luna. He said something very important with his family is happening, and he'll be delayed longer but will explain when he gets here."

"I got a text from him a little while ago." I checked my phone again, and when I saw I'd missed a call from him two minutes ago, my stomach tightened with anxiety. "Did he say what it was about?"

Sam shook her head. "He asked Beau and me to hang out until he arrives. Cord cryptically mentioned that whatever it is might involve me too."

I considered telling them they didn't need to stay, that we'd be fine, but the truth was I wanted them here, especially after Remi's unexpected visit.

"Thank you," I said instead.

Sam squeezed my hand. "Of course. We love spending time with you and Luna."

My father came in from the kitchen with coffee for everyone. "That man," he said, his expression dark, "is he…?"

"Remi Gilbert. He's CB Rice's manager."

"But he denied she was his," my father said under his breath.

"He did," I confirmed.

"And now, he knows." My father's tone was grim. "You should call your attorney."

"Dad—"

"Just a consultation," he insisted. "To know your rights. To protect Luna."

He was right, of course. If Remi decided to assert his parental rights now, I needed to be prepared.

"I'll call on Monday," I promised.

Holt arrived about an hour later. The tension in his shoulders and the furrow between his brows told me something significant had happened. He embraced me as soon as he walked in, holding me tight.

"Where's Luna?" he asked, glancing around.

"Upstairs with my dad. She was getting tired, so he offered to read her a story." I searched his face. "What's going on, Holt? Sam said something happened with your family."

He ran a hand through his hair. "We should sit down."

In the living room, Sam and Beau joined us.

"Bridger discovered something on the ranch that explains his odd reaction when I mentioned the charity's original name," he began in a low voice. "It was a grave hidden in a small clearing, marked with a simple headstone."

My heart rate quickened. "Whose?"

"My sister's." His blue eyes met mine. "A sister none of us knew existed. Scarlett Blanche Wheaton. She only lived nine months."

I gasped. "Scarlett's Hope."

"Exactly," said Holt.

Sam leaned forward and opened her mouth to speak, but when she didn't, Holt continued.

"We went back to the house after finding the grave, and Echo—Bridger's mother—was there. She told us that no one ever knew who the anonymous founder of the charity was, but she wanted us to know that it's directed millions of dollars into pioneering cancer research over the years."

He reached for my hand, his fingers entwining with mine. "Research that has dramatically increased survival rates—including for kids like Luna."

My breath hitched, and my eyes filled with tears.

Sam cleared her voice. "Cena, my great-grandmother and also Holt's great aunt, had a daughter named Blanche who died from leukemia."

Blanche. That was the baby's middle name. Clearly not a coincidence.

Holt continued. "While we still don't know who the trustee is, at least we now understand why the charity would be the beneficiary in the event one of us didn't fulfill the terms stipulated by the trust."

We sat in silence for a few minutes, and eventually, Sam and Beau returned to the kitchen.

"How are you doing?" he asked, pulling me into his arms.

"Okay," I murmured, unsure whether I should tell him about Remi in the midst of his news. However, I knew I had to. "Earlier today, when you took Luna to get ice cream, Remi confronted me at the concert. Then, he showed up here a little while ago. He pushed his way in when my dad tried to turn him away."

Holt's expression darkened. "What happened?"

"Bridger, Cord, Porter, and Beau intervened and told Remi to get away from me."

"How about when he was here? Did Luna see him?"

"She did but didn't appear to pay much attention. He saw her, though, Holt. He knows she's his."

Holt's jaw tightened. "What did he say?"

"Not much. He was in shock. I told him to call me tomorrow so we could talk."

"You're too kind, considering what he did to you," Sam said from the doorway.

"I'm not being kind," I corrected. "I'm being practical. He's her biological father. If he decides to pursue his rights now…" I trailed off, not wanting to say the words aloud.

"He won't get anywhere," Beau assured me. "Not after abandoning you and her."

I wished I shared his confidence. "My dad thinks I should call an attorney."

"I agree," said Holt. "It's important to be prepared. Not that I think Remi has a chance, given the history. It isn't like you kept her from him. You told him you were pregnant."

The sound of footsteps on the stairs made us all look up. My father appeared with Luna in his arms, her head resting against his shoulder, eyes heavy with sleep.

"Someone wanted to say good night," he explained, carrying her to me.

Luna lifted her head, brightening when she spotted Holt. "Mr. Holt! You're here. I missed you."

He smiled, rising to take her from my father. "I missed you too, Unicorn Girl."

"Will you tell me a story?" she asked, fighting to keep her eyes open.

"Tomorrow," he promised. "You need your rest now."

"Okay. But it has to be a long one."

"The longest," he agreed, carrying her upstairs.

"We should go," Sam said after she and Beau exchanged a look. "It's been a tiring day for everyone."

"Thank you for staying," I said, hugging them both.

"Hey, Sam," said Holt, returning downstairs. "The family is going to meet again tomorrow. Our plan is to see if we can get Six-pack to come to the ranch. We'd like you to be part of that meeting."

"Just tell me when."

After they left, my father retreated to the guest room, claiming fatigue, though I suspected he wanted to give Holt and me privacy.

Holt's expression was somber when he sat beside me on the sofa. "Luna asked if I was going to be her daddy now."

My heart squeezed at the words. "What did you tell her?"

"That if it was okay with her and you, then yes." He ran a hand through his hair again. "I hope that was all right."

"More than all right," I assured him, snuggling into him. "If I had to guess, I'd say it's what she's wanted since Christmas."

He held me close, his chin resting on top of my head. "I never thought I'd have this, Keltie. A family of my own. Someone to love and protect."

"No second thoughts?" I asked.

"God, no," he said, leaning to look into my eyes. "If anything, finding out about Scarlett makes me more certain we were meant to find each other."

I reached up to touch his face. "Even with all the complications? Luna's illness, Remi's involvement, your career?"

"Especially with all that," he said. "I'm here to support you in every way I can."

I kissed him then, a gentle press of the lips that conveyed more than words ever could.

"Stay tonight," I whispered against his mouth.

His arms tightened around me. "I wasn't planning to leave."

Later, as we lay in bed after making love, my head resting on his chest, I couldn't help but marvel at how quickly my life had changed. Now, I wore Holt's ring on my finger, and Luna had asked him to be her daddy. The universe, it seemed, had a far different plan than what I'd previously envisioned.

"What are you thinking about?" Holt asked, his fingers tracing lazy patterns on my arm.

"How none of this makes sense, yet somehow, it all does," I replied honestly.

As we drifted to sleep, he hummed a familiar tune.

"My dad used to sing me a lullaby like that when I was young," I told him.

He tightened his hold on me. "When I was standing by Scarlett's grave, I realized my mom did too."

"I suppose it's common enough to be a coincidence," I offered.

Holt shook his head. "Something tells me it isn't."

28

Holt

The small headstone remained fixed in my mind as I woke in Keltie's bed the next morning. My *sister* Scarlett—a whisper from the past that now haunted me in the most unexpected ways. The early sunlight filtered through the curtains, casting soft patterns across the room where I'd spent the night holding the love of my life close.

I turned to find her already awake, watching me with solemn eyes.

"I think we should meet with Six-pack today," I said quietly, reaching out to brush a curl from her face. "After the family meeting at the ranch. He could refer a custody attorney, help us prepare for whatever Remi might try."

Keltie's fingers laced with mine. "Good idea. I spoke with my dad this morning. He's taking Luna to the park again."

"She's feeling up to it?"

"She seems better than ever," she said, a smile finally breaking through the worry. "The resilience of children is incredible."

The sound of small feet racing down the hallway interrupted us. Luna appeared in the doorway, still in her pajamas.

"Mr. Holt! You're here!" She launched herself onto the bed, wiggling between us. "Are we having pancakes? *Abuelo* makes the best pancakes."

"Is that so? I thought your Mommy made the best ones." I said, tickling her side and grinning as she squirmed.

"She makes the best ones with *blueberries*."

Behind her, Keltie rolled her eyes.

"Ah, right," I murmured, winking.

The smell of coffee lured us to the kitchen, where Victor was already at the stove, pouring batter on the skillet.

"*Buenos días,*" he said. "Sleep well?"

"Very," I replied, accepting the mug he offered.

After breakfast and quick showers, Keltie and I got ready for the day. I'd brought a change of clothes when I came over yesterday, anticipating I might stay the night.

"I'll change, and then we can go," I said to Keltie.

Luna tugged at my jeans as I headed toward the stairs. "You're coming back, right?"

"Of course," I promised, kneeling to her level. "Five minutes. Max."

She shook her head. "I mean later."

"If there's ever a day, I can't, I'll tell you, okay? Otherwise, you can expect to fall asleep with me here and wake up to me too."

She beamed and followed Keltie and me up the stairs.

"Still nothing from Remi?" I asked quietly when we came back down.

"No," Keltie replied, sliding the phone into her pocket. "I don't understand. I thought after seeing Luna…"

"Hard to say what he's thinking." My words weren't as reassuring as I intended them to be, but with a guy like Remi, it was impossible to predict what he'd do.

After we'd said goodbye to Luna and Victor, Keltie and I headed to the ranch. The pressure of her hand resting on my thigh steadied me, reminding me once again that whatever came next, we'd face it together. Her for me and me for her.

I glanced at my watch. "When do you expect Six-pack to arrive?" I asked once we joined everyone in the living room of the main house, where they were gathered. While Flynn and Irish had taken down the Christmas tree a while ago, memories of those happy, magical days lingered in the place where Keltie and I had gotten to know each other beyond a bar owner and guitar player.

"Any minute," Buck said, checking his phone.

Flynn stiffened at the mention of our attorney, and I understood why. She was the only one who hadn't received a codicil yet. The fear that she might be forced to leave her husband and twin boys was evident in her eyes, though unspoken.

"Hello, everyone." Six-pack entered with his usual smug expression, briefcase clutched in his manicured hand.

"Let's get on with it," Buck said, foregoing any pleasantries.

"I wanted to touch base with you all about the recent developments with the trust," he said, opening his briefcase on the coffee table. His eyes swept across the room. "As I understand it, you've discovered information about a previously unknown sister, Scarlett Blanche Wheaton."

"That's right," I said, my voice harder than intended. "And the connection to Miracles of Hope Children's Charity."

"Which still doesn't tell us who's behind the trust," Cord added.

"As I've said more than once, until the trustee chooses to reveal themselves, there's nothing more I can do. I'm simply the messenger."

"And we're supposed to believe you have no idea who it is?" Porter's skepticism was evident.

"I've told you repeatedly that I don't," Six-pack insisted. "My instructions arrive anonymously. I've never met or spoken with the trustee directly."

"Convenient," Buck muttered.

Six-pack straightened his tie. "I should also remind everyone that Holt's year doesn't end until December 23, and there is still one sibling who hasn't been required to fulfill any stipulations."

Flynn visibly tensed, and Irish's arm immediately wrapped around her shoulders.

Anger flared in my chest. "That was unnecessary," I snapped. "We're all aware of the situation."

"Just clarifying the status of the trust," Six-pack replied, unfazed.

Looking at Flynn's anxious expression, I made a silent promise to myself. If another codicil arrived and it demanded she be separated from her family, I'd suggest we abandon the whole inheritance. The ranch was worth millions, but not at the cost of tearing my sister's life apart.

For the next thirty minutes, Six-pack fielded questions about the trust, offering nothing new or helpful.

"Before you go," I said, standing. "Keltie and I need to speak with you privately."

"Of course."

I led him and Keltie into a small room, which had once been our father's study, off the main hallway. The leather chairs and oak desk remained unchanged from when he'd summoned us here for lectures on responsibility and duty.

"What can I help you with?" Six-pack asked once the door closed behind us.

"We need a referral to a custody attorney," Keltie said. "Luna's biological father has reappeared after five years of absence."

Six-pack raised a brow. "Actually, family law is one of my specialties. I handle custody battles all the time."

I exchanged a skeptical look with Keltie. Six-pack wasn't exactly who I'd had in mind.

"What's the situation?" he asked, settling into one of the chairs in front of the desk. I motioned for Keltie to sit in the other. I remained standing.

Keltie explained Remi's sudden reappearance, his history of abandonment, and our concerns about his intentions, given Luna's illness.

Six-pack listened, his expression unreadable. When she finished, he cleared his throat. "I'll be direct. If he can establish paternity, he could potentially seek rights to visitation or even shared custody."

Keltie's face paled. "Even though he denied Luna was his when I told him I was pregnant? Even though he's had no contact with her for four years?"

"Unfortunately, yes." Six-pack tapped his fingers on the desk. "Courts generally favor giving biological parents a chance to establish relationships with their children, regardless of past behavior."

"That's absurd," I muttered.

"That's family law," Six-pack countered. "However, his abandonment works in your favor, Ms. Marquez. As does your established role as Luna's sole provider and caretaker."

"And Luna's illness?" Keltie asked. "How does that factor in?"

"It complicates things. On one hand, courts are reluctant to disrupt a child's life during serious medical issues. On the other, if he's providing medical assistance through bone marrow donation or financial support, that strengthens his case."

Keltie's shoulders slumped. "So we're damned either way."

"Not necessarily. We can establish clear boundaries through a legal agreement if he wants to be involved. But first, let's see what he actually wants." Six-pack handed Keltie his business card. "Call me when he contacts you. I'll be ready."

We walked him out.

After saying goodbye to my siblings, we drove to Keltie's house in silence.

When we pulled into her driveway, I cut the engine but made no move to get out. "I hate that you're going through this."

Keltie turned to me, her eyes shining with unshed tears. "He's a *sonuvabitch*."

I took her hand. "You got that right."

"I appreciate you so much, Holt. I don't know how I would've faced any of this without your support. I hope you know how much it means to me." She bit her lower lip. "And that…"

"What, Keltie?"

"I love you for it, but it isn't why I love you, if that makes sense."

"It makes perfect sense," I responded honestly. I felt it too. Our love wasn't about what we did for each other. It worked the opposite way. I loved her, so doing things for her and Luna felt right.

We got out of the truck, and as soon as we were inside, Luna's excited chatter cut through our serious mood. She raced toward us, waving a drawing. "Look what I made at the park!"

The picture showed a girl with wild curls holding hands with a tall stick figure wearing what looked like a cowboy hat. A smaller figure stood on the other side, holding the girl's hand.

"That's me," Luna explained, pointing to the figure in the middle. "And that's you, Mommy. And that's Mr. Holt. We're at the ranch with the horses."

Keltie knelt down, pulling Luna close. "It's beautiful, sweetheart."

I swallowed hard, fighting the emotion rising in my throat. In the face of Luna's innocent joy, our worries seemed less consuming. We'd protect this child, no matter what it took.

The next two days passed in tense anticipation, waiting for a call from Remi that never came. Keltie tried to focus on work while I split my time between the Goat and the recording studio, laying down tracks for my EP. But uncertainty hung over us, making even ordinary tasks tough to handle.

On the third day, Keltie's phone rang while we were having lunch at her kitchen table. Luna's doctor's name flashed on the screen.

"Dr. Robbins?" Keltie said, putting the phone on speaker. "Is everything okay?"

"Hi, Keltie." The doctor's voice came through. "I'm calling with an update on Luna's test results."

Keltie reached for my hand, squeezing it tightly. "Go ahead."

"Luna's response to treatment isn't as strong as we'd hoped. Her latest blood work shows higher numbers than we'd like to see at this stage."

The air got thicker, and Keltie's face went pale, but her voice remained steady. "What does that mean for her overall plan?"

"I've pushed the lab to process the bone marrow compatibility tests faster. At this point, I believe a transplant is Luna's best option for achieving remission."

"How soon would that be?" I asked.

"The preliminary results should be available tomorrow."

When the call ended, Keltie sat motionless, staring at her phone. "I thought she was doing so well," she whispered.

I moved my chair beside hers, wrapping my arm around her shoulders. "She still is. This is just the next step."

Keltie nodded mechanically, but her fear was palpable. We'd both allowed ourselves to hope that the initial protocols would be enough. Now, we faced a new, more challenging phase.

The second call from Dr. Robbins came the following afternoon. Keltie and I were at the Goat; she was going over the books while I sat at a nearby table with Luna as she drew pictures.

"Hello, Dr. Robbins," Keltie answered, her voice tight with anticipation. I stood, telling Luna I'd be right back. On our way into the office, I caught Miguel's eye and he walked over and sat with her.

"Keltie, I have the bone marrow compatibility results," the doctor said once the door was closed and Keltie let her know she was on speaker. "Neither you nor your father is a full match."

Keltie's face fell, and I put my arm around her.

"However," Dr. Robbins continued, "Remi Gilbert is."

The irony wasn't lost on either of us. The man who had abandoned Luna before she was born was now her best hope for recovery.

"He never called me," Keltie said after thanking the doctor and hanging up. "After seeing Luna that day, realizing she was his daughter, *he never called.*" By the time she finished the sentence, she was in tears.

I fought to keep my anger in check. "We need to reach out to him."

Keltie scrolled through her contacts until she found Remi's number. She hit the speaker button, and we both held our breath as it rang.

"I was wondering when you'd call." Remi's voice came through, unnervingly calm.

She shook her head. "Misunderstanding, I guess. I was waiting for you to call me."

"Right," he muttered as if Keltie was lying. It made me want to reach through the phone and punch the guy in the face a second time.

"We received the test results," Keltie said, her voice firm. "You're a full match for Luna's bone marrow transplant."

"Ah, so that's why you finally called."

I rested my hand on Keltie's arm when her body visibly tensed. "You're her only full match, Remi."

"What exactly does that mean?"

"It means you could save her life." Keltie's knuckles whitened as she clenched her fists. "The doctors need to harvest your bone marrow for the transplant. Without it…"

She couldn't finish the sentence. She didn't need to.

The silence stretched for several seconds.

"Will you do it?" Keltie finally asked, desperation creeping into her voice. "Please, Remi. She's just a little girl."

He exhaled heavily. "Yes."

His straight answer caught us both off guard. I'd expected resistance, negotiation, or flat-out refusal. Keltie's eyes met mine, cautious hope flickering in their depths.

"Thank you," she said, her voice softer. "I'll have Dr. Robbins contact you with the details."

"There's something we should discuss first," Remi said, his tone shifting.

"What?"

"I want to be acknowledged as Luna's father."

And there it was. The catch.

"What exactly do you mean by 'acknowledged'?" Keltie asked.

"I want my name on her birth certificate, and I want visitation rights." His voice hardened. "I'm the reason she'll survive this, Keltie. I think that entitles me to be part of her life."

Keltie's face flushed with anger. "You denied she was yours when I told you I was pregnant."

"People change," Remi replied smoothly. "Seeing her the other day… affected me. She looks like my mother, you know. Same eyes."

I bit back a retort. The manipulation was so transparent it made my skin crawl.

"We can discuss arrangements after the transplant," Keltie said, her tone making it clear the conversation was over. "Luna's health comes first."

"Of course," Remi agreed too quickly. "I'll be waiting for the doctor's call."

When Keltie hung up, she sagged against me. "He's using her illness as leverage. Except, if he cared so much about her, why didn't he get in touch with me like he said he would?"

"Let Remi do or say whatever he wants," I said, keeping my voice low. "It doesn't mean it'll happen. Luna needs this transplant. That's the first step."

Keltie squared her shoulders. "I need to call Dr. Robbins."

"I'll check on Luna."

She studied the screen of her phone.

"You'll be okay?" I asked.

"With this part, yes."

I drew her into my arms, and she rested her head against my chest. "We're gonna make it through this, darlin'. You, me, and Luna," I said, watching as she dialed the number before stepping out and returning to the room.

When I sat beside her bed, the sweet little girl who'd captured my heart looked up with a smile, pushing a crayon toward me.

"Want to color with me, Mr. Holt?"

"Absolutely," I replied, picking up the blue crayon. "What are we drawing?"

"Space adventures," she said matter-of-factly. "We're exploring the moon."

I smiled, adding stars to her galaxy. "That sounds like fun."

Luna's expression was so serious I had to cover my mouth to keep her from seeing my smile. "They can jump super high there because there's no *grabity*."

"Gravity," I gently corrected.

"That's what I said," she replied with the confidence only a four-year-old could muster.

Keltie returned, her expression a mixture of relief and anxiety. "We're all set."

Luna looked up from her drawing. "Why do you look sad?"

Keltie forced a smile. "We're not sad, sweetheart. We were talking about the medicine you need to take soon."

Luna wrinkled her nose. "The yucky kind?"

"I'm afraid so," Keltie replied honestly. "But it's going to help you feel better."

"Do we have to go to Denver again?"

"We do."

"Can my toys come with me?" she asked.

"Of course they can," I said, watching as relief washed over Keltie's face at Luna's easy agreement.

"And will you come too, Mr. Holt?"

My heart swelled with love for this child who had somehow become as essential to me as breathing. "Wild horses couldn't keep me away, Unicorn Girl."

Luna smiled and kept coloring. I watched her small hands carefully select each crayon, oblivious to the storm gathering around her.

"Dr. Robbins is scheduling the transplant," Keltie said once we were at the house and upstairs in the bedroom while Luna stayed in the kitchen with Victor. "It will be done at Children's Hospital in Denver. Luna will need to undergo something called conditioning first—a process that lasts seven to ten days to prepare her body."

"What is it?" I asked.

"High-dose chemotherapy, possibly radiation," Keltie explained, her voice dropping. "It destroys the cancer cells and suppresses her immune system to prevent rejection of the donated cells."

The reality of what Luna would face hit me anew. More hospital rooms. More discomfort. More fear masked as bravery from a child too young to understand why this was happening to her.

"When do we need to go?" I asked quietly.

"They want to begin next week," Keltie replied. "Dr. Robbins says moving quickly gives Luna the best chance."

I reached for her hand. "Then, that's what we'll do."

We were on our way downstairs when my phone vibrated with a text. I swiped the screen and saw it was from Ben.

"I'll catch up with you in a sec," I said.

"Everything okay?" she asked.

Saying yes aloud would've meant I'd be breaking my promise never to lie to her, so I nodded once.

I reread the message. *Remi told Phil that he lawyered up. Wants full paternity rights and primary custody post transplant. Says getting tested proves he's committed to being a father.*

I deleted the message, my heart hammering against my ribs. The battle for Luna's life had begun. The battle for her future loomed right behind it.

29

Keltie

The Denver skyline appeared ahead as we crossed the city limits. Luna slept peacefully in her booster seat while Holt drove, his hands gripping the wheel a little tighter than necessary as I gazed out the passenger window.

Familiar dread settled in my stomach—heavier this time, knowing what awaited us. The medical procedures that would ravage my daughter's tiny body were necessary, but terrifying, nonetheless. And somewhere in this city, Luna's biological father awaited the call to donate his bone marrow—a connection I wasn't ready to acknowledge but couldn't avoid.

"She's been out for almost an hour," I whispered, glancing at my daughter. Holt's eyes met mine briefly in the rearview mirror, his face drawn with the same anxiety that clawed at my insides.

I was unable to speak around the lump in my throat. Behind us, I caught my father's concerned gaze from the car carrying him, Sam, and Beau. Our convoy to what felt both like salvation and doom.

My hands trembled when the hospital's familiar facade came into view. Luna stirred, blinking drowsily as she took in her surroundings.

"Are we here, Mommy?" Her small voice broke through the silence.

"Yes, baby. We're here." I forced a brightness into my tone that I didn't feel.

Luna sighed, clutching Bunny tighter. "I don't want more medicine."

"I know, Luna-bug." My vision blurred with unshed tears. At four years old, my daughter had endured more pain than most people faced in a lifetime.

Holt's hand squeezed mine, anchoring me to the present. "One step at a time," he murmured the phrase that had become our mantra.

The apartments Beau had arranged were even better than our previous accommodations—spacious two-bedroom units with full kitchens and living areas. My father, Sam, and Beau took one, while Holt, Luna, and I settled into the other.

"This place is fancy," Luna declared, exploring every corner despite her fatigue from the journey. "Look, Mommy! The bathtub has jets!"

I smiled at her excitement, treasuring these moments of normalcy.

Later, after Luna had fallen asleep in the bedroom she'd claimed as her own, I collapsed beside Holt onto the sofa, my head dropping to his shoulder.

"Seven to ten days of conditioning," I whispered, the medical term for what amounted to systematically destroying my daughter's immune system. "Then the transplant."

Holt's arm tightened around me. "We'll get through it. *She'll* get through it."

The procedures necessary to prepare my daughter for the transplant were worse than I'd imagined. Each day, Luna grew weaker as the chemotherapy and radiation ravaged her small body. Her nausea became so severe she could barely keep down water. Yet somehow, she still found moments to smile—usually when Holt was telling her stories.

On the fifth day, I was sitting beside Luna's hospital bed, watching her sleep fitfully, when a nurse appeared in the doorway.

"Ms. Marquez? There's someone asking for you at the nurses' station."

Ice formed in my veins. I knew before I even left the room. My father had gone to pick up fresh clothes from the apartment, and Sam was getting coffee with Beau in the cafeteria. Holt had stepped out to make a call to his siblings.

Remi stood at the desk, impeccably dressed in a tailored suit that seemed grotesquely out of place among the medical scrubs and worried parents. A slim portfolio was tucked under his arm, and the smirk on his face made my stomach lurch.

"Keltie," he said, as if we were meeting for drinks rather than discussing our daughter's life. "You look tired."

"What do you want, Remi?" I demanded, keeping my voice low for Luna's sake.

He pulled documents from the portfolio, sliding them across the counter toward me. "Just making things official before I proceed with the transplant. My lawyer drew these up. They're quite straightforward."

I stared at the papers, not touching them. "What are they?"

"The agreement we discussed." His tone was casual, as if we were negotiating a business deal. "I provide the bone marrow, and in exchange, I get full acknowledgment as Luna's father—on her birth certificate, legal documents, everything."

I grabbed the papers, scanning the first page, and my blood turned from ice to boiling as I read further. "This isn't what we discussed. This says you want primary custody once she's recovered."

Remi shrugged, straightening his jacket. "I've been thinking about it. She needs a stable environment—financially secure, with the best schools, best opportunities. I can provide that."

"You've never even spoken to her!" I hissed, rage building in my chest. "You don't know her favorite color or the stories she loves. You denied she was even yours!"

"People change," he replied smoothly. "Besides, it's not like you have much choice. I'm her only full match. Without me, her chances drop significantly."

Something inside me snapped. The calm I'd been desperately maintaining for Luna's sake shattered like glass.

"Nurse," I called, my voice shaking. "I need to speak with Dr. Robbins immediately. It's an emergency."

She must have heard the desperation in my voice because she picked up the phone without question. In under a minute, Dr. Robbins appeared, her face etched with concern.

"Keltie? What's happening?"

I turned to her, aware of Remi shifting behind me. "Luna's father has decided against doing the transplant."

I felt rather than saw Remi step forward. "That's not what I—"

"Shut the fuck up, or I swear to God I'll kill you." Holt's voice came from behind us, low and deadly. I hadn't even realized he was back.

Dr. Robbins looked between us. "Perhaps we should discuss this privately."

"I'm a half match," I said, the words tumbling out before I could stop them. "Use me instead."

Dr. Robbins hesitated, then motioned to me to follow. "My office. Now."

I clutched the papers in my fist, aware of Holt physically blocking Remi from following us. Once the door closed behind us, I slammed the documents onto her desk.

"He wants to take my daughter," I said, my voice breaking. "In exchange for his bone marrow, he wants my daughter. He's never even had a conversation with her!"

Dr. Robbins picked up the papers, scanning them quickly. Her expression hardened as she read.

"Sit down, Keltie," she said gently.

I sank into the chair, my legs no longer able to support me. "Can you do it? Can you use my cells instead?"

She sighed, setting the papers down. "While a full match is preferred, a half match *will* work. Particularly given the circumstances."

Hope flickered, fragile but present. "Thank God."

"Bone marrow transplants from half-identical family members have been performed more frequently due to the challenges in finding a fully matched donor," she explained. "Treatment advances help the body accept the new cells, regardless. In this case, I believe it's in Luna's best interest to proceed with you as the donor."

She leaned forward, her expression more personal than professional.

Tears spilled down my cheeks. "Will it hurt her more? Be harder on her?"

"The risks are slightly higher," she admitted. "But Luna is strong, and frankly, her connection to you—her trust, her comfort with you—those factors matter in recovery."

I wiped away tears. "When can we do it?"

"I'll need to run more tests, but we can begin harvesting your cells tomorrow. The procedure itself isn't pleasant—you'll be sore for several days—but it's nothing compared to what Luna's going through."

"I don't care about the pain," I said. "I'd give her my heart if she needed it."

Dr. Robbins smiled. "I know you would. That's why I believe this will work."

When we returned to the hallway, Remi was engaged in a tense standoff with Holt and my father, who'd created a physical barrier between Remi and Luna's room.

"You're no longer needed," I said, my voice steady for the first time in days.

Remi's face darkened. "You can't do this. I'm her father."

"No," I replied. "You're a sperm donor who abandoned us both. A father is someone who shows up, who loves unconditionally, who puts his child's needs above his own." I glanced at Holt, drawing strength from his presence. "Luna already has that person in her life."

"This isn't over," Remi warned, gathering the papers I threw at his feet. "My lawyer will be in touch."

"Get out," I seethed.

Rather than watch him leave, I turned to Holt and my dad, whose faces reflected the same mixture of concern and relief I felt.

"Dr. Robbins says I can do it," I told them. "My cells. My donation."

My father's arms felt strong around my shoulders as he embraced me. *"Mi hija valiente,"* he murmured. "My brave daughter."

When he let go, Holt pulled me against him, his breath warm against my hair. "I love you so much."

How did he know those were the exact words I needed to hear?

The bone marrow harvest was as painful as Dr. Robbins had warned. I lay face down on the operating table while they extracted marrow from my pelvic bone with a long needle. The local anesthetic dulled the worst of it, but nothing could completely eliminate the strange pressure and discomfort of having part of my body literally sucked out through my bones.

It meant nothing compared to watching Luna's struggle. The conditioning had left her so vulnerable that even the slightest infection could be deadly. She was isolated in a sterile room, the visitors limited and required to wear masks, gloves, and gowns.

The actual transplant was anticlimactic—a bag of cells, not much different in appearance from a blood transfusion, dripping slowly into her veins. I held her hand throughout, telling the same stories Holt did, of magical forests and cloud kingdoms where unicorns danced among the stars.

"Your super cells are going inside me?" Luna asked drowsily, her eyes heavy from the medication.

"That's right, Luna-bug," I said, squeezing her fingers gently.

She smiled, her eyes drifting closed. "Then, I'll definitely get better. Your cells are strong, like me."

The next few days were the most terrifying of my life. Every temperature spike sent panic through me.

Every blood test held the potential for devastating news. Luna's body might reject my cells, attack them as foreign invaders, or simply fail to integrate them.

But somehow, miraculously, neither happened. Seven days after the transplant, Dr. Robbins entered Luna's room with the first genuine smile I'd seen since we arrived.

"Her blood counts are improving," she announced. "The engraftment is beginning to take hold."

I sagged against Holt, who had been my constant shadow throughout the ordeal. "So it's working?"

"It's early," Dr. Robbins cautioned. "But yes, so far, it's working exactly as we'd hoped."

That night, when we were at the apartment while my father stayed with Luna, the stress of the past weeks crashed over me like a tidal wave—the fear for Luna's life, the battle with Remi, the physical toll of the donation, all of it.

Holt held me through it. "You saved her," he murmured against my hair. "Not only from the cancer, but from him too."

I looked up at him through tears. "We're not out of the woods yet. She has a long recovery ahead of her, and Remi's threat still hangs over us."

"Let him try," Holt said, his voice hardening. "He's going up against you, me, and an entire community that loves Luna. He doesn't stand a chance."

Our moment was interrupted by a sharp knock at the apartment door. Holt frowned, crossing the room to answer it. Ben Rice stood in the hallway, his expression grave.

"Sorry to disturb you this late," he said, stepping inside when Holt gestured him in. "But I have information you both need to hear immediately."

I straightened, instantly alert. "About Luna?"

"It's about Remi." Ben's jaw tightened as he sat across from us.

Holt's eyebrows shot up. "What about him?"

Ben ran a hand over his face. "The lead singer of the band that opened for us on the East Coast contacted me yesterday. He said one of his sound engineers is accusing Remi of sexual assault. She's also saying she wasn't the only one." Ben's expression darkened. "Liv, the rest of our band, and I have been on the phone with everyone Remi's worked with, every band we've toured with. In the last twenty-four hours, more women have come forward with similar stories."

"My God," I muttered. "He *assaulted* them?"

"That's right. Every one of the women said they were afraid to speak up because of Remi's position and influence. He threatened to ruin their careers." Ben met my eyes directly. "When you disappeared from the tour, I should have questioned it, especially given how abruptly you left."

The validation after all these years brought unexpected tears to my eyes. "You couldn't have known."

"I should have," Ben insisted. "When I confronted him about these new allegations, he became defensive, started ranting about 'ungrateful women' trying to ruin his life." Ben shook his head in disgust. "Then he made the mistake of bringing up Luna."

"What did he say?" I asked, my stomach tightening.

"He implied that if these allegations came to light, he might need to 'explore all his options' regarding her." Ben's expression hardened. "He didn't explicitly threaten custody, but the implication was clear—he was planning to use her as leverage to silence the accusations."

"That fucking *sonuvabitch*," Holt seethed.

"Here's the thing; I recorded the entire conversation," Ben continued, pulling out his phone. "His veiled threats about Luna and his response to everything else. It might not be admissible in a court of law, but if these women are willing to press charges, knowing they have my backing, along with that of other powerful people in the music industry, we wouldn't need it for evidence."

My breath caught in my throat. "Do you think they will actually press charges?"

"Two already have. The police picked him up an hour ago. He's in custody now."

"For how long?" Holt asked.

"With multiple charges coming in from different jurisdictions, his lawyer will have a hard time getting bail." Ben's expression was solemn. "I came here as soon as I heard. I wanted you to know that Luna is safe from him, and so are you."

I pressed my hand to my mouth, overwhelmed by the sudden turn of events.

"I know this must be a lot to process," Ben said gently. "But I wanted you to hear it from me directly. I'm doing everything in my power to make this right—not only for you and Luna, but for every woman he's hurt."

Holt stood, extending his hand to Ben. "I don't know how to thank you."

Ben shook his head. "I'm so sorry…"

After Ben left, I found myself standing by the window, watching the Denver lights flicker against the night sky. Holt's arms wrapped around my waist from behind, and he rested his chin on my shoulder.

"What are you thinking?" he asked softly.

"That sometimes the universe has a strange way of delivering justice," I replied.

My phone rang, and I answered it quickly when I saw Dr. Robbins' number.

"Dr. Robbins? Is everything okay?"

Her voice came through, professional but with an undercurrent of excitement. "Better than okay, Keltie. I've completed Luna's evening assessment and am happy to say her fever has broken and her latest blood work shows the strongest signs of engraftment yet."

Tears sprang to my eyes. "She's accepting the transplant?"

"Better than I dared to hope," Dr. Robbins continued. "The cellular integration is remarkable. It's like a perfect match, after all."

I turned to Holt, who was watching my face anxiously. "Luna's improving. The transplant is working."

He pulled me into a crushing embrace, his own tears dampening my hair. "Our girl's going to be okay."

Our girl. The phrase encompassed everything I'd ever wanted—a family bound not by biology or legal documents, but by love, by choice, by fierce protection of one another.

"I should return to the hospital," I said, already gathering my coat.

"We both should," Holt agreed.

As we drove through the quiet streets, my mind kept circling around to the unexpected resolution. Remi's threat had disintegrated under the weight of his own misdeeds. And Luna was healing, growing stronger with each passing hour.

At the hospital, we found my father dozing in the chair beside Luna's bed. Her color had improved dramatically, and her breathing was deep and even. I approached quietly, not wanting to wake her. But her eyes fluttered open as I took her hand.

"Mommy," she whispered, her voice stronger than it had been in days. "I had a dream about you."

"Did you?" I smoothed her cheek with my thumb. "Tell me about it."

"You were wearing a long white dress and a veil," Luna said, her eyes drifting to Holt, who stood beside me. "And you had on a suit."

"What else did you dream, Unicorn Girl?" Holt asked in a shaky voice.

"I was between you, wearing a long purple dress, and the three of us walked down an aisle together while everyone clapped." She glanced up at Holt. "And you told me that I could call you Daddy."

"That sounds like a very happy dream," I said, not even bothering to stop my tears.

Luna smiled, her eyelids growing heavy again. "Not just a dream, Mommy." She glanced at Holt a second time. "Right, Daddy?"

"That's right, Luna-bug. It's a dream come true."

30

Holt
July

The ranch looked different today. Not because anything had physically changed—the butte still framed the horizon, the big trees still spread their branches across the eastern field, and the main house still stood proud against the Colorado sky. But something had shifted in the way I saw it all. Today, this place wasn't only our legacy or where I'd grown up. Today, it was the place where Keltie, Luna, and I would begin our new life as a family.

I stood beneath the white wooden arch my brothers and I had built last week, watching as Keltie walked toward me across the grass. She wore a white dress that flowed around her, catching the July breeze. No elaborate cathedral, no hundreds of guests, no pageantry—just us, our families, and the land that represented far more than we'd ever dreamed.

Her smile caught the sunlight as she approached, her hand tucked in her father's arm. I'd never seen anything more beautiful than her wild, curly, dark-brown hair framing her face and her gorgeous amber eyes filled with joy.

When she reached me, those eyes were bright with unshed tears. Happy ones, I knew. We'd cried enough of the other kind to recognize the difference.

"Hi," she whispered, taking my hands.

"Hi, yourself," I whispered like she had.

The ceremony passed in a blur. I remembered the important parts—the promises we made, the rings we exchanged, the kiss that sealed it all. But mostly, I remembered how it felt to stand there, surrounded by everyone who mattered, pledging myself to the woman who had shown me the best of what life could be.

Luna stood between us, like she'd dreamed, wearing her long purple dress and beaming with pride. She occasionally waved to everyone as if she were the star of the show—which, in many ways, she was. After all, she was the one to dream this day into existence.

After the celebratory cheers died down, I squeezed Keltie's hand. We'd planned this moment carefully.

"Before we all head to the reception," I said, raising my voice so our gathered family could hear, "Keltie and I have an announcement."

She stepped forward, her hand drifting to rest on the swell of her belly, visible now if you knew to look for it.

"We're having a baby," she said, her voice steady and clear in the summer air. "Due in December."

The second round of cheers was even louder than the first. My brothers and Flynn were the first to reach us, pulling us both into tight embraces. Luna danced around us, shouting that she was going to be a big sister.

Later, as the celebration continued under the twinkling lights strung across the yard, Keltie found me standing aside, watching our families together.

"Happy?" she asked, slipping her hand into mine.

I pulled her close. "More than I ever thought possible." I pressed my hand gently against her belly. "When you said yes to marrying me, I didn't think life could get better. And then this somehow happened…"

She laughed. "Somehow? I believe my exact words were, 'Let's start our family now.'"

"Best decision ever," I murmured against her hair.

A few days after the wedding, Dr. Robbins called. The hospital was holding a ribbon-cutting ceremony for the new research lab, funded largely by Miracles of Hope, along with significant private donations.

"They specifically asked that we all attend," my brother Buck said after hanging up the phone. "And mentioned that Luna will be the guest of honor."

"Of course she will." I smiled. Wasn't she always? Hadn't she more than earned it? Not only because of her struggles, but from her positive outlook on life.

So we went—Keltie, Luna, and me, along with my siblings. Beau and Sam, who'd flown in from New York for our wedding, stayed an extra week.

When we arrived at the hospital, I was surprised to see Ben and Liv Rice already there, chatting with Dr. Robbins.

"There they are," Dr. Robbins said warmly as we approached. She knelt down and gave Luna a big hug. "You're looking very pretty today, Unicorn Girl."

Luna beamed up at me. "That's what my Daddy calls me."

The ceremony itself was brief. Dr. Robbins spoke about the importance of continued research into childhood cancers and how the new lab would focus specifically on the type that had affected both Scarlett and Luna. Then she unveiled the plaque beside the entrance—*Scarlett's Hope Research Laboratory.*

Underneath, a smaller plaque listed the major donors. I felt my throat tighten when I read that both the Rice family and the Barrett family had made significant contributions in Luna's name.

After the ceremony, as people mingled with refreshments, Ben walked over to Keltie and me. "I bet he didn't tell you that all the proceeds from Luna's song helped build this too."

Keltie's eyes were wide when she looked up at me. "You did that?"

"No, darlin'. *We* did it. Remember?"

A week later, we arrived at the Roaring Fork, where we joined my family for a walk to the memorial garden my siblings and I had created around Scarlett's grave. Luna ran ahead of us, carrying a small bouquet of wildflowers she'd insisted on picking herself.

"For Scarlett," she explained as she carefully arranged them at the base of the small headstone.

My siblings gathered around us and shared a moment of silence. Then Keltie squeezed my hand.

"We have one more thing to share," she said, looking at my family. "We found out a couple of days ago that we're having a girl."

Luna looked up from where she was kneeling by the flowers. "And we decided to name my baby sister Scarlett," she announced before either of us could continue.

I felt the breath catch in my throat as I looked at my siblings, realizing this was something I should have discussed with them first. But before I could speak, I saw tears in Flynn's eyes and Buck smiling.

"It's right," Porter said quietly.

"Scarlett is the perfect name," Cord added, brushing away his own tears.

I'd planned to make another announcement today, but decided it wasn't necessary to. Yesterday afternoon, Luna had officially become my daughter. Remi, who was in jail, facing several counts of sexual harassment and assault, had relinquished his parental rights, making it possible for the adoption to move forward.

I felt a small hand grab mine as I brushed away yet another tear of happiness.

"Are you okay, Daddy?"

"Never better, Unicorn Girl," I said as my eyes met Keltie's. I looked beyond her to Buck, who stood with TJ and Buckaroo, Cord with Juni, Porter with Cici, and even Sam and Beau. The Roaring Fork Trust had brought love into each of our lives when what we'd all expected was pain and uncertainty.

I looked up at the sky. "Mama, if you had a hand in all this, thank you. I hope we've made you happy."

The clouds parted then, and a ray of sunshine bathed the garden in light.

Flynn raised her face and closed her eyes as the warmth settled over her.

I had no idea what else the trustee would demand, but for the first time since our dad died, I believed that whatever it was would bring more joy, more happiness, and more love into all our lives.

Keep reading for a sneak peek at
the next book in Heather Slade's
Roaring Fork Ranch series,
Roaring Fork Rooker

**He left her to honor a promise made in blood.
She survived his abandonment
but carries secrets of her own.
Together, they must confront the past that
tore them apart and the truths that
could destroy their future.**

JW

Thirty years ago, I left Echo without an explanation, choosing a dying family member's desperate plea over the woman I loved. I told myself I was protecting her by disappearing, but I shattered both our hearts. Now, my family obligations are complete, and seeing her again at a small-town parade reminds me that some wounds never heal—and some loves never die. I want a second chance, but first, she needs to understand why I vanished and why I can never let her go again.

ECHO

JW destroyed my world when he disappeared without a trace. One day, we were planning our future; the next, he was gone, leaving me to pick up the pieces of my shattered life. I survived by building a career helping families through crises, convincing myself I'd moved on. But when he walks back into my life after three decades, every defense I've built crumbles. He says he can explain everything, that there were secrets bigger than our love. What he doesn't know is that I'm hiding secrets of my own—ones that could destroy not just our second chance, but everyone we both love.

1

JW

Standing on the wraparound porch of Sangre Vista's main lodge, I watched the road that wound through the pines toward the entrance gate. The December air bit through my sheepskin jacket, carrying the scent of pine and the promise of more snow before evening.

Today was important. The Warrick family would be arriving this afternoon, and everything needed to be ready.

I pulled my jacket tighter and began my morning rounds. The walkways around the lodge had been cleared and salted twice since yesterday's snowfall. Ice could form quickly at this elevation, and the last thing I wanted was a guest taking a fall.

Inside the lodge, I made my way through the great room, where overnight embers still glowed in the massive stone hearth. I added fresh logs, watching as flames caught and danced against the river-rock chimney that stretched two stories to the vaulted ceiling. Fresh wreaths and evergreen garlands adorned the main entrance, and pathway lights created pools of warm illumination leading to the guest cabins.

My boots crunched through snow when I walked to the stable complex at seven. Inside, twenty-six horses stirred in their stalls, some already munching hay.

Rick, our stable manager, looked up from where he was measuring grain into buckets, pushing his hat back on his graying head.

"Morning, JW. You're here early."

"I wanted to check the road conditions before our guests arrive," I said, though we both knew I could have done that with a phone call to the county highway department. "How are the horses this morning?"

"Good to go. Kit and Carson are ready for sleigh work if you need them, and the riding horses are sound. Weather's supposed to hold for the next few days."

I walked down the center aisle, checking each stall. Fantasma, our quarter horse stallion, stretched his neck over the door for attention. I obliged, running my hand along his neck while he snuffled at my jacket pockets, hoping for treats.

"The new guests have young children. Twin boys, about three years old, and an infant daughter."

Rick nodded. "I'll keep the gentler horses close to the barn. Maybe set up some supervised visits if the boys are interested. Kids that age love seeing the big animals, even if they're too small to ride."

"Good thinking. And, Rick?" I paused at the stable door. "This family is important. I want everything to go smoothly."

"You got it, JW. We'll treat them well."

Walking back toward the lodge, I detoured through the equipment barn, where Michael, our maintenance guy, was already at work.

"Morning, Michael. Everything running okay?"

"Yeah, all good. Pueblo Moon's holding temp fine."

"Good. I want you to do another walk-through this morning—check the faucets, test the lights, and make sure the fireplace is working right."

"Already on my list," Michael said. "Anything else?"

"They have small children. I want child-safety latches on the lower kitchen cabinets and outlet covers throughout. Also, check for sharp corners at toddler height and loose rugs that could cause slips."

"I'll have everything childproofed within the hour."

By seven-fifteen, I was reviewing the day's schedule with Sarah, our front-desk manager.

"The Warrick family's file," I said.

She pulled up the reservation on her screen. "Party of five, arriving today. Welcome packet ready with maps, activity schedules, and emergency contacts."

"What about their special requests?"

"Organic milk, decaffeinated coffee always available, and family-friendly meal options. Chef Alton has everything ready."

"Weather can be unpredictable in December. Make sure we have plenty of indoor activities ready—books, games, maybe coordinate with the kitchen for some cookie-decorating sessions if the boys get restless."

"Should I handle check-in when they arrive?"

"No, I'll greet them personally. But please be available in case they need immediate assistance."

At eight, I convened the morning staff meeting in the main dining room.

"Good morning, everyone," I began, consulting my notes. "Today, we welcome our only guests for the next month. We're closing the ranch to all other reservations during their stay."

Alton leaned forward. "Any dietary stuff?"

"Simple finger foods for the children—they'll prefer familiar options. We'll check with the mother in the event she needs anything special for the baby."

"I'll prepare a welcome basket with local honey and some of my softer cookies for the kids."

Our activities director, Lisa, raised her hand. "Shall I look into activities for the toddlers, or do you have something specific in mind?"

"The boys might enjoy seeing the horses, though they're far too young for riding. Supervised visits to the stable, maybe some gentle interaction with our calmer animals. Sleigh rides if weather permits, but with extra blankets and shortened routes."

"What about hiking trails?" she asked.

"Unlikely with an infant and toddlers, but the easier paths around the lodge might work for short family walks."

Jim, the head of security, spoke from his position near the door. "Any specific considerations on my end?"

"Privacy is essential. No staff should approach their cabin unless requested. All maintenance and housekeeping should be coordinated in advance."

I noticed the questioning looks my staff exchanged when they thought I wasn't watching. In the years since I'd transformed Sangre Vista from a working ranch into a luxury guest operation, I'd built a reputation for high standards but reasonable expectations.

But today felt different. Today required my personal attention in ways I couldn't explain to my employees.

After the meeting ended, my next stop was Pueblo Moon itself, situated on a ridge overlooking the valley. It offered breathtaking views while maintaining privacy from the other accommodations.

Michael was already there with his toolkit. "Latches are installed," he reported. "I've also added padding to the corners of that coffee table—it's the height where a running toddler might hit his head."

The main living area was spacious and welcoming, with a stone fireplace flanked by comfortable leather furniture. Large windows framed the mountain vista, while warm wood floors were softened by thick woolen rugs.

"I also set up the baby crib in the third bedroom," Michael continued.

I walked through each room. In the master bedroom, fresh flowers sat on the dresser, beside a bottle of sparkling cider and gourmet chocolates—adult treats to balance the child-focused preparations.

The second bedroom had been transformed into a welcoming children's space. Twin beds with colorful quilts faced a window overlooking the stable complex. Between the beds sat a basket of toys—wooden horses, picture books, and soft building blocks designed for small hands.

Cora, our head of housekeeping, entered with an armload of supplies.

"May I help?" I asked.

"I'm all set, JW. I've stocked the refrigerator, and Sarah will check with the family at arrival about how often they'd like housekeeping."

"Outstanding work."

She paused in the doorway, her expression thoughtful. "Javier? Is there anything else you want to tell us about these particular guests?" In fifteen years of working together, Cora had developed an ability to read my moods and motivations.

"Every guest who chooses Sangre Vista deserves our best efforts. Some require more coordination than others when traveling with small children."

She raised a brow, but wisely let it go. "Oh, by the way, Sarah asked me to mention that the Warricks sent a message saying they expect to arrive around two o'clock."As I left the cabin and turned to the main lodge, I took a deep breath and let it out slowly. This was going to be a memorable month—for all of us.

About the Author

USA Today best-selling author Heather Slade writes shamelessly sexy, edge-of-your seat romantic suspense.

She gave herself the gift of writing a book for her own birthday one year. Sixty-plus books later (and counting), she's having the time of her life.

The women Slade writes are self-confident, strong, with wills of their own, and hearts as big as the Colorado sky. The men are sublimely sexy, seductive alphas who rise to the challenge of capturing the sweet soul of a woman whose heart they'll hold in the palm of their hand forever. Add in a couple of neck-snapping twists and turns, a page-turning mystery, and a swoon-worthy HEA, and you'll be holding one of her books in your hands.

She loves to hear from her readers. You can contact her at heather@heatherslade.com

To keep up with her latest news and releases, please visit her website at www.heatherslade.com to sign up for her newsletter.

MORE FROM AUTHOR HEATHER SLADE

ROMANTIC SUSPENSE

K19 SECURITY SOLUTIONS TEAM ONE
Razor's Edge
Gunner's Redemption
Mistletoe's Magic
Mantis' Desire
Dutch's Salvation

K19 SECURITY SOLUTIONS TEAM TWO
Striker's Choice
Monk's Fire
Halo's Oath
Tackle's Honor
Onyx's Awakening

K19 SHADOW OPERATIONS TEAM ONE
Code Name: Ranger
Code Name: Diesel
Code Name: Wasp
Code Name: Cowboy
Code Name: Mayhem

K19 ALLIED INTELLIGENCE TEAM ONE
Code Name: Ares
Code Name: Cayman
Code Name: Poseidon
Code Name: Zeppelin
Code Name: Magnet

K19 ALLIED INTELLIGENCE TEAM TWO
Code Name: Puck
Code Name: Michelangelo
Code Name: Typhon
Code Name: Hornet
Code Name: Reaper

K19 GENESIS CONSORTIUM TEAM ONE
Blackjack's Ascent
Dagger's Shield
Sundance's Trail
Nomad's Compass
Preacher's Decree

K19 SENTINEL CYBER TEAM ONE
Code Name: Admiral
Code Name: Dante
Code Name: Grit
Code Name: Tank
Code Name: Atticus

K19 SENTINEL CYBER TEAM TWO
Code Name: Kodiak
Code Name: Paragon
Code Name: Vex
Code Name: Shredder
Code Name: Jagger

PROTECTORS UNDERCOVER TEAM ONE
Undercover Agent
Undercover Emissary
Undercover Savior
Undercover Infidel
Undercover Shadow

ROYAL AGENTS OF MI6
Make Me Shiver
Drive Me Wilder
Feel My Pinch
Chase My Shadow
Find My Angel

THE INVINCIBLES TEAM ONE
Code Name: Deck
Code Name: Edge
Code Name: Grinder
Code Name: Rile
Code Name: Smoke

THE INVINCIBLES TEAM TWO
Code Name: Buck
Code Name: Irish
Code Name: Saint
Code Name: Hammer
Code Name: Rip

THE UNSTOPPABLES TEAM ONE
Code Name: Fury
Code Name: Merried

MORE FROM AUTHOR HEATHER SLADE

WINE COUNTRY ROMANCE

BUTLER RANCH
Kade's Worth
Brodie's Promise
Maddox's Truce
Naughton's Secret
Mercer's Vow
Kade's Return
Butler Ranch Christmas

WICKED WINEMAKERS
CENTRAL COAST
FIRST LABEL
Brix's Bid
Ridge's Release
Press' Passion
Zin's Sins
Tryst's Temptation

WICKED WINEMAKERS
CENTRAL COAST
SECOND LABEL
Beau's Beloved
Cru's Crush
Bit's Bliss
Snapper's Seduction
Kick's Kiss

WICKED WINEMAKERS
RUSSIAN RIVER VALLEY
FIRST LABEL
Bas' Blend
Hux's Harvest
Wolf's Want
Oak's Vintage
Cooper's Claim

COWBOY ROMANCE

COWBOYS OF
CRESTED BUTTE
A Cowboy Falls
A Cowboy's Dance
A Cowboy's Kiss
A Cowboy Stays
A Cowboy Wins

ROARING FORK RANCH
Roaring Fork Wrangler
Roaring Fork Roughstock
Roaring Fork Rockstar
Roaring Fork Rooker
Roaring Fork Bridger

SANGRE VISTA RANCH
Thorn's Stand
Stetson's Storm
Maverick's Reckoning
Cinch's Wager
Flints Chance